BECOMING
BROOKLYN

BECOMING BROOKLYN

AMANDA DEICH

BECOMING BROOKLYN

© Park Bench Publishing 2021
Cover design by Sarah Anderson

ISBN 13: 978-1-7361601-2-1

To the three thousand souls who perished in the attacks of 9/11, to the thousands more who survived, and to their families who carried on:

YOU ARE THE REAL HEROES.

1

God bless America,

The first blast came from behind the flag at the front of the room, shattering the silence we'd assumed during the patriotic song. It could have killed us, but it only succeeded in throwing me sideways, making me land sharply on the edge of the buffet table.

Land that I love!
Stand beside her, and guide her...

A hand reached toward me. I clung to it desperately as it tried to pull me out of the chaos, away from the explosions and the deafening spray of gunshots.

Through the night with the light from above.

Three short breaths – two blinks – and we were hit again.

This time from the back.

Sticky warmth ran down the back of my neck and between my bare shoulder blades. The tight dress I wore to the memorial gala trapped me as I tried to escape.

From the mountains,
To the prairies…

I gripped the hand that had grabbed mine. The owner of it was ripped backwards, succumbing to the crowd, his fiery red hair sticking out among the mass. With all my strength, I threw him in front of me, and together, we sprinted toward the exit.

To the oceans,
White with foam!

Camouflaged men lining the back of the room aimed past me as we ran.

They opened fire on a target I didn't know.

God bless America!
My home, sweet home!

'Didn't know'?

That was a lie. I knew who he was.

He was the monster who killed my dad on the attacks of 9/11, the one who sentenced my mom to a lifetime of grief and pain.

God bless America!

The entire country knows him, and they know him well.

My home....

His name?

Sweet...

It's Hate.

Home.

2

I COULD SEE THE FLASHING LIGHTS AROUND ME,
but I didn't hear the sirens that accompanied them —
didn't hear the incessant shouting of the adults around me
trying to control the situation, either. I just saw a man's
mouth moving as he yelled to another, a woman's arms
frantically waving to get the help she needed. Their eyes
flashed from me, then to another victim, then to another
and another, as if they were caged animals themselves,
pacing the corners of their quarters, searching for an
escape or a rescue.

I wondered if this was trauma: the stripping down of your
senses until you experienced only the amount you could
handle.

"How are you feeling? Are you okay?"

Oh. Questions. I could hear again.

The medic held a thumb up in front of his chest,
pointing it down, sideways, and up. His face was inches
from mine, but his voice came from miles away, past the
high-pitched tone that filled my ears.

I didn't know how to respond at first. Was I okay? Would I ever be?

"You have some blood on your back," he said, studying that area of my body closely. "But I don't see a wound. It must have come from someone else."

Blood from someone else.

I was going to be sick. I tried to focus on a spot on the sidewalk and breathed deeply, counting to ten.

"Miss, are you okay?" he asked again.

I gave him a timid thumbs up, then looked past him as he moved down the line to the other people sprawled out in their formal attire.

On a normal evening I'd see some of the iconic buildings that lined New York City's Park Avenue, but tonight I couldn't see anything but armed policemen, the crowded sidewalk, and flashing lights. The sound of hovering helicopters echoed beyond the turmoil.

I pushed my palms against my ears and squeezed my eyes shut.

I stayed that way – silent in my solace – until I recognized the familiar scent of my mom's perfume. Her tiny frame – dwarfed by mine – somehow held me in her arms like I was a baby all over again.

"Oh, Brooklyn," she moaned, rocking me in an almost maniacal fashion. "Not again. Not again. NOT AGAIN."

The strength of her embrace held me captive as she repeated the words, and I willingly disappeared behind the curtain of her long black hair.

Everything about what had happened made me want to regress to young childhood – to the moments like this, where my mom's lap was my entire world, and in that world, nothing evil existed.

But that wasn't the world I was born into.

I was a 9/11 baby.

I was born into a battle.

3

Two Days Later

WE'RE FAMOUS, YOU KNOW: 9/11 BABIES.

We were all still developing in our mothers' wombs when we were given that name, when our fathers died as a result of the terrorist hijackings.

We weren't babies anymore, though.

I studied the others seated beside me. There were five of them, and they were my age, nineteen or so. They'd all had the dumb luck of being seated at my table the night of the memorial gala. Thankfully, we'd received only minor injuries from the incident two nights ago. You could barely even tell we'd been attacked.

The memorial had been held every year since the infamous attacks, on the Fridays prior to September 11th. It'd always been a somber event, but never violent. Never unsafe. It'd never led to an attack, to an armed and heavily-guarded press conference a couple days later.

The mics poised in front of us were turned off now.

We'd given our statements – some political and impassioned, but most just sad – and now the questions from the press were being hurled at the podium, where the White House press secretary was responding rapidly.

"Do we know who's behind the attack?" a lady from NBC asked.

"Not at this time," was the answer. "The perpetrators' deaths are unfortunate, in the way that they leave us with a lot of questions. But we are following all leads, and we are carefully monitoring all known terrorist networks."

"How many gunmen were there? How many detonated devices?" I couldn't tell who had asked.

"Five gunmen were involved, all taken down by our military personnel who were present that night. We believe there were twelve homemade explosives that went off during the attack as well," the secretary continued.

"How many victim casualties were there?" A woman from the back.

"Surprisingly, none. We were lucky."

My mind flashed back to the intense fear I'd had during the onslaught.

Lucky, she'd said. I sure didn't feel it.

A man wearing a CNN lanyard rose. "The memorial in honor of the victims has been held annually since the attacks of 9/11," he declared. "Can it possibly continue, given the events of Friday night? How can we ensure the victims' families won't be targeted again?"

I searched the exits for an escape, from the attention and from the comment, but this particular conference room in the Waldorf-Astoria Hotel had its exits in the back – furthest away from my seat.

And I knew I had to wait it out, anyway. As my mom had told me earlier, it was the honorable and courageous thing to do.

The press had moved on quickly after the brief statement I'd given at the start. It was obvious that some of the other "babies" were much more comfortable in the limelight. Their words were eloquent and their demeanor, refined.

Not me, though.

I wasn't made for this.

I'm a lot like the city I was named after: Brooklyn.

That part of the Big Apple isn't sophisticated, but it's got a strong will and stubborn personality. And those are the same traits I have, the same traits I inherited from my dad.

Based off the umpteen-million stories I'd heard about him my whole life, I was sure he would have hated this publicity, too.

According to my mom, my dad hated everything I hated: speaking in public (speaking in general, actually), having to dress up in anything besides workout gear, and engaging people in small talk. Even though he was a software engineer, Rex Blackburn had looked more like a UFC fighter when he was alive, or maybe even a Scandinavian bodybuilder – like one of those lumberjack types I always saw on the World's Strongest Man championships on TV.

"Your dad would actually wince as he got dressed for

9

work," my mom had told me as she helped me change my bandages and get ready earlier that day. "His company was located on the 74th floor of the south tower, and he would wait until he was in the elevator before he'd knot his tie. He said it always felt suffocating."

"Then why did he wear it?" I'd asked, not even trying to hide my bitterness. I was thinking about my own situation, having to tell the vultures in the press what had happened the night of the memorial.

"Because," my mom said, answering my question with a sympathetic squeeze of her hand. "He was born brilliant. Gifted, really. And people respected him. He always made it a priority to show others respect in return. That kind of leader was exactly what people needed."

"Even people he didn't know?" I asked, still annoyed she was making me to go the press conference.

"Especially people he didn't know," she'd replied. "Every single citizen in this country deserves to have their questions answered. It doesn't matter who they are. They deserve that respect. And we deserve to live our lives without fear."

Angela Blackburn, relentless patriot. I could see that pride in her now, swelling up in her tiny five-foot-three frame as she stood in the back of the crowded makeshift press room.

She was the opposite of me in almost every way. She was short and petite, classy and refined. She looked like the stereotypical Italian, while I resembled the Norwegian ancestors on my father's side.

My older brother, Bryce, was seated toward the back as

well, just in front of my mom. He caught my gaze and crossed his eyes. I smiled slightly, grateful for the levity that always seemed to accompany him.

Even though I was a year younger than my brother (and a girl, for crying out loud), I was as tall as him: five feet, nine inches. I had broader shoulders than him, too — probably because of all the sports I played.

We were opposites, for sure. But that didn't stop me from wishing he was sitting next to me. If he were up here, I'd be able to hide under his protective wing as he freakishly commanded the room, just as he'd done the last eighteen years.

But he was in the back, and I was stuck in this seat until the assigned personnel allowed us to go.

Which seemed like it'd be any minute.

My heart stopped momentarily as I recognized one of the "babies" who was speaking. He had dark red hair and ruddy skin. His emerald eyes had looked so scared the night of the attack when he'd grabbed my hand, yet had looked determined as well. He had done everything he could to save me.

And I'd done everything I could to save him, too.

We were strangers. I'd never spoken to him and didn't know if I ever would. But the moment of vulnerability and immediate intimacy we'd experienced made me feel like we shared a mutual best friend — or the same enemy. I didn't know whether to approach or avoid him. Being this close to him again, I felt an odd combination of gratitude and fear, comfort and dread.

He was seated next to a girl, and I instinctively knew

11

they had to be twins. They shared the same color eyes and hair, but my hunch went beyond that. They acted too comfortably around each other to not be related.

The girl was animated and seemed to dominate the speaking, but the boy was a perfect complement to her, chiming in when appropriate to explain something in more detail.

Even though there were six of us answering the reporters' questions, I felt particularly drawn to the pair, attracted by some invisible magnet. I told myself all survivors of an attack felt that connection, too, but my heart knew different.

I was drawn to them because of him: the boy who'd saved me at my weakest, and who'd allowed me to save him, too.

4

WHEN THE PRESS CONFERENCE ENDED, THE SIX of us were shuffled from our places in front of the cameras to a quieter part of the hotel. I was weaving my way through the last security point when I saw an officer in the army looking at me expectantly. He was standing behind the long cardboard panel that served as a backdrop during the press conference and was dressed in military garb: not camouflage, but the navy, red, and white dress uniforms I noticed soldiers wearing at respectable events. His dark brown hair was graying slightly and fine wrinkles outlined his hazel eyes, which widened as I approached.

"Brooklyn?" he asked. "Brooklyn Blackburn?"

I nodded. "Yes?"

I hadn't meant for it to come out like a question.

"My name is Major McCoy. I'll be escorting you to a brief meeting," he advised. "Military protocol to ensure your protection. You can stay here while I gather the others."

I assessed him carefully. He was straight-backed in a no-nonsense kind of way, and while he didn't exactly appear welcoming, he didn't intimidate me, either. A guard stopped to salute him as he walked past, and even though I wasn't in the Army, the underlying respect shown in the action made me question whether or not I should do the same.

"Um. Does my mom know about this?" I asked. You could never be too careful these days. Creepos were everywhere.

"She does," he replied nonchalantly, pointing across the room. I followed his gaze and saw my mom, who nodded, looked at the officer, and gave me a grin and a thumbs up.

Weird. My mom hadn't let me out of her sight since the attack. For her to be so trusting of a complete stranger was disarming.

"Isaac?" The officer asked, stopping a tall, thin, black guy as he left his spot at the front table.

"Yeah?" he answered.

Major McCoy introduced himself again, adding, "I'm going to need to see you, too," before instructing him to stand beside me.

The boy named Isaac looked even more suspicious than me. His brown eyes narrowed as he arched a brow and leaned down to my level.

"What's this all about?" he asked.

"'Standard protocol', apparently," I replied, immediately feeling more relaxed – probably because I wasn't alone.

"Liam and Bree?" Major McCoy asked, interrupting the twins' departure. The girl nodded back, her burgundy hair billowing behind her. The boy looked at me and smiled shyly.

His name was Liam.

Any sense of relaxation I felt just moments earlier disappeared, and a nervous tingling took its place. I smiled back just as shyly before my eyes found the floor.

"I'm going to need you to join us as well."

The twins joined Isaac, and I did my best to appear busy, which took all of my concentration. I knew I'd stammer through any conversation with them, so I watched Major McCoy instead and avoided the three of them altogether.

He flagged down two other young people: an insanely beautiful, smaller-framed girl with long black hair and brown eyes; and a tiny, pale boy with black hair and rimmed glasses.

I remembered them from the gala because they'd been seated at my table. The boy had arrived alone and was much smaller than the rest of us. He had played with his silverware most of the night, reenacting juvenile fight scenes, so I hadn't spoken to him.

The girl was dressed more casually today than she was at the gala. Her dark hair reached her lower back, immediately reminding me of the hair featured in Instagram ads for hair growth supplements. At the gala, it'd been tucked into a classy updo, complimenting the dress she'd worn perfectly, her light brown eyes easily picking up its golden hue. When she'd started talking to me that night, I remembered feeling like I was a tween playing dress up. She'd seemed so much more sophisticated for her age. Just after she'd spoken to me, the explosions had started.

The pale boy with black hair stood by the twins. He was incessantly twirling a fidget spinner, and I allowed myself to get lost in its constant motion, grateful for the distraction so I didn't have to look at any of them for too long. I caught the eye of an older guy in a suit who was standing behind the group. He was trying unsuccessfully not to check out the girl with long dark hair.

Ew.

"I'm Adrianna," the girl began. She held out a petite hand- one my man-hands would swallow up in an instant.

"Brooklyn," I replied, weakly offering the man-hand to her.

"Ready, Jacob?" Major McCoy interrupted, clapping the back of the small kid.

"I-I guess so," he replied, stuffing the fidget-spinner back into his pocket and pushing his glasses up the bridge of his nose.

The officer turned to the rest of us. "This way," he commanded. "The sooner we get there, the sooner you can be briefed."

"Briefed?" I asked, whispering the question to the group. Isaac shrugged. Adrianna and Bree shook their heads, and Jacob looked as if he were studying Major McCoy's face for clues. Liam was the only one who answered.

"I have no idea what's going on," he admitted. "But I'm glad I'm not finding out alone."

5

"TAKE A RIGHT, EVERYONE." MAJOR MCCOY extended his hand, inviting us to enter into the quiet lobby of the Waldorf-Astoria Hotel and leave the commotion of the press room behind us. "We'll begin the briefing in the Presidential Suite."

"The briefing?" the girl who looked like a model – Adrianna – asked. "About what? The attack?"

He didn't answer. Instead, his gait increased in speed as we rounded another corner. Trying to keep up, I caught the sharp edge with my shoulder and cussed quietly.

Or so I'd thought.

"Are you okay?" Liam asked, staying back from the rest of the group. He nodded to my shoulder.

"I'm just clumsy."

He laughed, then looked down. "I'm Liam," he said softly. It took a beat for his green eyes to finally rise and assess my response.

"Brooklyn," I replied, acting like I didn't already have his name tucked away in my heart. "I was with you, you know, when they – when they attacked."

"I remember," he stated solemnly. "You saved me."

There was so much I could say about this, and yet the words all jumbled together in a big mess inside my brain, so instead, I said nothing. We came to a stop outside of an elevator. Major McCoy stepped inside and invited us to do the same.

We made an informal circle as the doors closed, the girls on one side and the boys on the other. It was like we were at some lame middle school dance. The silence was loud.

"How's your neck?" Liam asked me from across the space. He turned to the others, who were listening with piqued interest. "She got hit from behind when we were trying to escape."

"Hmmm?" I asked. I felt the bandages covering the graze on my temple and left wrist, but I was otherwise unscathed.

"It looked – uh – pretty bad – that night," he explained.

"Oh," I answered, recalling the medic's response. "It was…someone else's blood, they think."

The pressure of the small space dropped significantly. Isaac shifted uncomfortably from one foot to the other. Jacob and the two other girls stayed silent, but Liam raised a brow. "Huh. It looked like you were hurt."

Major McCoy cleared his throat as the elevator dinged and the doors opened. He led us to a room with a gold plaque on wall next to the door.

THE WALDORF-ASTORIA PRESIDENTIAL SUITE, it said. A FEW OF THE FAMOUS OCCUPANTS:

"Every President since 1931…" I read aloud.

Isaac let out a low whistle, lightening the mood. "Look at all those Kings and Queens," he said, shaking his head and turning toward Major McCoy. "How much does this room go for?"

"Around ten grand, but the government gets a good deal." He winked, opened the door, and gestured to the inside of the room. "Come on in."

Curious and excited, I bolted forward without looking. I bumped into the back of Liam's shoulder as we attempted to enter the doorway at the same time.

"I'm sorry," he apologized quickly.

"I'm —er…" I knocked into him again. Stupid broad shoulders.

He moved to the side and grinned sheepishly. "Ladies first."

I blinked, trying to clear my head of the dizzying effects of his attention, then darted inside, only to stop dead in my tracks a few steps in.

My jaw dropped in awe.

6

THE ROOM WAS BIGGER THAN I EVER IMAGINED a hotel room could be, and multiple doorways showed that it was actually a suite. A ginormous one.

Almost all of the furniture was dark, heavy wood – the kind my grandma always pointed out at antique stores. The walls were adorned with velvet curtains that swept across the classic wallpaper, and black-and-white pictures of past presidents highlighted the space between the windows. The fireplace was outlined with marble, and the fabric on all of the chairs was a soft white.

Besides the six of us and Major McCoy, there was only one other man. He was also in military attire, but was older than Major McCoy – probably in his fifties, or maybe even his sixties. His hair was grayer and deeper wrinkles lined his face. He looked pretty athletic, though: like one of those regimented officers in war movies – y'know, a Clint Eastwood or someone – and even his posture gave the impression that he didn't relax. That, coupled with his uniform looking absolutely perfect and formal, made me a little on edge.

Major McCoy saluted him, then motioned to the couches, an invitation for us to take a seat. After that, he silently stood at attention.

I was happy to get off of my feet, but nervous about the sofas. They were white, and I had a bad track record of ruining nice things. I sat on a rocking chair instead.

"That was President Kennedy's, you know."

Adrianna was smiling at me, her brown eyes even bigger than before.

"It's true," she laughed. "Look at the plaque!"

I turned my body to the back of the chair, to the place where her finger was pointing. Sure enough, there was a small sign verifying that the 35th president of the United States had sat on the very seat I was now occupying.

I hopped up right away, willing to take my chances marking the (hopefully) historically insignificant couches.

Isaac and Jacob had followed me to the seating area, both having a mock race to the arm chair and almost knocking over a vase of flowers in the process. I giggled and glanced at the twins and Adrianna, who brought up the end of our group.

They weren't in any hurry to sit, though. In fact, they looked like they were in the presence of the president, rather than a soldier. They nodded solemnly at the man in front of the room, then walked briskly to the other sofa and sat stiffly on its cushions.

Was I doing something wrong?

Jacob and Isaac looked as confused as I felt. I didn't have time to ask, though, before the man getting all the respect spoke.

"SECURE THE SITE!"

Before I could even process what was happening, several soldiers entered the room. Some were holding long, slender handles that looked a lot like beeping selfie-sticks, going over every wall, corner, and crevice in the suite. Others were sticking small, black orbs on different surfaces of the room. A small, circular robot that looked like one of those vacuum-thingies was zooming around the floor and shining a laser across every surface.

After about thirty seconds, it was over, and they were gone.

"I apologize for that," the older man said. "The Chinese own the hotel now, and we can never be too safe. We have to ensure we're not being bugged, or worse, targeted."

I made eye contact with the others, who looked as shell-shocked as I was. The atmosphere of the room had shifted as uncomfortably as I did on the couch.

"Adrianna. Brooklyn. Jacob. Liam and Bree. Isaac." He looked each one of us in the eye as he addressed us.

How did he know all our names?

"My name is General Richards." He remained standing, a proud statue of patriotism in front of us, and his gaze never shifted, just as ours didn't on him. "I don't have a lot of time with you tonight, and I have a lot of material to cover, so I'm afraid I need to cut to the chase." He paused for a moment, like he was a substitute teacher waiting for the class to calm down.

"I know you think we asked you to come here and participate in the press conference because of the attack two nights ago," he continued. "But we've been planning this meeting for a very long time."

I glanced at the others' faces to see their reaction, but their attention was rapt, their focus on the high-ranking officer.

"In fact," he added. "I think this meeting was the reason behind the attack in the first place."

7

"WHY DO YOU NEED TO TALK TO... JUST US?"
Bree asked, her stare critical and questioning. "Why not all the 9/11 Babies?"

The general nodded, acknowledging the fairness of her question. "You would probably instinctively group yourself with the rest of the kids who had parents die in the attacks of 9/11. And while the entire group of 9/11 Babies have been branded heroes – appropriately, I might add – the six of you are different than the others who attended the dinner the other night."

He brought his hands in front of him, clasped them together casually in front of his broad torso. "In fact, I've been assigned to talk with you all this evening regarding this difference. But before I begin, please know I am about to tell you something that is quite possibly the most sensitive, most valuable, most protected secret in our military today."

My heart picked up speed. Suddenly I felt like I was sitting in the principal's office, in trouble but not quite sure why.

"Sensitive, how?" Adrianna asked.

The general pursed his lips. "It may take a while to explain. If I may, I'm going to ask for your patience as I attempt to do so." He walked slowly toward us, clicking a button to lower a white screen behind him. It hovered above the fireplace as if it were a painting.

"I was thinking about the best way to inform you on the topic, and I decided I should start with what you already know: what you see in the papers and what you've learned in History Class."

Ugh. History Class.

The six of us took turns shooting uneasy glances to one another, and the general, like so many teachers, pressed on, despite our obvious lack of enthusiasm.

"Even before the terrorist attacks on 9/11," he explained, "the United States of America was the world's leader in stopping terrorism. We continue to fulfill this role today."

As if to prove his point, the screen behind him exploded into pictures of ongoing warfare. Bombs, tanks, and horrific blasts filled the screen.

"Terrorists know no geographical boundaries," he continued as the pictures ceased, "but neither do we, when it comes to humanitarian issues. When the U.S. was young, we were spoiled by our location. Oceans separated us from the rest of the world's conflicts, so we were primarily concerned with our own. But after the atrocities of the Second World War were exposed, we knew we needed to make a global effort to combat the evil that existed outside our borders."

"The way we did this was to develop our best, most gifted citizens. We identified them at a young age and used our training facilities to nurture their gifts, pushing them as hard as they could be pushed, and making sure those gifts weren't wasted. Soon, we had enough of these gifted warriors to form an elite military group. Its earliest members named it The Crest."

"And what does this have to do with us?" I asked. I mean, it was nice of him to give us a history lesson and all, but the anticipation of why we were meeting with a general was killing me.

"Patience, Brooklyn," General Richards replied, his tone implying he was losing his own. "I promised I'd explain, and I'm about to." He turned to address the whole group again.

"You are six of the so-called '9/11 Babies'," he began. "But you are a special six. The hundreds of other 9/11 Babies lost their parents heroically on that horrible day, and you did, too. But your parents were more than heroes."

He paused, making sure he had our undivided attention. We weren't breathing; we couldn't.

"You would probably think of them as *superheroes*, members of the very same group I described."

His gaze intensified. "They were part of our most secret, gifted branch of the military: The Crest: Chosen, Rare, Elite… Superhuman and Triumphant."

8

THE LOUD GUFFAW CAME FROM ME. I COULDN'T
help it. As a group, we looked around at each other and
let out a collective breath.

Isaac spoke first, standing up. "Wow, superheroes,
huh? Is that the best you've got? Do we have to learn how
to melt bad guys with our eyes?" He smiled, and Jacob
and I laughed.

"I'm afraid it's not like your comic books," General
Richards replied, interrupting our laughter. "I know it
sounds like science fiction, but I assure you it's not."

I looked at the others in the group. Liam and Bree
were sitting straight-backed on the couch, silent and
straight-faced – their green eyes wide with wonder – and
Adrianna was following suit.

"You're talking about all our parents?" I asked. "An
elite group? C'mon, General."

Almost immediately a picture of my father was
projected on the screen, next to some kind of symbol
resembling a bird. I'd never seen either one: the symbol or
the photo. My dad looked about the same age as he was
when he had died, but he was wearing army fatigues and

had a stern look on his face. In the pictures I'd seen at home, he was always smiling. But something else about the picture was even weirder.

"My dad wasn't in the Army," I stated. I'd never seen him wearing camo like he was in the picture, had never even seen a picture of him in a uniform.

"He was, Brooklyn," General Richards replied. "He just didn't make it known to your family." He clicked to the next slide.

"Rex Blackburn," he said pointedly, not even needing to read the information off of the screen. "Brooklyn, New York. Cover: Software Engineer. Gift: Strength."

The general's eyes were piercing, as no-nonsense as his tone. "Your father worked for the U.S. Army, Brooklyn. He was born with incredible strength, more than any other human has ever known."

I sat there with my mouth open, stunned silent. I couldn't deny that if superheroes existed, it'd make perfect sense if my father was one. Everyone knew he loved to lift weights and work out, that he'd won a ton of competitions, and he definitely had the body-builder physique. But superhuman strength?

"So how strong was he?" I asked, "I mean, was he like the Hulk?"

The general left his spot and walked over to mine. "Stronger than you can possibly imagine," he replied. "He could definitely break buses."

Breaching some kind of protocol, I'm sure, he extended a hand to my shoulder. "On September 11th, 2001, he was working on the 74th floor in the south tower."

That was true, and the fact that the general had that information so readily available in his mind – felt like a bucket of ice water in my face.

"When the north tower was hit," the general continued, "everyone in the second tower was told to stay put. Your father had called us to let us know he was prepared to use his gift as needed. In that moment, we couldn't see what was ahead, so he stayed."

"And then the second plane hit, just above your father on the 77th to 85th floors. He immediately contacted me again and told me how the building shook so violently he feared it would collapse. Only one stairwell was open; the other two were blocked because of the crash."

The general stared at the wall behind me, just above my shoulder, but faltered only slightly as he recounted that day. "He used his power to hold up the 74th floor – and everything above it, Brooklyn – so as many people as possible could make it down the stairs." His gaze left the spot on the wall and settled back on me. "For fifty-five minutes he did the impossible: he held up a skyscraper. And he saved countless lives in the process."

"Unfortunately, he couldn't hold it forever. People kept climbing up the stairs – not down – expecting a roof rescue that never came. So the weight your father held got heavier and heavier. The helicopters we had couldn't operate amidst the smoke, you see, so a rooftop rescue was impossible." He paused for a moment.

"More time passed, and even members of The Crest have their physical limitations. Your father did all he could do, Brooklyn, but eventually he couldn't hold the building up anymore, and the tower crumbled to the ground. If it wasn't for the efforts of Rex Blackburn, it would have fallen immediately after the impact."

The general placed his hand over my own. I tried my best to be composed, even though my eyes were tearing up, making my vision blurred and unfocused.

"He died saving people, Brooklyn. Fifty-four human souls from his floor alone were saved because of him that day, and hundreds more because they could evacuate while he held the tower up."

I'd been holding my breath – hadn't even realized it. I looked down to my lap, then up at the screen, at the picture of my father, who certainly looked like the hero this general had just described.

But looking like a superhero didn't mean he was one.

Right?

Was I crazy, even allowing myself to consider it? Could I honestly believe in something I once believed as a kid?

He'd always been perfect in my eyes: faultless because I'd never witnessed any imperfections. I'd conjured up the image of the best man possible whenever I thought of him. To even entertain the thought that he was a true superhero with more-than-human powers wasn't that different than what my heart had been doing all these years.

It was just my brain telling me it couldn't be true.

The picture behind General Richards changed again. The symbol of the bird remained, but instead of my father's picture, a Hispanic male, also in army fatigues, gazed unsmiling from the screen.

"Alberto Montoya," General Richards said, walking over to Adrianna. "Queens, New York. Cover: Firefighter. Gift: Endurance."

He held Adrianna's gaze with the same intensity he'd used to hold my own. "Your father died on duty that day as a firefighter, Adrianna. But he was also on duty for the Army. His gift was endurance. Alberto won marathons, slept only a few hours a week, and volunteered at multiple organizations on top of holding down a full-time job. He could do it all because he could function at an extremely productive level for much longer than any other human. On September 11th, 2001, he trekked up and down hundreds of flights of stairs, carrying twenty-six injured people to safety. He was carrying what would have been the 27th survivor – and surely would have saved more – when the south tower collapsed."

Adrianna blinked back at the soldier and swallowed thickly. I wondered what she was thinking.

Another click and another picture appeared on the screen next to the symbol: a smaller white man with black hair and a black goatee. "Maximillian Jay. Greenwich Village. Cover: Air Marshal. Gift: Prophecy."

He turned to Jacob. "We'd received intelligence Al Qaeda was trying to gain access to our commercial airlines, but we'd thought it was through their employees: namely, pilots. Jacob, your father, Maximillian, had the power of prophecy. Max could tell what you were going to do five minutes in advance. If you were second-guessing yourself, though, his power would be a little less accurate, only giving him five seconds of warning. Just prior to September 11th, your father assumed the cover of being an air marshal, honing in on the pilots' minds to make sure they weren't intending to harm their passengers."

The general paused, but only for a moment. "Jacob, on September 11th, 2001, your father was a passenger on United Flight 93. He was focusing his power on the pilots, not the passengers, but about thirty minutes into the flight, the hijackers became resolute about their plan, so determined that Maximillian picked up on their evil. He could see very clearly what they wanted to do. They wanted to kill all of our elected representatives in the Capitol building, to create mass chaos in the days after 9/11. Your father, Jacob – along with a few other incredibly brave civilians – made the decision to fight the terrorists. As a result, they saved the lives of our countries' leaders, but also sealed their own fate by losing altitude in the struggle. The plane went down in a field in Pennsylvania."

He knelt down, making sure he was eye-to-eye with Jacob. "He had the power of prophecy, Jacob. He could tell they wanted everyone on that flight, and everyone in the Capitol, to die. And he chose to sacrifice his life to make sure that didn't happen. It was an incredible act of heroism."

Tears welled in Jacob's eyes, and he looked into his lap, hiding them.

"Liam and Bree, the oldest of the group." The old man nodded respectfully to the siblings. "The miracle twins born on 9/11."

I looked at Liam and my heart felt heavy. "You were born the same day your dad died?"

"Our dad didn't die," Bree said. My blank stare must have explained how confused I was.

"Your fathers passed away while you were all developing in your mothers' wombs," General Richards

32

clarified. "But Liam and Bree didn't lose their father to the 9/11 attacks. They lost their mother."

Behind him the picture changed to a slight, stunning, red-haired woman with porcelain skin and emerald eyes. "Molly O'Dell," the general introduced. "New York City. Cover: Emergency Medical Technician (EMT). Gift: Healing."

General Richards approached the siblings.

"Your mother was called to the towers as an EMT in order to help the injured. She could heal anyone with a non-fatal wound, but her power had repercussions. She would heal others, but take on a portion of their injury or ailment herself. That morning, she saw more people suffer than she'd ever seen in her life, and she couldn't stand it, so she healed many more than she ever had before. As an organization, The Crest was more disjointed on that day than any other, and no one was overseeing her to make sure she didn't take it too far. Unfortunately, that's exactly what she did. She healed so many people – took on so much physical distress – that it was too much for her body to handle. Bystanders said she appeared to die of a heart attack, but the truth is, several of her organs stopped working when she healed the injuries of victims."

He met Liam and Bree's respectful gaze. "You two were born via emergency C-Section that very day. While we couldn't save your mother's life, we owed it to her to save yours." He let a smile escape, "And to see you, Liam, so tall and strong and thriving, is absolutely amazing. For a while, we thought Bree was going to be the only infant to pull through."

Liam's cheeks flushed crimson, at the compliment or the attention, I wasn't sure.

"And last, Isaac." General Richards continued after none of us spoke up. I wasn't sure I could handle another story. It was all so much to take in.

A picture of an older black man with graying hair, long and lean in body type, came on the screen. "You're the son of Demarcus Jackson. Demarcus was particularly effective in the Army. He was probably the most versatile of all The Crest members, working in basic training camps, international leadership summits, as well as interrogation rooms. Isaac, your father – the police detective – had the power of tranquility."

"Tranquility?" Jacob interrupted. He looked at Isaac apologetically. "No offense, but everyone else you've talked about had these crazy physical and mental capabilities. And Isaac's father had the job of … relaxing?"

"Don't jump to conclusions," the General warned. "Demarcus was one of our most valuable assets. While brute force, the power of healing and endurance, and mental telepathy are certainly formidable, emitting peace during times of warfare can be the biggest weapon of all. Demarcus was the main reason we never went to war with the Soviet Union in the late 80s, and he was one of the reasons our conflicts with other countries were settled peacefully as well. He had the most amazing ability to calm individuals, which worked in a few Presidents' favor during many tense meetings with leaders of other countries."

He turned his attention back to Isaac. "On September 11th, your father was called to duty with the NYPD, where he worked as a detective. Once on the scene, he saw people jumping from the buildings, which were going up in flames."

"They had no other choice," General Richards explained, noting the look on our faces. "It was burn alive or jump, and many chose the less painful death. Demarcus heard their shrieks, and running against the tide of survivors exiting the buildings, he sprinted up the stairwell in the south tower and got as close to the jumpers from both towers as he could – close enough so they could benefit from his power. Then he emitted pure peace from his soul so they could leave this life without fear. That's what he was doing when the tower crumbled to the ground."

The general punctuated the sad atmosphere with a thick swallow and clearing of his throat. "I'm sorry," he apologized. "What happened that day – the barbarianism and violence and suffering – it's still hard to talk about. It haunts me at night. So does the loss of your parents. You see, I knew all of them, had worked closely with them. To talk about them again, to relive their sacrifice, and to see their gifts in all of you…it's rather emotional."

"Wait," Adrianna interjected as she wiped away tears. "What do you mean, you 'see their gifts in us'?"

The general smiled slightly. "Very observant, Adrianna. I do see their gifts in you. And that's the real purpose behind this meeting."

9

"I TOLD YOU THE CREST WAS AN EXTREMELY elite group of highly trained and gifted individuals in the army," he divulged. "But unfortunately, it's a group that's dwindling."

He clicked to another slide. This time, pictures of hundreds of men and women in army fatigues shuffled past, so fast I couldn't study them. The last slide had one word:

MURDERED.

It was below the symbol we'd seen alongside our parents' pictures – the one of the bird.

Bree broke the solemn silence. "All those people died?"

General Richards nodded slowly. "Yes. We lost our best and brightest on 9/11, and since then, the international terrorist communities have banded together to target our remaining Crest members. To date, over two hundred of them have perished."

"Wait, so there are hundreds of these – uh, superheroes – in the U.S.?" Bree asked.

"Hundreds of Crest members? Yes," the general responded. "I know it seems like a lot, but when you consider the population of the United States is over three hundred million, the number of people working for us in The Crest is very few. And because they're being hunted, we're in a dire situation."

"We do have a few things working in our favor, though," he continued. "The vast majority of Crest members' locations and identities are still unknown to the terrorists, and they don't know all our secrets. Unfortunately, though, we believe they know about you."

"About us?" My voice was trembling, and so were my hands.

"We think that's the reason behind the attack on Friday night, that they detonated different devices to dispose of you. Thankfully, they made a few mistakes, but you also made it nearly impossible. You're too fast. Too strong." His eyes met mine, and I tried unsuccessfully to calm my heart rate.

Dispose, he'd said.

Of us.

The general walked to the empty chair by the fireplace and sat. He laced his fingers together and rested his elbows on his legs before he continued. "They don't know everything about you, though. For example, they don't know the powers of The Crest are completely innate, that you're born with them. They believe we are producing our Crest members in a laboratory, that we're creating humans with these powers to use in biological warfare."

"Of course, they're wrong," he continued. "All of the members of The Crest got their powers by the age of twenty, and their superhuman abilities are present in their lineage: inherited from their parents or grandparents. It's the reason we chose a phoenix to represent the members of this secret division." He pointed to the symbol on the screen. "When others die, their children rise from the ashes and become heroes themselves. Their powers are in place by the time they become adults, and most showed signs of their power long before that."

"Your father, for instance," he said, nodding to Adrianna, "was a cross country and long distance swimming champion in high school. And your mother," he added, nodding to the twins, "she used to sneak into hospitals to cure people. She knew she had a gift even when she was in middle school."

The general sat straighter in his chair. "You're here today because we think it's quite possible all of you have inherited the same gifts as your parents."

The room was quiet, and I wondered if the other five were thinking the same thing as me.

Were they also recalling their own achievements, their own gifts?

In a span of a minute, I remembered them all:

I remembered lifting a full bookshelf in preschool so I could grab a toy that had fallen behind it.

When I was in third grade, I was riding home on the bus one day when the most athletic boy in my older brother's class challenged me to an arm wrestle. I creamed him without even trying.

I thought of my championship medals from all of my swim meets, the school records I held in pushups and the flexed arm hang.

I thought of the night of the attack, when I threw Liam ahead of me as we fled. Could that have been more than just adrenaline?

Sure, I showed the same athletic prowess as my father. It was something I'd always been proud of.

But could I really have superhuman strength? The same superhuman strength my father had?

Was this even all true?

I closed my eyes and let the words of General Richards sink in, let the image of my father and the other parents be seared into my brain.

And I knew.

Everything I'd been told throughout my childhood, every story I'd ever heard about my father were half-truths: alluding to his full capabilities, yet never truly revealing them.

I knew what the general had said about him had to be true, because, deep inside, it was the truth about me as well.

"What do you need from us?"

My voice, unlike the rest of me, was weak.

General Richards' face relaxed. "We need you to become soldiers in the U.S. Army and join The Crest as soon as you can. You have to start training immediately, to hone your gifts and sharpen your skills, and we'll need to identify your weaknesses and make sure you can compensate for them as well. A terrorist organization is after you and has identified you as a threat." He drew a deep breath. "I can't emphasize this enough: Another attack is imminent. Your country needs you *now*."

"But make no mistake," he added, almost as an afterthought. "By agreeing to help us in serving your country, you're putting yourself at risk, too. You'll be the first line of our defense, like our infantry units. Unlike them, you'll be hidden in the shadows of the United States Army, protected above all other soldiers. But even with our highest degree of protection, you are still risking your lives to be on the front lines in our battle against evil. You are willingly leaving behind the title of being the infants of 9/11, and becoming U.S. Army Infantry instead."

10

THE ELEVATOR DINGED, ANNOUNCING OUR
arrival to the main floor. It'd been a couple hours since
we'd left the press conference, so I figured the hotel
would be emptied. Sure enough, the atmosphere was
quieter, and only a few people were left in the lobby. We
stepped onto the marble-mosaic flooring, still in a daze, as
our family members met us with congratulatory hugs and
squeals of delight.

"WEST POINT!" my mother exclaimed. She framed
my face with her hands and squealed. "I CAN'T EVEN
BELIEVE IT!"

I blushed and looked at my toes. "Mom, stop," I
requested, knowing she'd ignore me. She tried
unsuccessfully to drape an arm over my shoulder. Even
on her tip-toes, she couldn't do it, so she put it around my
waist, instead. We walked that way toward the exit, leaving
the others behind us.

"This is a huge opportunity," she gushed. "HUGE."

The doors opened automatically in front of us. The
blast of cool autumn air was just what I needed. I glanced
nervously toward the bellman stationed at the entry,

hoping he hadn't overheard my mother spouting her pride. Our training at the prestigious military academy was supposed to be a secret.

Our living parents didn't know about the possibility that we had *powers*, and they didn't know about the powers of our late parents, either. They'd been told we were attending West Point because we were exceptional.

And while we were exceptional, none of us were exceptional enough to attend the academy itself. We didn't have the grades, the leadership skills, the athleticism, or talents the academy demanded.

In reality, it was the academy that had what we needed: the tools and space we needed in order to train properly, in private. So while attending West Point was our cover, it would never be my Alma Mater because I hadn't earned a rightful place in their ranks.

"Don't worry, I didn't tell a soul." She reassured me with a dismissive wave of her hand after seeing the horrified look on my face. "Not even your brother! He went home before I could share the good news. But I can't believe you didn't even tell me you applied!"

"I – uh – didn't really *apply*, Mom. It's more of a special program they're offering for me," I explained weakly. "My grades haven't been great, and that matters a lot when going to West Point."

My mom clicked her tongue. "Grades, schmades," she said indifferently. "I always knew your intellect couldn't be measured the same way as other kids'."

Right, I thought. Where was that motto during the last round of report cards? I'd been grounded for a week for getting Cs and Ds.

"Anyway," she said, looking up to me as we made our way down Park Avenue. "Your dad would be so proud," she said sincerely. "He went to West Point, you know."

I stopped dead in my tracks. "I didn't know that," I replied honestly. I forced myself to walk again. "You never mentioned it before."

"Well, it was in his earlier years," she said briskly, with another wave of her hand. She whistled loudly for a taxi.

"I wish you would have told me," I commented, almost whispering. "It would have been nice to know that about him."

"Oh, honey," my mom replied, placing a hand on my elbow. "I'm sorry. I didn't think it was a huge thing to tell you about. He only spent a few years in the Army. Then he met me and settled down." For a second, her stare blanked, and her eyes looked past me to a place I couldn't see.

"Anyway," she said, focusing on me once again, "Tell me more. What do you think? Do you want to go? You've never acted like you wanted to before, but I know you'd like all the…the sports-stuff they do there."

The sports-stuff. Right, Mom. I want to attend the most prestigious military academy in the world so I can play a pick-up game of basketball. It's not like I need to save the world from terrorists or anything.

Or protect myself and my family from a future attack.

I bit my tongue and swallowed the sarcastic remark.

"I do love the sports-stuff about West Point," I mimicked, trying to feign pride as much as possible. "The pay stipend is awesome. And they'll help me get a good job after I graduate, which is cool, too."

My mom beamed. "West Point is soooo hard to get into!"

She must have known a little bit on the admittance process, but it was obvious she had no clue how freaking hard the application process actually was.

Most cadets spent years building their portfolio and working hard to prove they were deserving of the honor.

I was going there by default, and truth be told, I kind of felt guilty about it.

But General Richards said there were always extenuating circumstances when it came to Crest members going to West Point to train.

Like the fact that none of us had wanted to become soldiers.

Or the fact that Bree and Jacob claimed to have absolutely NO athletic capability.

Or the fact that I was on academic probation at my school.

But the general didn't seem to think it'd be an issue. "Exceptions have been made in the past," he'd explained. "And they'll be made again. Desperate times call for desperate measures."

Which meant lying was okay. Right?

"I guess my athletic ability and the fact that Dad died in the September 11th attacks allowed me to be considered," I whispered.

"Wow," my mom said, obviously spellbound by the gift the government had just given us. A taxi came to a stop at our feet.

"Yeah."

"Well, how many of you are going?" she asked after getting into the vehicle. "I understand they offered the deal to six of you?"

"Yeah, there were six of us there. But I don't know if they'll all say yes," I answered. "I guess they're probably talking it over with their families, too."

She reached for my hand, but I jerked my head toward the cab driver, hoping she'd take the hint and stop talking in front of him. I've never been one to talk in front of strangers, and it felt like an even bigger deal now.

My mom understood. "Should we talk over the details tomorrow?"

"Sure," I replied, relieved to be done with the conversation. I turned toward the window and leaned my head on it, embracing the coolness of the smooth surface. My alert and somewhat-scared expression gazed back at me.

Maybe I was made for this life, whatever it was I was signing up for. Maybe I was made to be pushed, to sacrifice for the good of the country. It was honorable and courageous. I should feel proud.

But I was still uncertain.

Liam, Bree, and Adrianna had been ecstatic about telling their families. The twins' dad was active military, and Adrianna's uncles and grandpa were too. They knew their families would be supportive.

Isaac and Jacob weren't so sure. Their moms weren't anti-military by any means, but they were definitely pro-peace.

"I don't know what my mom's gonna say about me leaving school to go and train to fight," Isaac had told me as we were waiting for General Richards to sign off on our application.

"Just tell her who will be in charge of us," Adrianna advised.

"Why would that make a difference?" I asked.

"General Richards?"

She'd waited for my reaction. There was none. "Come on guys. He's the highest ranking military official in the U.S. He's on the news all the time."

"Oh," I replied simply, turning to Isaac. "That explains it. I don't watch the news."

Liam chimed in. "That's okay," he said, smiling his gorgeous smile. "Neither do we. But our dad's a captain in the Army, so we know the rankings. We saw the insignia on his shirt and knew we weren't being called for something minor. Whatever it was he had to talk to us about, it had to be a big deal."

So that explained the reaction of the twins and Adrianna when they walked into the Presidential Suite, and it probably explained why they seemed so happy-go-lucky about the prospect of joining the military themselves.

Why couldn't I be that sure?

It wasn't like I was sad to leave my home, or even my friends from school. In fact, I was kind of excited for a change. But leaving my home behind meant leaving normal behind, too. Even though I'd always known I was different, I'd always been able to fake it. I allowed myself to excel at sports, but only to the point where I'd barely win, barely get a record. By agreeing to go to West Point – by allowing myself to be pushed – I was going to be shoved right out of my old life and into a new one where everything was scary and unfamiliar.

General Richards had told us not to take the decision lightly. He explained that at West Point, cadets were expected to excel in academics, athletics, and perform duties in the Army, and while we weren't interacting often with the cadets, we were expected to behave like them.

"You won't have the free time college kids do," he cautioned. "You study to learn content before class, not after. And you are ready at 7:00 a.m. every morning. You can't talk in the hallways, or be loud in the mess hall. An ongoing joke is there are more rules at West Point than there are at a maximum security prison." He smiled. "It's only funny because it's true."

"So what happens if we break those rules? Ten to twenty in the pen?" Jacob joked.

"You won't want to break them," was the general's curt reply as he turned to leave. "Let Major McCoy know what your decision is tonight – before you leave, if possible. We're in a dangerous situation as a country. We need you. And to put it bluntly, you need us, too."

They needed us. Our country was in danger.

And we needed them, because we were in danger, too.

That thought plagued me on the way home. It followed me into my house, up the stairs, and into my bedroom, as I tried desperately to fall asleep.

11

I HAD TO BE READY BY NOON – MY PICK-UP time by West Point officials.

I didn't even bother to set my alarm clock, knowing I only needed a couple of hours to pack my 'essentials', eat some breakfast, and say my goodbyes.

My mom had stormed into my room a little after nine, flicking my bedroom lights. She sat on my bed, her eyes wide and scared.

"Why do you have to leave now?"

"Mmmmmm?" I yawned. It wasn't because I was tired, although I hadn't fallen asleep until almost three o'clock. I was stalling. I needed to wake up fully and think before I spoke. General Richards had stressed the importance of being careful with our answers.

"I just got off the phone with a West Point Officer."

"Really?" I asked, propping myself up with my elbows. "But it's early…" I searched my nightstand. "It's only nine o'clock."

"They said they had to call early," my mother answered, "Because you are leaving today. Today! But didn't the school year already start? After all, it is a military college, right? Why wouldn't the exams you passed pertain to next year? Why this year, after the classes have already started?"

Because we need the protection, I thought.

"It *is* a college, Mom," I replied smoothly, pulling the covers back over my head, praying the lie I was about to tell would be believable. I'd thought they had told her this the night before.

"I'm not taking the courses most of the cadets take. All six of us are seniors, so we'll be taking college entrance courses. Think of it like a high school on steroids, preparing me for the courses that will get me college credit. Those prep courses aren't available at most high schools." I took a shaky breath and exhaled heavily into my pillow. "Major McCoy will be able to tell you all about it."

We had been told to keep our explanations as simple as possible, that he'd speak with each concerned parent individually if they were suspicious. And I definitely had a suspicious parent.

She was silent, so I pulled the covers back down to see if she bought it.

She nodded, and I turned my back to her again, relieved.

"And what about basic training? Isn't that something you need to complete?"

"We're doing that at the same time," I replied, almost too quickly. "The easier classes will make it possible for me to do both. It'll save me time in the long run, which is why being accepted at this time with the scholarship and the stipend and everything was such a huge deal."

That wasn't a complete lie. We were undergoing physical and survival training at the same time as taking classes. The difference was our classes were going to be used to hone our skills, not work toward a degree or prepare us to be regular officers like the real cadets. And we'd be taking the classes either individually or within our group of six, separated from the college-like courses the rest of them took.

"Are all of the kids who passed the exams taking the same courses as you?"

"I don't think so." I could respond to this honestly. "I think just me and a couple of others will be getting extra help."

My cheeks were flushed because I hated lying. But my mom must have thought they were red because I was embarrassed of my weakness, of how poorly I'd done in school so far this year. She immediately saw my story as believable once again, and her whole face brightened.

"Then this is a great opportunity for you, Brooklyn. You get to go to one of the best schools and get the extra help you need in order to stay there. I hope you realize how lucky you are."

Translation: Don't blow it.

"I understand," I assured her.

I waited for her to leave, then ran to the bathroom in the hallway to brush my teeth and take a quick shower. I pulled on a pair of sweats and, seeing it was now ten o'clock, decided to have some breakfast before packing.

My hand slid down the painted wooden banister as I made my way down the stairs into our living room.

Bryce was sitting on the couch with a gaming headset on, his eyes fixed on the flat screen in front of him. An open bag of chips lay on the coffee table, its entrails leading to his lap. The TV's volume was turned way up, assaulting my ears with a spray of make-believe bullets. It was so loud it temporarily drowned out all my other senses.

But it only took a couple of seconds for my brain to register there was another boy sitting in my living room. It was my brother's friend, Jace.

Who happened to be my ex.

We had dated for an entire year, up until six months ago. He'd been my first boyfriend, one I wasn't afraid to be myself around, one I swore I would marry someday.

But he broke my heart. I'd shown up at a mutual friend's party to see him making out with another girl.

And not just any other girl; he was kissing the freaking head cheerleader and Homecoming Queen.

What was he doing here?

He knew my worst insecurities. He knew how awkward I felt, being the height I was and having the strength I had. He knew how I sometimes wished I could be one of those cute, petite girls who men seemed to flock to.

I'd confided all of this to him, and afterwards he would always assure me I was perfect just the way I was. And I actually believed him – until I saw him making out with a five-foot-nothing head cheerleader.

And just like that, I went from being completely in love to completely heartbroken. I refused his phone calls, burned his letters, and even changed the route to my classes in order to avoid seeing him. I made my brother promise to never let him in our home, had even requested he un-friend Jace altogether for what he'd done to me.

51

But here he was. In my house.

"Hi Brooklyn," Jace said, his face stoic, his baby blue eyes trying their best to melt me into a puddle all over again.

My mouth in a thin, straight line, I gave my brother a look I hoped would hurt and sprinted back up the stairs.

12

TEARS STUNG MY EYES. I WAS RIPPING MY clothes from their place in my closet and throwing them into my oversized duffle bag when I heard a knock.

"You can't come in!" I yelled.

The door opened, anyway.

"I said you're not welcome here," I snapped at Bryce. "Maybe you should learn to use that phrase, too."

"Brooke," Bryce began.

"That's not my name," I interrupted. "I hate being called that. Which you would know, if you even tried to give a damn about my feelings."

He sighed. "This was the first time he's come over since you guys broke up. I thought you were over it, and since you usually sleep in, I didn't think it'd hurt anything to have him here."

"Well it did," I retorted. "It hurt me to have you betray me. You're supposed to be my big brother! The big brother I *wish* I had would never let anyone in his house who had hurt his sister. Ever."

"I didn't invite him over to hang out, Brooklyn." Bryce let himself in and sat on my bed, next to my open bag. "It's mid-morning, for God's sake. I just needed help with my Xbox, and he's good with that stuff." He paused for a brief moment. "It's been six months, Brooklyn. I thought you were getting better, so I didn't think there was any harm in asking if he'd come over. That's it. He'd honestly just finished fixing it when you walked in."

I rolled my eyes and began furiously packing again.

"And what's this I hear about you leaving?" he said.

"Not that you even care," I said, still feeling sorry for myself, "But I just got accepted to West Point."

"West Point?" He laughed. I threw him another death stare. Not only was he going to make sure my heart was trampled on today, but he wanted to make sure my ego was crushed, too.

He cleared his throat immediately. "Wait, seriously? The military academy? So Mom's for real?"

"Yep."

"Well, how did you? I mean, how could you even – "

"I took a test, Bryce," I said, continuing to ice him with a glare. "And I passed. Aced it, actually. Turns out I have potential to be a killer soldier, no pun intended. Lucky for you, they said I could start training right away."

"Brooklyn." My brother rose, eye to eye with me. "You're leaving? Seriously?"

"Yes."

"But why go now? Why can't you wait until the next semester starts?"

I sighed. "They want me in a remedial program to bring my academics up to par."

"Why? You're smart."

"Well, duh," I said, cracking a smile. "But y'know, my grades weren't great my last semester."

For a while, the break up messed me up. I couldn't concentrate on anything, and I'd skipped school almost every day. My biggest fear was running into Jace or his new girlfriend. I wanted to hide in my room forever, but Bryce had helped me come up with the idea of alternative routes to my classes so I could avoid running into them both. It helped me cope with being in school, but my concentration in classes definitely suffered right along with my heart. I'd always been an A or B student, but after the breakup, I either failed or almost failed all of my classes.

Bryce grabbed my elbow. "So this is what you want? To go to a military school? You never acted like it was something you wanted to do before."

I shrugged. "I haven't ever known what I wanted, Bryce. But maybe I do now. Maybe I want to be known for being more than a 9/11 baby. Maybe I want to learn how to impact this world rather than sleepwalk my way through it. And maybe going to West Point is a way to do that."

He fell silent. I continued packing, and he kept me company with his quiet self as I finished. When I was done, I heaved the bag onto my shoulder and made my way to the door.

"I know you're probably doing the right thing," Bryce said, rising to meet me. "But something isn't sitting well with me about all of this." He shook his dark hair out of his eyes. "Do what you have to do, Brookey. But be careful, k?"

He must have meant it. I hadn't heard this level of emotion come from him since he started playing video games all the time, and honestly, I think the last time he called me "Brookey" was when I was in elementary school.

"Thanks Bryce," I said, giving him a one arm hug. "I'll miss you."

"I'll miss ya, too, Sis."

And with that, I went to the living room to wait for the van that was coming to deliver me to West Point, an hour and a completely different life away.

13

THE VAN WAS PLAIN WHITE, WITH NO
lettering or design on it whatsoever. Major McCoy
hopped out of the driver's seat to load my bags so I could
say goodbye to my family.

"Why didn't they send you a school van?" My mom
asked, looking unsure and all skeptical again. I wasn't sure
how much longer I could make up lies. Luckily, I didn't
have to.

"None were available," Major McCoy interjected
smoothly. "Our athletic teams are held in high regard at
West Point, and this weekend the vehicles were used in a
few different competitions. Monday's the day they're
cleaned and readied for the next week, so we had to rent
this van today to bring the cadets in for Beast training."

"Beast?" my mother asked, shifting her eyes
momentarily on me.

Crap. Guess who forgot to use that term?

"Yes, Beast," Major McCoy replied, smiling. "I'm sure
Brooklyn forgot to mention it in her excitement last night.
In fact, I'm sure this is all incredibly strange and stressful

for you." He extended his hand. "I'm Major McCoy, and I'll be working with Brooklyn quite a bit once we arrive at West Point."

After shaking my mom's hand, he reached into the van and retrieved a file folder. "I'd love to speak with you more regarding her acceptance into West Point. Do you have a few minutes?"

My mom nodded and followed him over to the steps in front of our brownstone house. Bryce followed, too, acting all overprotective of me. They all spoke for a few moments while I stared down my street, trying to sear all my memories from my childhood into my mind.

My eyes roved two houses down, where Martha McClanahan baked fresh cookies every Sunday. For this reason, we looked forward to Sundays more than any other day, when the sweet smell of melted chocolate would waft its way to our open windows. When I was little, I was audacious enough to ring her doorbell and ask her for some. As I grew up and learned more about what's appropriate and what's not, I had stopped asking. Before long, we found a small plate of cookies in our mailbox on Sunday nights. Since then we'd referred to the treats as our 'Sunday mail.'

I was going to miss getting those cookies. I closed my eyes and breathed deeply through my nose, hoping to smell them just one last time. But I only smelled the stench of exhaust from the tailpipe of the van, and as if on cue, a horn blared a couple of blocks over, jolting my senses back to the present.

"Here's all the information you need regarding Brooklyn's stay at West Point," I heard Major McCoy say from behind me. I turned toward him, my mother, and my brother as they rose from the stairs and headed back toward the van. Major McCoy handed my mother a thick folder.

"If you have any doubts or any concerns whatsoever, you can get ahold of me," Major McCoy continued. "My contact information is here." He pointed to a sheet of paper in the folder. "Brooklyn's contact with you will be spotty because of how much time she will be putting in to catch up with the other cadets," he continued. "See this website? And see the personal code below it?" He pointed to the bottom of the card. "Just visit the site and enter the code to view pictures of Brooklyn doing various activities: classes, physical examinations, survival skills training - all that stuff. You'll also be kept up to date with her progress."

For the first time all day, I saw my mother's face brighten.

"Thank you so much, Major McCoy," she gushed. She turned to me and held the sides of my face with her warm hands. "You take care of yourself," she said firmly. She brought her petite frame up to whisper in my ear. "And no matter what they say, you can leave, Brooklyn. Always."

I wondered if she was right. The contract we'd signed last night seemed binding.

She quickly kissed my cheek and headed back into the house. In a trance, I hugged Bryce goodbye as he told me the same thing, and then I got into the van.

Adrianna and Jacob were already there, taking up the opposite sides of the back seat. It was silent, the air electric with the anticipation of what was to come. Even though I was wearing my go-to Sunday sweats, I felt as uncomfortable as I had at the dinner on

Friday night. I sat in the seat in front of them. Nodding to them and receiving a curt nod in return, I retrieved my phone from my backpack, put my earphones in, and found my favorite workout playlist. I let the angst-filled lyrics scream at me. Call me weird, but when I get all worked up, that kind of music calms me down.

I replied a quick "Love you, too" to my mom's text when it popped up, but shoved the phone back into my pocket so I could ignore the rest of my notifications. Might as well get used to it — my phone would be taken from me as soon as I checked in at the academy.

Before I knew it, we were in the thick of the city. Traffic crept and people scurried about as if they were ants at a picnic. Everyone was always in a rush to get somewhere, to do something, even on a Sunday in NYC. It was one of the reasons I usually opted out of going downtown. I preferred a calmer environment.

We pulled up next to a tall building, complete with a doorman out front. Liam and Bree exited and excitedly hugged an older man, probably their father. He was tall and well-built: almost like an older Liam, but with darker skin and eyes. He was following behind them and beaming proudly.

But when Major McCoy surfaced, his demeanor became more rigid. After a much shorter exchange than the one he had with my mother, the twins' dad waved his proud goodbye as his children heaved their duffle bags into the back and got in, sitting ahead of me.

They were so excited, so full of positivity. The opposite of me.

"Hey," Liam breathed as he sat directly in front of me, showcasing his friendly grin. I nervously pulled out my ear buds.

"Hi," I said simply. Suddenly I was annoyed I wasn't wearing any makeup. I never regretted not wearing makeup. I brought a hand up to my face to shield my imperfections and my unwanted embarrassment.

"You think you're ready for this?" he asked, nodding toward the front of the van, where Major McCoy was navigating through heavy traffic.

I shrugged. "As ready as anyone else would be, I guess," I answered. "You know, if they were leaving high school to become superheroes."

His grin broadened. "Right," he said. "Superheroes." He shook his head. "It's such a trip, isn't it?"

I swallowed nervously and nodded, looking into my lap at my hands. I couldn't think of anything to say.

My emotions about everything – finding out who my dad was, who I was, leaving my family behind, joining the Army – all of my feelings about what had happened in the last twenty-four hours… they were stronger than any words I knew.

Bree, Adrianna, and Jacob seemed to feel the same way. The atmosphere changed dramatically after Liam's question, his broad generalization about how crazy our situation was.

I put my earphones in again, trying to drown out the unknowns with sheer volume. We drove for a long time, and I stared out the window, focusing on the music traveling up the wires to my ears, fast and loud.

Before I knew it, we had made our way out of the city, its skyscrapers a scenic backdrop to our van on the freeway. Isaac was the only one we hadn't picked up, and I wondered how far away he lived. We traveled next to the Hudson, and as the river went south, we made our way north, where the houses got bigger and the land in between them more rural.

Eventually we veered left, crossing the Hudson over a small bridge. Major McCoy slowed the vehicle, turning into a town called Stony Point. We pulled in front of a modest two-story home, situated far from the quiet road we were on.

Isaac was already on the front porch when we slowed to a stop. Behind him were a man and a woman, with four small children hugging their legs. I pulled out my earphones. Somehow, I thought I'd get a better look without them in my ears. The windows in the van were down, and my clammy body welcomed the breeze coming from Isaac's yard to the stifling vehicle.

It was like a scene from a postcard, or the perfect ending to a sappy movie. Isaac loaded his bag into the back of the van and returned to his family, where he hugged each adult and tossed each child up in the air. They giggled hysterically and begged for more, and he promised he would continue the game as soon as he returned. He waved a general goodbye once he left their sides and climbed into the front seat.

"Hey guys!" he breathed, smiling widely.

"Hey," we all said in unison.

"Good trip so far?" He directed the question at all of us.

"Sure," Liam and I replied.

"Yep." That was from Jacob in the back seat.

"It's pretty here!" Bree chimed.

He nodded.

"Are those all your little brothers and sisters?" Bree asked.

"Yep."

"How old are they?' I interjected.

"The oldest is five. The twins are four, and the youngest – Maurice – is two."

"They're adorable." It was sappy, but the kids were seriously cute, and they were a good distraction from the adventure we were about to embark upon. And actually, I was thankful for their interruption and the lift in the atmosphere that followed. Up until we came to Isaac's house, we'd been tense and edgy – all of us – preferring silence over chatter.

Wait.

My eyes widened.

"Isaac," I said, my voice almost accusing. "You already have your gift, don't you?"

"Excuse me?"

"Your gift!" I looked at Adrianna and Jacob behind me. "His dad had the power of tranquility, remember?"

"Yeah," Jacob said, realization kicking in. "We were all quiet and freaked out by all of this, and then we came here, and we're happy." He leaned forward toward Isaac, sitting straighter in his seat.

Isaac beamed back. "I guess," he said, shrugging his shoulders. "Truth is, I've had it for a while." He smiled broadly. "Why else do you think my mom and stepdad had four kids, only being married five years? They're happy all the time, even when it's chaos at the house." He shook his head.

We laughed.

"That's like, the best power ever," Liam said, giving him a friendly slap on the shoulder. "So people just want to be around you all the time? Cuz you make them feel so happy?"

"Not happy, not all the time," Isaac said. "But yeah, I can make them feel relaxed. If you're feeling all stressed, then feeling relaxed can make you feel happy." He turned my direction again. "Remember how I said I wasn't sure how my mom was going to feel about me going?"

I nodded.

"I kinda had to lay my gift on real thick these past few hours. That's why you guys are so damn happy, too. You just got my biggest dose."

I giggled.

Major McCoy shook his head as he turned onto the highway, sandwiched between the Catskill Mountains and the Hudson River. "That's a helluva gift, son," he said.

It may have been Isaac's presence, but the beautiful scenery around me amplified my good mood as well. Lush trees were everywhere, in all shades of green, and the mountains – more like giant, rolling hills – were the perfect backdrop to the river.

Before I knew it, we came to a stop at the entrance to West Point, next to something that looked like a tan castle turret. It was about two stories high with a few small windows. On each side, there was a simple gate that lifted up and down, like ones you would find in parking garages, letting select people in and the other side letting people out. A couple of guards stood underneath the bronze insignia identifying it as Thayer's Gate. We pulled up next to the tower and Major McCoy rolled his window down and showed his military ID. Immediately the gate in front of us buzzed and lifted, and we made our way through the first part of the grounds.

A vast green field was to our right, and a few small buildings with colonial charm — red brick with white accents- were scattered on my side of the van. I took a closer look at the signs in front of them.

"There are stores?" I asked, taking in as much as I could through my side of the window. "And a movie theater?"

Small streets, parking spots, and sidewalks ran in front of the buildings, making it look like any other small town in America. People in regular clothes were walking casually in front of the shops, even going to normal-looking cars. I don't know what I expected (Barracks? Tanks? Marches?), but this wasn't it.

"Yep. All the other military bases have them, too," Liam answered, peering out his own window. "Bree and I grew up on them. There are restaurants, a post office, a bowling alley, even a grocery store."

"We call them commissaries," Bree interjected.

Liam nodded in agreement. "Yep. Anyway, they're a lot like small towns. Most stuff can be done on a base."

"Up here to the left is where most of our sports are played," Major McCoy pointed out.

A huge stadium dominated the area, but there were large brick buildings for the indoor sports, too. I was comforted by thoughts of fun games played in the evenings, and then by lazy Sunday afternoons fishing and canoeing as we passed a lake on our right.

My reverie was interrupted, however, as we entered what Major McCoy called the "central area".

"Some people call it the cadet area," he explained, "Because the first part of campus caters to visitors and tourists. This is the part of campus where the cadets live, compete, learn, and improve."

The collegiate sport scene was left behind. It was a different world than the medieval one in front of me. The scene I was staring at was like a painting you'd find in an art museum in Europe, the artist choosing dark and neutral colors for the buildings to contrast sharply with the bright colors in the vegetation and sky.

It was beyond beautiful. Beyond striking, even. If America were to have royalty, I'd imagine this is where they would dwell: at the base of green, gently rolling mountains, next to a vast river, in buildings both intimidating and enthralling with their architecture, resembling gothic castles.

They dominated the picture, and the patriotic statues between them complimented them nicely. Most of the buildings were grey-and-black and granite – all large – but still varying in size. Sprawling fields and lawns were scattered intermittently between the looming beasts, and even the cadets littering the campus looked as if they were placed there on purpose by the artist, wanting to add just the right touch to the perfect scene he just painted on a canvas.

Major McCoy parked the van next to a building with a statue of a man on a horse in front of it.

"Washington's Monument," Adrianna told me as I got out.

I actually knew. My middle school history teacher had showed us a picture of the statue during our American History class.

"George Washington was a man who didn't have to earn the respect of his soldiers," Mr. Morgan had told us. "He just came by it naturally, maybe because of his large size, but mostly because of his no-nonsense attitude and overall strength. Here's a story that's well-documented: Two soldiers had gotten into a fight during the Revolutionary War. When he saw them fighting, Washington flew off his horse and had them both by the necks in less than a few seconds. Men respected that kind of strength."

Strength. My gift.

Maybe Washington was gifted like I was: a member of The Crest before it even existed.

I stared at the statue for a while before I realized I was being left behind.

I hurried to catch up with the group, who had made their way to a huge area of green space. "The Plain," Major McCoy said, waving a hand in front of him, as if it were an introduction. "It's where we congregate, where we celebrate."

Hundreds of cadets – uniformed and moving together in groups – were everywhere on the humongous field. Unlike the scurrying ants in the city, these people knew exactly where they were going, who they were going with, and how they were going to get there. They marched as one, not exactly the same, but as if all of them were parts of a working clock.

I was in awe of the perfection in front of me and unsure of my worthiness to be a part of it as I shifted my bag to my other shoulder.

Isaac came to my side and without even thinking about what I was doing, I grabbed his hand. Almost immediately, I felt my heart beat proudly instead of fearfully. "I think you should stay with me for a while," I said, only half-joking.

He smiled back. "I'll stay."

And he did. For as long as he could, anyway.

14

I WAS DOING THE BEST I COULD TO MAINTAIN A
brisk walk toward my next destination: Lincoln Hall. I'd
been following the sharp orders that'd been flung at me
for almost two hours now. The sack I was carrying was
getting heavier, but as usual, lifting something this
substantial didn't seem to bug me.

A piece of hair escaped from my ponytail and I shook
it loose from my eyes.

"New Cadet Blackburn," I heard a female voice say.

I froze in my tracks.

"New Cadet Blackburn," the voice said again. "When
a higher-ranking officer acknowledges your presence, you
are to stop and acknowledge ours immediately. Do you
understand this, New Cadet Blackburn." It wasn't a
question; it was an order.

"Yes," I answered, facing the young woman with short
brown hair. She was also a cadet at West Point, but was a
firstie (a senior, according to every other collegiate
institution in our country). She was barely five feet tall and
would have looked cherubic with big brown eyes and
dimples, but her demeanor made her tower over me.

"New Cadet Blackburn," she demanded, coming within inches of my face. "I know you're not here for normal reasons. Maybe you didn't make the original cut into West Point because you're on the slow side. But even a child would understand the simple rule of stating the higher officer's rank when you address them."

Crap. She was right. They'd gone over these rules already. My heart was pounding in my chest. It was as if the girl in front of me was daring me to fight, and she was fearsome and fearless: a powerful combination despite her tiny physique.

"New Cadet Blackburn, are you a child?"

She hadn't even given me a chance to answer. I knew I needed to address her the right way. I knew I should be speaking. I knew I should talk to her right now, say anything. But-

"Can you not even grasp this simple concept of respect?" she continued, staring me down as she paced to my other side. "Or do I need to teach you?"

"No, Ma'am. I understand respect, Reg...Regimental Commander." I said, finally remembering her rank. One of the things Major McCoy said we couldn't forget was to address all higher-ranking cadets – the third or fourth year students, especially - as 'Sir' or 'Ma'am,' greet them by their rank, and salute all officers, even if they are simply walking past us.

"My name is Regimental Commander Tessa Harlowe, New Cadet. Now state my name and my rank again."

"Yes, Ma'am. You are Regimental Commander Tessa Harlowe."

She stood back on her heels, a predator tired of messing with her prey. "New Cadet Blackburn, your hair

is falling in your face. You have two choices: you can cut it short, or wear it in a bun at all times. The bun is not to touch your collar or your hat. Do you understand your choices, New Cadet?"

"Yes, Regimental Commander Harlowe."

I shuddered at the thought of cutting my hair. I mean, I was already tall and muscular. Short hair would make me look even more masculine. I quickly twisted and pinned my hair, secured it with a ponytail holder, and once again picked up my large bag.

She nodded curtly. "Continue." With that, she turned away, searching for new victims.

Adrianna and Liam were behind me somewhere, on their way to our next station as well, where more necessities and supplies would be handed out to make our bags even more full. I had no idea where Isaac, Bree, and Jacob were, and I sent up silent prayer asking an angel or guardian or - or *something* to warn and encourage them.

We'd all shown up with a single duffle bag of various personal items and had been told the Army would give us everything we would need for our living quarters. For some reason, I thought we'd arrive in our rooms and they would already be filled, like some well-stocked refrigerator at a fancy hotel.

I couldn't have been more wrong.

In June, the other cadets who were new to West Point had something called R-Day. "Since you missed it," Major McCoy had said, "You are going to have your own R-Day activities."

The "R" stood for reception, but trust me when I say, so far the reception had been horrible.

As we walked into one of the gray brick buildings to begin our R-Day, two upper classmen were introduced to us: a boy and a girl. I was polite, but didn't pay any particular attention to them; I didn't think it was important. But as soon as they were done with their rapid-fire introductions, Major McCoy took on a domineering, authoritative tone, demanding that we repeat their names and ranks. Adrianna and Liam and Bree could, but I couldn't even remember one. I stumbled through it eventually, but not before I was berated by all of them, told I was disrespectful, and warned I should hope I wasn't part of their companies.

Thank God we wouldn't be joining them.

A large sack was thrust into my hands, and I'd been carrying it ever since, filling it up with different items that would be necessary for us to have at West Point. It sounds like this would be simple, but it was one of the hardest things for most cadets to do. Besides all of the personal items I'd need for things like hygiene, I was given a heap of other things: army fatigues, boots, shoes, PT (physical training) clothes, dress uniforms, and hats.

The two upper classmen had made it their job to make our day hell. There were only six of us receiving items, yet we still had to go to numerous buildings to collect all of it. We'd only been taken on a brief tour. I had no idea where the different buildings were located as they hollered instructions, but they expected us to be experts already. For the past hour, they'd been screaming at us to listen and hurry up, shouting, "Where are you going?", "Pay attention, New Cadet!", and my favorite: "Do NOT drop your bag, New Cadet, or we will make sure you get the exercise you need to handle the work!"

Thank God I was strong; the physical toll of carrying my bag was nonexistent. The only things I had to focus on were the directions. The others hadn't been so lucky.

Jacob had been leading us at one point and took a wrong turn. Immediately Regimental Commander Mick Johnson harangued him for five minutes straight. I made the mistake of interrupting him once to say we were sorry and didn't mean any disrespect, and had forgotten to address him by rank again, so got a verbal lashing of my own.

I didn't have it as bad as Jacob, though. After he was done with me, Mick – I mean, Regimental Commander Mick Johnson – continued his onslaught on him. Jacob didn't respond at all to the verbal backlash. His fists clenched and his whole body shook as if it were a dam holding the tears back. I stood next to him, forced to hold my tongue as Jacob was told he was a runt and didn't know how to listen, that he was undeserving and didn't belong here.

My mind wandered to him now, as I turned at the end of one hallway to go up the stairs. I hoped they were leaving him alone. Suddenly I heard someone above me, and when I rounded the corner, I saw Bree, who – struggling under the weight of the bag and drenched in sweat – let it slip from her fingers. The contents spilled out, making a ton of noise.

I looked behind me and didn't see Mick or Tessa. I looked at Bree.

"Catch your breath," I ordered, and I picked up her things and slung her bag over my shoulder as well. "Come on," I prodded, and her eyes welled up as relief spread across her face. We quietly followed the blue line and left the stairwell behind us. We rounded the corner together, only to hit a human wall.

It was him again: Regimental Commander Mick Johnson.

"New Cadet O'Dell," he said, inches from Bree's terrified face. "Is there something wrong with your equipment?"

"No, Sir," Bree replied after a short intake of breath, meeting his stare. "There's nothing wrong with my sack."

"Is there something wrong with your body? Are you injured?" His voice dripped with distaste.

"No, Regimental Commander. I'm not injured," Bree answered, looking at the floor and still breathing heavily.

"Then why are you allowing another cadet to carry your load?"

"You're right, Regimental Commander," she replied, snatching her bag from my hands as quickly as she could.

"Not so fast," he said, holding his hand out in front of her as she tried to make her way around him. "Drop and do twenty. Pushups," he clarified flamboyantly, as if speaking to a child.

Her jaw dropped, then closed. She must have realized complaining was no use. With a single tear rolling down her cheek, she set her bag on the floor and took the pushup position. Her exhausted body seemed limp, despite her efforts, and her arms were already shaking. Letting a breath out, she began.

"One," Cadet Prick – I mean, Mick – said, providing an unnecessary commentary.

"Two," he continued as she let herself down again.

At three, Bree's butt inched up in the air. "Uh, uh, uh!" Mick interrupted, shaking his head. "Bad form, New Cadet O'Dell. Try again!"

She lowered her butt, and then her body. Her arms shook even more violently under the weight of even her slight physique.

And then gave out entirely.

"Three? No, wait — not even three…two pushups, New Cadet? You think you can make it through West Point doing two pushups?" His sneer dripped with arrogance. "Guess we better practice."

Bree was sobbing now.

"Knock it off!" My cheekbones burned and my heart wanted to beat its way out of my chest to punch the grin off his face.

It may as well have; the grin was completely gone as he slowly turned toward me.

"Do you think you're some kind of hero, New Cadet Blackburn?" He shook his head. "It's not that easy. The rest of us have been training years to lead our country. Years. Do you think you can just show up and — poof! — deserve to be in West Point, just like that? Do you think you actually belong here?"

He practically spat out the words, then looked around and leaned in closer to me. "I don't know what you all think you're doing, but this isn't some kind of game. You come here to work. It's not vacation." He straightened. "Speaking of work," he sneered, "You're not leaving this spot until you complete fifty pushups. And they have to be perfect. If not," he nodded to Bree, "This one has to do them in your place."

I glared at him, hoping my blue eyes would ice him over. I assumed the pushup position without breaking his stare.

"One!" he called out, and I called it out louder.

"Two!" we hollered in unison.

"Three!" I yelled, this time without him, watching his face turn a deep shade of red. And I continued calling out the numbers myself as I counted up to fifty.

"Fine," the cadet said, the muscles in his face still tense, obviously surprised I was able to complete them. "You can get up now, New Cadet Blackburn."

But I was still in my pushup pose.

"Fifty-one!" I shouted, doing another. "Fifty-two!"

"Cadet Blackburn, you are DONE. You've completed your fifty!"

But I didn't listen. Instead, I held his gaze as I counted to eighty. Hoping I'd given Bree enough of a break, I hopped to my feet and saluted him.

"Fine. You want to show off? Do eighty more." He leaned against the wall and crossed his arms, smug and arrogant.

"My pleasure, Sir!" I yelled.

And it was. Watching him try to mask the disbelieving look on his face as I pumped out another eighty pushups with hardly any effort was worth every ounce of effort I'd put in.

"You're dismissed, New Cadets." He turned and left. If he had a tail, it would've been between his legs.

I was sure I'd pay for my disrespect at some point, but for now, beating that jerk at his own game felt good. Damn good.

And if that wasn't enough of a reward, Bree's broad smile as we made our way to pick up the last of our items was.

I made myself walk slowly as I approached our barracks to shower and change for drill and marching instructions. I wasn't sore or anything, but I was all revved up and didn't want to lose my temper again. I wasn't sure Major McCoy would keep me here if I pulled another stunt like that.

But what else should I have done? I hated bullies and jerks. Back home, I fought them. Or, at the very least, I went and told the teacher – or whoever was in a position of authority – about them. But this was a different situation than I'd ever been in before.

It was like living in a different world, one where no individual rights existed, yet here we were learning how to protect the individual rights of everyone else. All inalienable rights I'd ever learned about were thrown into question, and it'd only been one day. This place was foreign to me, and I wondered how much I was going to let it change me.

And if it did change me, I wondered if I'd ever be able to go home as "Brooklyn" ever again.

I doubted it.

Under the careful monitoring of Regimental Commander Tessa Harlowe, I unpacked my large sack into my dorm room, paying close attention to the order in which my uniforms were to be hung, the exact angle of my blanket's fold on the bed, and the precise position of my pillow, among other things.

I'd been warned of consequences if anything was out of order.

I changed into fatigues for the first time – the army camo I'd always seen on TV – and made my way to the edge of the central area, where Major McCoy said he'd teach us the basics of marching after a quick late lunch. I was starving and glad for the short break. I'd need to focus intently on learning this stuff. We were told how crucial it was for us to blend in.

Like it or not, I was in the Army now.

15

IT WAS LATER THAT SUNDAY EVENING, AND somewhat shocked by my own choice of what to do with an hour of free time, I made my way across campus to Crandall Pool. As far as I knew, the others had chosen to stay in their rooms. If they were like me, they were contemplating how they had gotten to this point, what we'd gotten ourselves into.

Arriving at the water's edge, the familiarity of the endless painted lanes before me under fluorescent lights soothed my soul. So did the fact that I was alone. Major McCoy had said the facility was not used by teams at this time of night, but I didn't realize my need to have some solitude until the double doors slammed shut behind me. I exhaled heavily, letting the stress of the day leave with the breath.

I threw off my robe and stared into the Olympic-sized lap pool, taking the time to adjust my swim cap, ensuring none of my hair would escape as I plunged into the water. My body welcomed the warmth of the liquid silk as I dove in, and I settled into a rhythmic freestyle swim. It was evening now, just an hour before our curfew, and with no one else around, I simply relished my solitude.

I went back and forth, over and over again, letting the familiar, monotonous task of swimming, flipping, and pushing off the opposite wall wash away the overwhelming chaos that had invaded my mind through the course of the day. Each new word and rule I'd learned today was important, and I made my mind organize them through the rhythm of my arms carving their way in the water. It helped make sense out of the chaos.

Plebes… plebes…plebes….

That's what we were called. At West Point, plebes were like college freshmen. A senior cadet (called a firstie) named First Sergeant Austin Stovall, who had helped with the tour, told us that plebes typically show up in June for basic training. "It's called 'The Beast'," he explained with exuberance, reminding me of the overachieving Student Council president at my high school.

And The Beast was aptly named. We'd had only a taste of what it was like today as we pushed our physical capabilities to the limit and followed the directives of our superiors. Because of our gifts, our training would be different than it was for the other plebes: done in isolation from the rest of the cadets who had already completed it.

Duty…Honor…Country…

First Sergeant Stovall had pointed out this phrase numerous times on our tour. It was displayed all over the campus. "When things get so tough you want to quit," he'd said, "this motto will remind you why you agreed to come in the first place."

I'd already had to think of the motto on a few different occasions today. Major McCoy had pulled me aside after we were dismissed and reprimanded me for my behavior toward Regimental Commander Johnson earlier. "It's not about you and him, Brooklyn. There's a bigger mission here. Those firsties don't know why you're here, and you can't give them any hints as to why. You just pumped out a hundred and sixty pushups without sweating. Don't you think that stuck out to them? Watch yourself. You can't do anything to give your gift away again."

And I wouldn't, even if I were baited – even if it was Major McCoy who was doing the baiting. He had informed us he'd have to behave differently toward us whenever other officers or cadets were present. So in a way, we were all soldiers, but we were actors, too.

For the good of our duty, honor, and country.

Long…Gray…Line…

All West Point graduates belonged to this exclusive club. It got its name from the gray uniforms we had to wear. It was kind of cool to be considered part of this club, but at the same time, it scared the crap out of me. A lot of "big-deal" kind of people came to West Point. Their statues were all over the place.

Like presidents and well-known generals… congressmen, and even leaders of other countries.

And I was just… me.

I wasn't sure I belonged here. Why did they want me, again?

Strength…Strength… Strength…

The words catapulted themselves from my mind to the rest of my body, and my strokes took the verbal cue and became longer, stronger, and more determined. My heart picked up its pace, too, and the energy that surged its way through my muscles was electrifying: exhilarating, even.

Knowing I've never pushed myself to the limit, and realizing that today I was a brand new... me, I pushed harder...as hard as I could.

And I went faster, flew through the water quicker than I ever had before.

I knew I had to be booking it. Each motion was so simply done, but the force of the water on the top of my head was more than I'd ever felt. One stroke launched me halfway across the pool. I spun at the end and did it again, forgetting my goal of trying to learn the things I'd been repeating in my mind.

Because I was having too much fun to learn.

It was as if all the adrenaline my body ever held – after years of being trapped behind a dam – was now gushing through my veins. I could do anything, be anything. My muscles, working at full capacity, could make myself be anywhere. Even the threat of choking on the spraying water couldn't keep me from laughing as I came up for air between strokes.

I practically leapt out of the water, still laughing as I shook my hair free from my cap.

"Ahem."

Crap.

I straightened quickly, remembering Major McCoy's words, his warning that I was always supposed to be a normal soldier-in-training outside of our private classes. Very slowly, I turned around.

And saw Isaac and Liam: Isaac with his arms crossed in front of his body and Liam smiling broadly.

I almost tripped, they caught me so off-guard.

My cheekbones seared with heat, either because I knew they had seen me swimming a little too fast to be human, or because they were both shirtless and muscular in only their swim trunks.

I tried my best to ignore the latter.

They both sat stiffly on the bench, obviously sore from the day's taxing physical demands. I was sure the fluorescent lighting was making me look hideous and the thought made me back up to the bench, where my large towel could work as a curtain over my body.

Isaac spoke first. His eyes were amused, and his mouth, as usual, was smiling broadly. "You liar!"

"What?" I asked, feigning innocence.

He nudged Liam with his elbow. "In the van, she acted like I was the only one with powers. And then she comes here and does like ten laps in thirty seconds."

I rolled my eyes. "It wasn't that fast." I turned away from them to retrieve my towel, then suddenly turned back around. "Was it?"

Liam laughed out loud, and the sound of it was almost as gorgeous as his smile, momentarily distracting me from my embarrassment. "Uh, yeah, it kind of was." He shook his head, then held my gaze with a serious stare. "It was insane, actually. How did you even move through the water like that?"

I shrugged, trying my best to be nonchalant and confident, rather than a shy, insecure puddle of a teen. "I kinda let loose, I guess."

"Pssh." Isaac waved his hand dismissively. "Like you didn't know that was going to happen."

"I didn't!"

"Right."

"Seriously guys," I said, shaking my head and wrapping myself in a towel. "I've never really made myself compete before." I looked down, adding in a muffled whisper, "I've always been kind of scared."

"Scared to be amazing." Liam stated with his mouth open, like he was a fan in awe of his favorite football player or something. I blushed again and looked away.

"So you didn't know you had your gift?" Isaac pressed.

"I've always known I was strong," I explained. "I just never felt like I should push myself completely. I didn't know what would happen, what kind of freak I would be."

And there it was: that awkward silence I hated, the moment where I had to wait and see if they would agree with my self-depreciating comments or assure me I was okay.

"Well," Liam said. "Take it this way: If you're a freak, he's a freak, too." He nodded jokingly to Isaac.

"Ha. Ha. Ha." Isaac replied dryly.

I laughed, pulling my gray USMA sweats over my swimming suit.

"You leaving already?" Liam asked.

"It's late. Curfew's in thirty minutes and I've still got to pick up my room." I didn't want to get caught having my room out of order. I didn't need the extra work that went with it.

I quickly waved goodbye and turned to leave. But just as Isaac cannon-balled into the pool, Liam put a hand on my shoulder and sent a shiver down my spine. "Hang on," he said.

It was against my "fight or flight" nature, but for some reason, I obeyed.

He turned back to Isaac, whose head had just broken through the water's surface. "Sorry, man, I gotta go, too. Brooklyn made me nervous. My room's a mess."

"Dude," Isaac said, shaking his wet hair and then doggy-paddling in his careless way. "Your dad's in the Army. You know how these things work. Before we came here, you just sat in my room and watched me clean up. And it didn't even occur to you that you should be picking up your own mess?" He shook his head in mock disapproval.

Liam shrugged. "Guess I better get my act together like you and Wonder Woman, huh?"

Wonder Woman. I tried to shake the blush away that I felt reddening my cheeks.

"Or else," Isaac threatened jokingly, pointing an index finger up at Liam.

"Have fun," I commented awkwardly to Isaac, and Liam held the door open for me to leave.

16

I SWALLOWED NERVOUSLY AS WE MADE OUR way out of the sports complex. The air was chilly and gave me an excuse to hug my arms to my body. We walked silently for a minute or so, under the soft haze of the lanterns lighting the path to our dormitory.

"You do that a lot," Liam observed, nodding to me.

"What?" I asked.

"Cover yourself up. Like you don't want anyone to look at you."

My blood rushed to my cheeks and I looked down, watching one foot go in front of the other.

"You do that a lot, too," he laughed. "You know, get embarrassed and blush."

Damn him.

In a half-hearted attempt to prove him wrong, I made eye contact, and he was shaking his head. "Thanks for letting me walk with you back to the barracks," he said. "I've, uh, been wanting to get some time alone with you ever since the news conference."

My cheeks got even hotter, and I tried to look at anything but him.

"I want to say thank you, Brooklyn."

My head shot up. "For what?"

"For saving me," he replied. "The night of the gala, during the attack."

I had a sudden lump in my throat, and my heart sank to the pit of my stomach as I remembered.

I'd been watching him earlier that evening, laughing with Bree across the table. Liam had met my gaze briefly and had offered a shy smile. Moments later, we were running from bombs and gunfire. The crowd fleeing had nearly trampled him.

"You pulled me out of the crowd," he recalled. "And threw me ahead of you somehow." He shook his head in apparent disbelief. "That night, I'd thought I'd been a part of this crazy shot-of-adrenaline-during-a-crisis story, but you were just being…you."

We were outside, but the air felt thin somehow as I tried to breathe deeply and relieve the constriction in my throat. "You're welcome," I said simply. But I wanted to say more.

I could feel him studying me, could see him shake his head out of the corner of my eye. "It's just crazy to me." He laughed nervously. "Look, you're still covering yourself up. I mean, haven't you ever been told how strong you were? How pretty?" He added, and a touch of pink kissed his cheeks.

"I- uh….I don't really like to focus on those things." I replied honestly.

"Yeah, I can tell," Liam said. "You're not like any girls I know."

This time it was my turn to shake my head. "That's not a good thing," I explained, deciding I might as well give it to him straight. "When you hang out with me, it's like hanging out with one of your guy-friends. I don't like to get all dolled up. I hate doing my hair and wearing makeup. And I'd rather be in detention than be stuffed into a dress. Give me sweats and Nikes any day." I motioned to my current ensemble.

Liam looked at my outfit, then quickly glanced away, clearing his throat. "You can make anything look good."

I forged ahead of Liam slightly with my strides. I wasn't trying to leave him behind; I was just trying to temporarily escape his uninhibited adoration and make my heart rate slow down. I wasn't used to this feeling, and I needed it to stop.

I was here to be trained, not tempted.

The silence was thick between us.

"So what do you think about all this? Being in the Army?"

This time, Liam's question was innocent, a welcome intrusion because the topic had nothing to do with me. I joined him at his pace again. I looked around his beautiful face to the buildings that littered the area behind him. Some housed classrooms, I surmised, because their windows were darkened at this late hour. Others were lit up, a sign the building was a barrack. I thought of the other cadets who were in those rooms, studying and practicing – the ones who had worked so hard to be here – and felt ashamed.

"I guess I still can't believe I'm here," I answered honestly. "I mean, just a week ago I hadn't once even thought about joining the military, and suddenly, it's the only thing I can think about."

"You never wanted to join? Never even thought about it?"

"No," I answered honestly. "I've never seen the appeal. I mean, you join. You get bossed around, given impossible tasks. And why? Just so you can sacrifice everything for people you don't even know?"

Liam clenched his jaw slightly and looked up to the stars as we walked, as if he were searching them for the words he needed.

I hoped I hadn't offended him. I knew he was raised on army bases and probably had "duty, honor, and country" told to him as often as I'd had bedtime prayers recited to me.

"It's not that I don't appreciate what soldiers do," I explained rapidly. "It's just...I'm not sure if I was made do it, if I can sacrifice as much as they do."

His face broke out in a huge grin. "I was just thinking of a way to say how I was feeling," he said. "But you did it perfectly."

"Really?" I was genuinely surprised.

Liam was a military kid. Military families tended to stay that way for a reason. They were born into a culture we weak civilians couldn't understand. I mean, we handed down recipes and quilts. They tended to hand down new generations of brave soldiers. It wasn't hard to see which was the more honorable cause, which bore the deeper mark of pride and sacrifice.

"Yeah," he said, shrugging and sighing deeply. "I've always thought about becoming a soldier. I admire all of them, because I've seen firsthand what they have to give up and how brave they have to be. But signing up for it— especially if you end up being a lifer, like my dad — it's giving up a lot. I think that's why he's never pressured me to follow in his footsteps. But especially after seeing how proud he was of us before we left, I guess he always hoped I would."

"So you've talked about it with him before?"

He shook his head and smiled. "Not even once. I avoided the topic like the plague. I didn't even want to consider joining. Last week at this time, I was all set on going to USC to be a normal college kid."

"Really?" I questioned, my eyebrows raised.

"Really," Liam replied simply.

I forged ahead again. "USC would probably be amazing," I said, a little too loudly, a little too awkwardly. "You'd do well in southern California." Hollywood, in particular.

He laughed. "I'd better. That's where I live."

"What?" I asked incredulously. I stopped in front of him. "But we picked you up in the city today."

"Yeah," he agreed. "That's where our hotel was. We take a trip to New York every September for our birthdays and for the memorial dinner. We visit my mom's gravesite and a few relatives, too. But we actually live in San Diego. And before that, it's been Florida, Virginia, South Carolina, and we spent a very interesting year in Kansas," he explained, ticking the places off of one hand with his forefinger. He smiled wistfully. "Just another day in the life of an Army brat."

"Huh," I uttered, an admittance of civilian ignorance.

We walked in silence for a few steps.

"Was it hard?" I asked. "You know, moving around all the time?"

He shook his head. "Not really. It was our version of 'normal'. Army families tend to stick together, and we always lived with them on base. And all of my friends knew what it was like to have active duty parents, too." He paused, but only for a second. "Sometimes it was even like we spoke our own language. We used military lingo to do everything, from tell time to describe the status of dinner."

He took a deep breath. "Nah, the hardest thing about it was when my dad was deployed and we had to live with my grandparents. Living with people who were old and weren't used to kids, going to school with kids who didn't get it, waiting to hear from a dad who was fighting overseas...it wasn't fun. That's for sure."

"Where do your grandparents live?" I asked, genuinely curious.

"In New York City."

I raised a brow. "But you stay in a hotel when you go there?"

He nodded. "Yep. And that's why. Bree and I don't mind going back there to have dinner with them or something, but we hate staying there for too long. Too many depressing memories of living with people who didn't understand us. Too many memories of missing our dad." He breathed in deeply. "That's why we didn't even hesitate to come here, you know." He leaned in closely, as if he was telling me a secret. "I mean, I probably would have come. But Bree would have passed. The only reason she's here is because my dad is getting deployed again, for at least a year. We would have had to stay with our grandparents again if we hadn't signed up."

I studied him for a second. There was genuine depth to him, so much he'd already done, so much he'd already given up.

"You say you're afraid of being a soldier," I commented, almost whispering. "But you've always had to make sacrifices. You guys are way more heroic than me."

He smiled shyly, and I realized it was the first time I'd given him any verbal form of adoration, which seemed crazy because I had drooled over him in my mind.

That's a good thing, I reminded myself. *Keep the wall up and stay focused on the reason I'm here.*

"Thanks," he said. "To tell you the truth, though, what Bree and I do is way different than what soldiers have to do." He clenched his jaw. "I've heard way too many stories about wars from my dad."

He didn't offer any more on the topic, and I was grateful. I didn't want to hear him elaborate.

"I have no idea if I'm cut out for being here," he continued. "But you, Brooklyn," he said, nudging my shoulder lightly with his own, "You were born to be strong."

I fought the urge to smile and looked away, thinking about the short conversation I'd had with Major McCoy about the same topic.

Before signing the rest of the necessary paperwork to enter, I had asked him if he thought I could really be a soldier. He had done his best to placate my fears.

"A lot of people aren't sure if they can make it," he'd said, his hands on my shoulders. "Coming here is tough. Abiding by the stricter rules and meeting the increased standards is hard. But you're different than most people. You were born for it."

And I hadn't argued back.

Because even though I wasn't raised in the Army like Liam or Bree, in a weird way – as much as I didn't want to admit it – I knew he was right.

I was born with exceptional strength – a rare power no one else would ever know. And because of this power, I had a duty to use it. It kind of reminded me of that line in the Spiderman movie: *With great power comes great responsibility*. It didn't mean I had to like it.

"What about you?" I asked, wanting to change the topic. "Do you think you have your gift?"

Liam paused. "Not yet, not in the way my mom did. I definitely feel the need to fix things, though, to heal people. I've always felt it. I was going to be a Pre-Med major. I know I have the interest; I'm just not sure I have the superpower. You know?"

I nodded. "I guess we'll all get a chance to see how gifted we really are."

And we would. We weren't taking classes with the other cadets on campus: just with each other, to ensure our gifts would remain a secret. We also didn't have to have roommates or even stay in the same area of the barracks as the other cadets. They had us in the Sherman barracks, which were far more isolated and easier to get in and out of undetected so we could meet with Major McCoy. With any luck, our whole stay at West Point would be understated. That's why it was so important we learn the ways of the cadets, so we wouldn't stick out whenever we were around the others.

We'd made it to the side entrance to our barrack. I fumbled around in my hoodie pocket, searching for my card-key to get into the building, but Liam had found his before me. Two quick beeps, and the door clicked, ready to be opened. Liam stepped to the side, holding the door open for me and gesturing for me to go in first.

I had to remind myself he was my age, that we were both newbies to this life, learning together. He seemed so much older than I was, having already made so many grown-up decisions. And yet he always felt the need to praise and compliment *me*.

I wondered how long it'd take him to realize how inept I really was.

Bree and Jacob were in the small lobby that greeted us, and Bree's initial expression was inquisitive as Liam and I entered together. But she quickly turned back toward Jacob, who was sitting cross-legged next to her on the couch. Their facial expressions – the whole mood of the room – told me they were probably commiserating with each other.

Adrianna peeked her head out of her door, somewhat flushed, like she was nervous or something. She nodded her approval when she saw me. "Good," she said. "I was afraid you all would break curfew on our first night. Where's Isaac?"

"Still swimming," I said. "But he knows it's almost curfew time."

She nodded her approval again and turned to Liam. "Don't forget we have to be up by five-thirty. We have to run the Flirtation Walk trail tomorrow."

"Flirtation Walk?" Unlike everything else about this place, it sounded pretty un-military.

Liam flashed a grin. "Yeah." He leaned carelessly against the concrete wall behind him. "My dad told me about it. He went to West Point, too. It's this private, rocky trail that's like, a mile long. It runs right along the Hudson. It was named 'Flirtation Walk' a long time ago because it was the only place on campus where cadets wouldn't be written up for holding their girlfriends' hands, or for kissing them or whatever when they came to visit."

Kissing. Liam. Gah, I'd have to work to get that out of my head. Damn him.

"Seriously?" I asked instead, arching a brow. "Why have a designated area to break the rules?"

"I guess even rule-breaking is considered a tradition at West Point," Liam said with a shrug.

"Yeah," Adrianna agreed. "As long as it's regimented and structured, too."

I laughed.

"There's even a rock monument there," Liam continued. "Legend has it if you don't kiss your girlfriend when you pass under it, a rock will fall and crush you both."

"Well, we all know who shouldn't run next to each other tomorrow then," Bree had said, sneaking up on us with Jacob in tow. She elbowed her brother in the ribs as I nervously tucked a strand of hair behind my ear.

"So, uh," I stuttered. My eyes averted Liam's stare and found Adrianna's. "We're being timed, right?"

She smiled back, her eyes gleaming. "Yes! I can't wait!"

I was kinda excited, too, believe it or not. Running hadn't necessarily been my forte in the past, but after being able to swim faster tonight, I was wondering how my leg muscles would react to being pushed harder.

The door opened and Isaac walked in, his hair still wet from swimming. "Well, guess I better get some sleep," I told the others quickly, not wanting to miss curfew, and really not wanting to be present if my gift was brought up. "Goodnight."

"Night," I heard from all of them.

I scanned my key-card again at the next door down the hall and entered my room. I quickly showered and changed into my running clothes, hoping to save time in the morning since I wasn't used to getting up at the butt-crack of dawn. I brushed my teeth and hair, set my alarm, and lay in bed.

Images from the day milled around in my head, along with the faces of the new friends I'd made. One face, in particular, stood out, but I tried to force him to the back of my mind. I didn't need the distraction. I had a job to do, and our national security was at stake.

The swim, as fun as it was, succeeded in tiring me out. Despite the overwhelming changes that had occurred that day, after only a couple minutes, I fell asleep, oddly comfortable in my strange new world.

17

"HMPF." I ROLLED OVER AND PULLED THE
pillow over my head.

As if the incessant beeping of my alarm clock wasn't
annoying enough, the LED lights with the giant digital
numbers FIVE: ZERO-ZERO blinked in cadence with
the noise. It was borderline assault, and for a second, I
wondered if throwing the clock against the wall was a
kind of self-defense.

Somewhere beyond my concrete walls I heard another
alarm. And then another. It took those alarms to remind
me why I was making an appearance before the sun,
where I was and what I needed to do.

It was my first morning at West Point, and I had to wake
up before the bugle call stirred the normal cadets because it
was also my first day of PT: Physical Training. This
morning's agenda: a timed run on the Flirtation Walk Trail.

I rolled back over and stretched my arm out, using
my fist to attack the different buttons on the small box,
waiting for one to respond to my punches. The fifth try
did the trick.

"Rise and shine," I told myself in a yawn. My mom said the same thing every morning when she woke me up. Saying it to myself felt nice.

I stretched my muscles and made my way over to the sink. Not bothering to brush my hair, I yanked it back into the simple bun the academy required. I used water to rub my eyes awake and straightened my T-shirt and shorts. After a quick brush of my teeth and throwing on my sneakers, I made my way out my door and to the small rec room, where all of The Crest members-in-training were waiting. Isaac tossed me a granola bar, a banana, and a water bottle.

Breakfast of champions.

Adrianna let out a sigh. "Good. We're all here. Everyone ready?" She nodded to the others, who looked even more tired than I was.

We reluctantly made our way out to the campus. The only exception was Bree, who hovered in the lobby. She looked incredibly on edge and extremely pale.

"You okay?" I asked her.

She nodded, then shook her head back and forth furiously. "No, not really. I'm sore. And I hate running and everything else having to do with sports." Her eyes widened and she swallowed thickly. "I keep wondering when they're going to realize I don't have a gift and send me home."

"Don't worry about it," I urged. "None of us are here based on the usual standards, remember?"

"But you have your power, and so does Isaac," she insisted. "Liam told me." She paused. "I'm gonna look dumb."

"Nah," I said, trying my best to assure her. "Your brother saw me swim. I'm way worse at running."

My insistence that I was going to suck seemed to make her feel slightly better, and she joined us outside. As we made our way through campus, past the library on our right, The Plain and the baseball field to our left, I thought about whether or not it was true.

Would I be fast?

I'd never stood out in races before, but like I'd said, I'd never really tried. The Flirtation Walk was three-fourths of a mile long, and we had to run both to the end and back along rugged terrain.

I guess it was time to find out.

As we walked, the pre-dawn gray took its hold on our surroundings. We passed three more barrack buildings, and as different lights flicked on, I thought about the other cadets. It amazed me that they came here with no prodding to do so, with no incentive other than to serve their country and better themselves. For the umpteenth time in less than a day, I felt ashamed of my self-centeredness, how I'd never made any big sacrifices in my life.

We finally arrived at the start of the Flirtation Walk, a rocky outcropping with the scenic Hudson River behind it. The sun was just peaking over the horizon as Major McCoy addressed us in an informal line.

"I hope you all had a restful night's sleep," he said, with even more fervor than he'd had yesterday. "Because today, you're going to need it." He walked in front of us, back and forth, as he continued. "Each one of you says you've never been pushed. Well, you're about to be. You all say you've never honed your gifts. You're about to. And some of you have no clue what your weaknesses are." He stopped to look at Bree. "You're about to find out."

She winced.

"You have seven minutes to finish this run," he said succinctly.

Wait, my brain told me. Seven minutes? Seven *freaking* minutes? To run a mile and a half, with rocks and turns and animals and holes and lord-knows-what-else to slow us down? I couldn't even run a seven-minute mile on a nice, flat track last year in PE. Granted, I hadn't pushed myself, but how was I going to run a faster time during a longer run with more obstacles?

"Seven minutes to finish," Major McCoy repeated, obviously enjoying our disbelief and discomfort. "And if you don't finish in that time, you'll stay with us for a while longer to get more practice in."

Bree groaned.

"You have ten minutes to get loose and ready."

With that, he left us.

MY LUNGS WERE ON FIRE, MY LEG MUSCLES rubbery and numb. I had just finished running for the fourth time. The Flirtation Walk Trail was going to kill me. If I had the happiness or even the energy in me it'd take to laugh, I would do it. It was certainly laughable I'd thought I would excel in running after doing great in the swimming pool.

"Surprised?" Major McCoy asked in a mocking tone as I threw up after the third run. "Gotta think biology, Brooklyn. Bodybuilders don't make good runners for a reason. Their muscles aren't built for endurance."

"Stick to the weight room," he sneered as I'd run past him this last time, shaking his head as he showed me my time of twelve minutes. It was an entire minute slower than my last attempt.

He was way cooler before R-Day. Did all drill sergeants turn into big fat jerks as soon as new soldiers entered the Army?

I braced my hands on my knees, trying to control my breathing. I stole a glance at the other members of The Crest and realized it could very well kill all of us.

Bree was crying, which was causing her to hyperventilate. Major McCoy was at her side, instructing her to breathe into a paper bag.

Liam was stretched out on his back with his hands behind his head, his face etched with a painful grimace and his grey shirt drenched in sweat.

And Isaac held his body in a similar way, except he was upright, walking back and forth in a pose my middle school track coaches had instructed us to take after a race. He had finished each time in a slow jog, as if he didn't have a care in the world, and he didn't seem like he was in pain at all, which made me wonder if he was even trying.

Jacob hadn't even made it past the finish line yet.

It was almost noon and none of us could run the trail under the impossible standard of seven minutes.

All of us but Adrianna, that is.

She'd passed on the first try. It was incredible watching her. She didn't even run past us. I swear to God, she flew. And she never ran out of energy. Like some kind of streak through the air – a person lifted directly off of a comic book page - she bounded off boulders that tripped up the rest of us, and it seemed like she got stronger with each lengthy stride she took.

And even though she'd finished the race impossibly fast, she continued to run with us, slowing to our pace. At first I thought she joined us to show off, but then she ran past me and the others, encouraging us to do our best. She was definitely the "big sister" type.

While the rest of us were taking humongous gulps of air, she was breathing steadily through her nose. All of our clothes and hair were drenched with sweat, and she had a slight glow, making her even more beautiful than before, more beautiful than I thought anyone could be after running so long and fast.

At the moment, I'd have given anything to trade her powers.

And looks, but that wasn't a priority at the moment.

My wishful thinking was interrupted by a terrified scream by the tree-with-purple-leaves, the informal finish-line marker. It was Bree and Major McCoy, and they were kneeling next to a body.

Jacob.

Bree's shrieks pierced the air like panicked bullets, and each word a barrage of frightened feelings. "HE'S NOT BREATHING!" She repeated it over and over again, even as we all leapt from our positions to help.

If we could help.

I didn't know what to do with those words. What was I supposed to do with them? I searched around me for something, as if things found in nature would help in this situation.

Major McCoy was holding Jacob's head, titling it back in an attempt to clear the airways. I ran to their side. Jacob's lips were blue and his eyes were closed.

"Wait!"

It was Isaac. "Sir," he said. "He's not choking. He can't breathe. But it's because he's asthmatic."

Major McCoy considered it and then shook his head. "None of his medical records indicated he has asthma."

"He and his mother had them changed, Sir," Isaac stated. "He was afraid you wouldn't let him come if you knew. He told me yesterday." He paused. "Please. Let me help him."

Major McCoy held his gaze for a second — which seemed much longer — then lay Jacob on the ground again and nodded curtly to the teen who was even taller than him. Isaac approached Jacob quickly, knelt beside him, put a hand on his chest, and closed his eyes.

And just like that, the tension surrounding this surreal moment seemed to evaporate. All the anxiety I felt about having a dying boy in our midst diminished, and then completely disappeared as I heard Jacob coughing and saw him open his eyes.

We all met the others' gazes with happy tears, and Bree scrabbled to envelop him in a hug.

Liam put a hand on Isaac's shoulder. "How'd you do that, man?"

"I relaxed his airways," he said simply. He smiled slightly at the purposeful underplaying of his ability.

"You're amazing," I told him, and he couldn't hold my gaze.

"Training is dismissed for the morning," Major McCoy said, once again authoritative in his tone.

He didn't have to tell us twice. We hadn't been to the mess hall yet, but as long as it had chairs and warm food, I was sure it'd be my favorite place yet.

18

MANNERS WERE DEFINITELY A MUST AT WEST
Point's cafeteria, so despite having four thousand plus
cadets seated in one room, there was a hum of quiet
conversations at all of the tables. The six of us got to sit
with each other, of course, at our own table on the
outskirts of the other cadets in our company.

Yesterday, there had been occasional glances our way
- curious looks from the others. But our plan to blend in
as much as possible must have worked. It was dinnertime,
and as we sat down for our second meal at the mess hall
that day, most of the curious glances seemed to dissipate.

We'd spent the afternoon in the basement of Jefferson
Library, going over a small book called *Bugle Notes*, otherwise
known as the Plebe Bible. It was a small book that included
songs, chants, facts about the campus, and quotes from
famous West Point grads. Its intent was to make cadets reflect
on the honor and character required of a soldier at the
academy, to instill pride in what we were doing. And honestly,
it worked. Considering today's date, I was savoring the
contents.

It was September 11th.

I'd completely forgotten about it until we had come together that afternoon.

I blamed my amnesia on the excitement of the last two days, and was grateful Major McCoy had reminded us as he passed out the books. Reading through the patriotic notes, I couldn't get the impact of the 9/11 attacks off my mind.

I still couldn't.

The ongoing buzz of voices around me did nothing to divert my thoughts as I picked absentmindedly at my plate of spaghetti.

No matter how hard I tried to see life from the perspective of others, I just couldn't fathom why those towers had to fall, why those planes had to crash.

And trust me, I'd thought about it a lot throughout the years.

It crossed my mind every night at supper, where my family filled only three out of the four chairs at my kitchen table. Each time a story was told about this man I resembled yet never met, I questioned why he had to die. And every time I played a sport as a child, as I'd glance up at the stands and see only one parent there, I'd wonder why I had to be cheated out of these moments with him.

At times I was angry. Other times, sad. But I always felt cheated.

I stole a look at the other Crest members, wondering if the weighty topic was heavy on their hearts, too.

Liam and Bree were sitting across from me, Liam looking so good in his uniform my heart almost hurt. I did my best to ignore it. Catching my assessment, he smiled at me before Bree elbowed him. They surreptitiously exchanged small boxes between them.

"Whatcha doing there?" I asked.

Liam's eyes danced and Bree broke out in a guilty grin. "Nothing," he said, pushing whatever it was below the table onto his lap.

"Let me see," I insisted.

Bree looked to her left and then to her right, then nodded quickly in her brother's direction. He feigned exasperation and rolled his eyes. At last, they both brought their objects just slightly above the level of the table.

Each twin held a small present.

"So… you're celebrating your acceptance and arrival into West Point?" I guessed.

"No," Liam beamed. "We're not congratulating each other. But today is something to celebrate."

I raised my eyebrows. "You guys exchange presents on 9/11?" It seemed borderline inappropriate. I mean, their mom died on this day, for crying out loud.

Bree's skin flushed. "We do. Not because it's 9/11, though." She paused. "We do it cuz it's our birthday."

Of course. Their birthday. They had to be delivered via emergency C-section because their hero-mother died healing people.

I was *such* a moron.

I was sure my skin reddened even more than Bree's as I stuttered an apology. She put a hand up to stop me. "Honestly, stop," she said, giggling. "It *is* kinda weird. It was worse when we were younger. Dad didn't know whether to be sad all day or celebrate. But now we've kind of learned how to balance it all."

"Well," I began, not knowing what else to say. "Happy birthday, you guys."

Their eyes gleamed in appreciation, but just for a moment. Then they promptly looked down, forcing their still-wrapped presents under the table.

"New Cadets," I heard behind me, and I recognized the voice immediately. I doubted I'd ever be able to forget the male Regimental Commander. "New Cadets O'Dell," Mick Johnson sneered.

I tried to busy myself with my food. The last thing the twins needed was for me to get involved. They'd be running for weeks.

Both Liam and Bree stood up, at attention. "Regimental Commander Johnson," they addressed in unison.

"What is that you're holding, New Cadets?" Mick leaned back on his heels and crossed his arms in front of his chest, as if he were a bouncer at a nightclub or something. "We haven't handed out today's mail yet. And I'm pretty sure you haven't been granted clearance to go off grounds to purchase anything…"

He brought a hand to his chin, mimicking a man in deep thought. He didn't come by it naturally and was a horrible actor. I forced myself to swallow the reckless comment I wanted to make.

"Maybe I should take these packages, just in case," he finally spat out. "Make sure you're not doing something illegal." He held out a hand, palm up, as if he were royalty who was bored of his lowly servants. He clearly expected Liam and Bree to hand over their presents.

They hesitated.

Not even skipping a beat, Mick went on with his soliloquy. "You can never be too careful, you know. Rules are rules." He looked at them sternly. "And they're rules for a reason."

Bree opened her mouth to speak, then closed it quickly. She looked to Liam for guidance.

He was looking at me, though. His jaw was clenched as tightly as his fists. I could tell he was wanting to fight.

Very slowly, very subtly, I shook my head. *It's not worth it*, my mind was screaming. *HE'S not worth it.*

"New Cadets."

This time the sound came from behind me. I recognized the high, cherubic voice. Regimental Commander Tessa Harlowe came to a stop at Mick Johnson's hip.

We all stood to salute her.

"At ease," she commanded after our show of respect. She turned to the twins. "It's my understanding that today is your birthday."

"Yes Ma'am," Liam replied.

"New Cadets," she addressed again. "Is that why you were hiding presents under the table?"

Bree swallowed nervously. "Yes Ma'am." She dropped her present on the table. Liam followed suit.

The tiny Regimental Commander left Mick's side and approached them. Mick's face darkened, and the twins shifted uncomfortably.

"New Cadets," she began, speaking softly this time, so only our table could hear it. "It's also my understanding that you lost your mother on this day, nineteen years ago, that she died serving our country during the 9/11 attacks."

"Yes, Ma'am," Bree replied.

"New Cadets." She paused indefinitely, allowing both of the twins time to meet her gaze.

Instead of addressing them, she snapped both feet together and brought a hand to her forehead.

She was saluting their very entry into the world.

Before I knew it, she left. Mick left, too – scurried after her, more like it – and met the other Regimental Officers in the middle of the Mess Hall. And there was another familiar face among them.

General Richards.

As the cadets seated in the closest proximity to our table gawked, unable to fathom why a Regimental Commander would be saluting a plebe, Liam and Bree found their seats.

But their presents stayed on the table, momentarily forgotten.

"What do you think he's here for?" Adrianna asked, shifting my attention back onto the general.

"I have no idea," Jacob answered.

Isaac leaned in and whispered, "He's real tense, Brooklyn. I wonder what's up."

I straightened in my chair so I could follow the highest-ranking cadets, who gave the highest-ranking officer in the room a salute. They flanked him as the entire group marched up the stairs to the balcony overlooking the entire hall.

"Why are they on the poop deck?" Jacob asked.

I stifled a giggle. Seriously, the *poop deck*?

Adrianna gave me the same kind of nudge my mother used to give my brother and me when we got loud in church.

"That's where big announcements are made," she explained. "The ones that affect the entire group, or even the entire military or the country as a whole."

A hush spread across the mess hall as General Richards took his place in front of the podium. He spoke clearly into the microphone as the entire mass of students stood to salute him.

"At ease, cadets."

We quietly returned to our seats. He took a moment to meet our expectant stares. "Today I want to speak to you as a fellow American and soldier, with less regard for rank or military protocol."

I gave Adrianna a side-glance. Was he for real? Adrianna maintained her straight-backed posture, her attention respectful and rapt. Every other cadet I could see made no changes in their demeanor, so I didn't, either.

"On this day, nineteen years ago, our nation changed," he began. "Prior to that day, war was something that happened on foreign soil, something we hadn't had the horror of experiencing for generations. America – thanks, in large part, to its military – had established good relationships with a fair amount of other countries. Most of you were babies or toddlers in 2001. You have no direct memory of what happened that day. But I can tell you that for the first time in decades, each and every citizen in this country felt vulnerable and under attack."

"In the years that followed," he continued, "we launched military campaigns against countries harboring terrorists. We countered their assault with attacks of our own, and used our intelligence to arrest those who were guilty of plotting their acts of terror."

He paused. "It's a worldwide crisis we continue to face today."

The atmosphere amongst the cadets was electric, but not out of fear. Instead, a unique blend of pride and courage oozed out of every person in the room, every person who had volunteered to combat such evil.

"We were born into a fallen world where evil exists," the general continued, this time quieter than he was before. "And because of good men and women like you, we are able to keep it at bay." He nodded to the doors. "The world out there depends on the future leaders of our country, and believe me when I say, I am incredibly honored to be in the presence of such leaders today: men and women who put their youth on hold for the good of people they've never met, and leaders who found their gifts to be so profound that they knew they had to use them to protect our citizens."

His gaze momentarily fell on our table.

"We are a different world than we were pre-9/11, I'm afraid. Nothing is sacred anymore, and civilians are as much of a target as any soldier wearing a uniform. Terrorists care about one thing only: planting a deep seed of fear into our hearts and using any means necessary to make us scared. For years they've used the internet, videos, social media, propaganda, and any weapon at their disposal to threaten us or do us harm, but now they have gone too far."

He stopped for a moment, braced himself against the podium as his chin rested on his chest, as if he was gathering strength from somewhere deep inside.

"Intel is confident these terrorists are no longer satisfied with threats. They're trying to take away our future, too." He held our stares with the utmost sincerity. "Reliable sources relayed information to us this morning, telling us of an impending attack at one of our military academies. They want to attack our youth."

Protocol broken, a buzz went around the large room. The general cleared his throat, garnering our attention once again.

"We don't know which military academy they are targeting; it could be one of any of our armed forces. But know this, West Point cadets: They have messed with the wrong Americans. You all," he said, waving his hand across the room, "You are the best and brightest we have. We will stop at nothing – nothing – to protect you. Trust that we have taken the proper steps to make sure you are – and will remain – safe." He straightened. "And God help the sonofabitch who by some miracle does invade these walls, because I know you'd give him hell."

A reverberating cheer went up around the room, and it was as if the sound were part of the building itself as the cadets welcomed the challenge. It took minutes for the officer to quiet them down again.

"I know you will always put your duty, your honor, and your country above all else," he stated. "In any moment of battle, I know you'd be available. But you are here to learn the tactics of war, cadets. And part of that is keeping your eyes and ears open to unusual things and reporting them to senior officers. It's about stopping trouble before it can truly start."

Once again, he paused. "You need to know this, soldiers: there may be a spy within the walls of one of our academies, someone who is funneling information to the terrorists. This could be information about who is attending, what weaknesses are on the campus for entry points, and even what our own cadets' individual strengths are." He made eye contact with me. My heart sank while my shoulders rose.

"This, of all days, is a day to remember our duty, to think about why we're here. Never forget, cadets. You are here to defend our freedom, our country, and all citizens. You. Are. Here. To. FIGHT!"

If I thought the building was shaking before, we might as well have been in the middle of an earthquake.

19

GENERAL RICHARDS' WARNING ON SEPTEMBER
11th didn't go unnoticed. For the next three weeks, as
September rolled into the start of October, the schedule
and atmosphere at West Point seemed to mirror nature
and its change of season. The air was heavier somehow.
The altered schedule meant the days were a little shorter,
and the demeanor of everyone was a bit more clipped and
icy.

Everywhere we went on campus, there were signs of
heightened security. Almost every day we had a drill of
some sort where we'd practice what to do in an
emergency, whether it was caused by an intruder, a
suspicious package, or even an air raid. The morning
inspections of our barracks (called AMIs) were more
intrusive, as officers searched high and low for what they
called "suspicious paraphernalia". More guards were
stationed at the entrance to the grounds, and every single
car was searched before it was allowed on the campus.
Rumors swirled that snipers were stationed in the woods
surrounding West Point, spying on our day-to-day

activities through their scopes, ready to pull the trigger if needed.

I was in the mess hall when I overheard some cadets saying two students – plebes – were questioned in the President's Office, suspected of espionage because they had provided "details of interest" in their letters home to their families.

I hadn't sent a letter home yet – I didn't want to. I knew my mom could follow my activities with the secured website Major McCoy had given her – the activities she was allowed to know about, anyway – and I didn't want to make myself homesick. For some reason, I thought writing a letter would make me wish I was with her in person, and I didn't want to set myself up for heartache.

So when Major McCoy personally delivered two letters and a medium-sized box to my barrack, I wasn't sure I wanted them. I felt a strange combination of excitement and remorse, especially when I saw the first letter from my mom. I did my best to steady my hands as I carefully tore the envelope open.

Her elegant, familiar scrawl beckoned me like a hug, and I brought the papers up to my chest, as if it really was one. Blinking back tears, I held it up again, ready to read.

It was filled with mostly mundane descriptions of what was going on at home. Her hours changed at the hospital where she worked. She was considering painting the living room. Our neighbors two doors down were moving. Normally, these things would hardly be considered newsworthy, but I didn't care. They were a welcome intrusion to the hundreds of changes my life had undergone in the last month.

And though the ordinary descriptions made me homesick, I didn't cry until I read the very last sentence my mom had written. The *I'm proud of you* was underlined three times and filled me with more happiness than I would have ever thought any group of words could bring.

I wiped my eyes and opened the next envelope.

Bryce, as usual, didn't write a lot, but he did say he missed me. And if Bryce said it, he meant it.

At the end, he added, *Jace wants to know if he can have your address. I won't give it to him unless you want me to, but he threatened to show up on a tourist bus if I didn't at least ask.*

Jace.

I thought back to what it'd been like to be with him... what I'd gone through when he'd cheated on me...how it had gutted me emotionally and isolated me from family and friends.

And the lack of emotion I felt now as I thought of him – it came as a shock. Before West Point, I'd felt everything when his name was mentioned: love and hate, happiness and sadness, bitterness and, oddly, even hope.

But I didn't feel that way anymore. I'd changed.

Because my future was here. At West Point. As a soldier in the U.S. Army. With Isaac and Adrianna and Jacob and Bree.

And Liam.

I had a new life – one I loved.

And hated.

I loved the new 'me', but missed the old 'me', too. Becoming a different person was the proudest, scariest, most exciting and petrifying thing I'd ever been through. I looked at myself in the mirror and barely recognized the person who wore a uniform. I wondered if my family would look at me the same way, or if they would be unnerved about how much I'd changed.

The rigor of each day had effectively kept my mind off of how much I missed them. Since my arrival at the academy, I'd folded their memory up as neatly and tightly as the clothes in my closet, shined my exterior to perfection, and had closed the door on that chapter of my life in order to concentrate on this life, this world.

A world that needed me.

I dropped Bryce's letter onto my mother's, which lay haphazardly on my tidy desk. I reached for the package, knowing from the handwriting it was also from my mom. The corners of the box had been dented in slightly, but the tape that held the flaps together remained intact.

I sliced it open and saw another note:

I found this in our basement the other day, Brooklyn. I'd never seen it before. I thought you'd like to plug it in and watch. You are so much like him.

Love, Mom

I set the note aside, and with shaky hands, I unwrapped the hard object my mom had put in the box. I tossed the crinkled packaging to the side, unveiling a camcorder.

A very old camcorder.

I plugged it in and studied the buttons a little further, recognizing the symbols on them as the same ones on my remote controls at home. From there, I figured out how to eject the black box inside – a videotape – and I opened a hinged screen that had been previously closed.

Whew. Breathe, Brooklyn.

I pushed PLAY. The small screen lit up almost immediately.

A stranger sprang to life on the monitor, fuzzy and far away. He was dressed in casual camo pants and an olive green t-shirt, lounging lazily on a cot in a room that looked markedly similar to the one I was sitting in.

"Pssst. Blackburn." The voice had come from behind the camera. The lens zoomed in to the lounging stranger, and for the first time I recognized him as my father.

He was lankier than most pictures and videos I'd seen growing up, but still pretty solid. When his eyes met the person's behind the lens, it felt like I was looking at some sort modified version of myself. Same color of eyes, hair, and skin. Same look of annoyance I had whenever I was interrupted. Just a different gender.

"Whaddya want, A.P.?"

His voice. It wasn't as deep or gritty as it was in those movies I'd watched from when my brother was a baby, but it was definitely him.

My heart beat faster and I didn't breathe. I held the screen so close it almost touched my nose.

"C'mon, man," the man behind the camera said. "It's about time you grant me an interview. It's been a whole two weeks since you saved me from that collapsing cave."

Teenage-dad tensed, swiveling around to make sure the door to his barrack was closed. "Dude," he said reprovingly. "Everyone can hear you. You gotta be careful."

The man behind the camera cleared his throat. "No one's gonna hear." Despite his nonchalant attitude, the man's voice was much quieter as he continued.

"So," he began. "Rumor has it you have the strength of all the Greek Gods combined. What do you have to say about that?" The interviewer – A.P. or whatever his name was – followed his question with a light chuckle.

My dad turned from the closed door and cracked a smile. "I can neither confirm nor deny my genetic superiority. Saving you? Well, it was just another day in the life of being awesome, man. Nothing too big for these guns to take on." He held up a curled bicep, and despite having just blinked away a tear, I rolled my eyes and felt a bit embarrassed at the display of juvenile chauvinism.

"So what's next?" A.P. asked. "Try to take over the world?" He was speaking in Brain's voice from *Pinky and the Brain*. My brother and I had watched the reruns when we were little. I pushed that memory to the back of my mind to focus on the imprint this new one would make.

My dad laughed, a deep resonating sound I tucked in and around my heart, the same way I'd always imagined him tucking me in when I was a little girl.

"Not quite," he answered. "Just trying to keep the world from being taken over by punks like you." He playfully shoved the man A.P., which ensued in what I can only assume was an epic WWE-esque wrestling match, based on the grunts and laughter I could hear in the background as the camera fell to the floor.

I waited for a beat, then almost turned the camera off when I saw it: the white board on the wall. I scrambled to press PAUSE.

The word "GOALS" was written on the board in sprawling, messy handwriting. About half of my father's face was plastered close-up on the camera's corner as he continued to play-fight, and I chuckled softly at his awkward, frozen pose before I studied the background more closely.

Under the heading, he'd divided the space into three columns and labeled them with the words *A Soldier*, *A Soul*, and *A Future Self*. I squinted until it almost hurt, wanting desperately to understand what inspired my father. I couldn't make it all out, but I saw the words "stronger" and "kinder" under the first column, "fire" under the second, and "wife and kids" under the third.

Had he eventually accomplished everything he'd wanted to before he died? Did he meet all of his goals? If he did, then is that why his time ran out? If he didn't, then was he bothered by it now? Did he feel like he had missed out? Was he mad at God for missing out on me?

There was something else that consumed my thoughts, though. It was the look on his face: the utter joy and pride that was all over it. He didn't have an ounce of hesitation or unworthiness that I battled every day.

Was that because I would never measure up to being the kind of soldier he was?

I turned the camcorder off and returned it to the box, curled up into the fetal position on my bed, and let the thoughts of what once had been and what could have been consume me.

SOMEONE KNOCKED ON MY DOOR. I WIPED away a couple of tears that had escaped and cleared my throat to make sure my voice wasn't blocked.

"Come in!"

Isaac entered, leaving the door open as he sat on my desk chair. West Point had strict rules about males and females, and one of those rules was we were not to be in any room alone unless the door was left open.

Initially I had welcomed the thought of him coming in. I was depressed, and he was the only sure thing that could lighten my mood. But as soon as he had a seat, it was obvious to me his power wouldn't benefit me in any way today.

Because Isaac had it the worst when it came to letters. His mom had sent him a letter every day, and each one read more anxious than the last. They weren't huge problems, what she wrote about, but reading them left you feeling like she was a woman who needed rescuing.

"Your mom?" I prodded as he sat in silence. I didn't mind pressing in to his feelings. It kept my mind off of my own.

He looked toward the ceiling, his arms crossed in front of him. "Sorta," he replied. "She's not handling life well at the moment. She and Jon are fighting more, and the kids are driving her crazy…" His voice trailed off, and he shrugged. "I didn't know she'd be like this without me."

"It's your own fault, you goof," I chided sarcastically. "You've graced her with your presence for the last sixteen years. She can't help but be miserable without you. Your very existence is an irreplaceable gift to the people around you."

"Really," Isaac said, letting a small smile escape across his stressed face. He sat straighter and brought his hands behind his head, lacing his fingers together in a relaxed pose.

"What's it like to be around me?" His question threw me off guard.

I blinked. "Serious?"

"Yeah," he replied. "I never get the benefit of my gift. I'd like to know."

"Hmmm," I began. "It's hard to describe."

He leaned forward attentively.

"It's like the antidote to adrenaline," I finally answered.

His brow furrowed and his hands flew palms up in front of him. "So I'm the opposite of exciting?"

I laughed at the wounded look on his face. "No," I answered, and then bit my lip, trying to think of the best way to describe it without offending him. "You know when you're nervous? Before a big test or something? And then the test is finally over, and you get the grade and you've passed with flying colors? That horrible feeling in the pit of your stomach is gone, and your heart rate is slow, and it just feels like all is right in your world again?"

"I think I know what you mean, but I'm surprised you do." His eyes gleamed mischievously. "Didn't you say you failed all your tests?"

I threw a pillow at him.

"Not true!" I insisted, then gasped.

The pillow had knocked him backwards toward the desk.

Crap. My gift.

I stole a glance at the hallway to make sure no one was walking by, then let out a small laugh of relief when no one was. I turned back to Isaac. "I've just sucked at test-taking this past semester. Before that, I'd always done well."

"What changed for you this year?" His eyes were wide with their questioning. Mine narrowed at the change in topic.

"Nothing that matters anymore," I commented curtly. He didn't need to know about what had happened with Jace. None of the people in my new life needed to know.

"Yeah, yeah, yeah," he said. "Got it. You've got this whole 'keep-the-focus-off-Brooklyn' thing going on." His eyes studied mine for a moment before he shrugged. "Guess I'll let it go, but just for today," he warned.

I smiled, appreciative. "So what'd your mom say this time?" I asked, sitting more erect.

Isaac shrunk a little. "This time she told me about Mo."

Mo was short for Maurice, his youngest brother.

"What's going on with him?" I questioned, genuinely concerned.

Isaac swallowed thickly and stared at his hands. "There's uh, this game we play, Mo and me. We call it 'Titan's Grip'. When he gets a little wild and too worked up to take a nap, he asks me to do it."

"What's it like?"

"It's kinda hard to explain," he began. "Can I show you?"

"Show me?" I answered. "Show me how?"

"Come here," he ordered, standing up.

"O-Okay," I stood on my uncertain legs.

"Come here," he commanded again, laughing and opening his arms.

"Like for a hug?"

"Yeah, like for a hug," he teased. Just backwards. Like we're snuggling."

Snuggling? The thought made my cheeks turn red. I didn't like Isaac like that or anything, but still. He'd said *snuggling*.

"The door's open," he rationalized. "And it's not anything inappropriate."

I let out a breath. "Okay." I scooted my way into his arms. Soon I was standing in front of him, my back flush against the front of his body. My heart rate picked up. My eyes focused on the doorway. Would another cadet walk by? Major McCoy? Then, an even worse scenario:

What would Liam think, if he walked by and saw Isaac holding me this way?

But why did I even care? I was here to train, not stress about boys.

"We're not doing anything wrong," Isaac assured me, but my body was telling me differently.

I closed my eyes and took a shaky breath.

"Cross your arms, like you're hugging your own body," he ordered, and I did as I was told.

"Good," he praised. He wrapped his arms over my own, enveloping my entire body with his. "Now take a deep breath in."

I did, and immediately, I was immersed in utter...calm.

I didn't hear anything: not Isaac's words, the ticking of the clock, the hum of the heater.

Nothing.

Blackness draped over all the things I had just had in my line of vision a second earlier, but it wasn't scary. It was welcome, a relief from all my anxiety - a reprieve

125

from the things that made me so restless. I felt myself take a deep breath in, and another, and then another. Each breath brought a taste or feeling or sense of something…intangibly good…with it. Like the best tasting dessert. Or the smell of Christmas.

Just…peace.

I opened my eyes, aware I was no longer in my previous state right away, because I could hear the intrusive daily sounds from before: the clock and the heater, and I could see the things that stressed me out the most, like the letters that were still spilled over my desk and the open closet with the uniforms in it that were still foreign to me.

"Wow." I was surprised I had even that word.

Isaac turned me slowly and backed me to my bed, sitting me down gently.

"So that's Titan's Grip," I stated. "I thought it would be more… I don't know… 'rough and tumble'?"

"Of course you'd think that, Little Miss I-Can-Bench-Press-Anything," He smiled. "But my power is different. It doesn't break you. It wraps around you like a blanket." He paused and glanced down at his shoes. "So it's good?"

I couldn't help but smile in return. "Yeah, it's good," I laughed. "You do that with Mo all the time?"

"Nah, not all the time," he said, staring out the window, past the Catskills to his home. "Just when he's wound up, or when he has nightmares and stuff." He continued to stare out the window, but his expression hardened. "And he's been having a lot lately."

He removed an envelope from his leg pocket, held it with one hand and slapped it a couple of times against the other. "My mom told me he hasn't been sleeping."

"What's bugging him?"

He turned sharply toward me. "Guess."

My heart sank. "It's cuz you're gone."

He looked out the window, his face fallen. I chose silence rather than words, trying to give him the space he needed to let his thoughts run freely.

"It just sucks," he said after a while. "I know I'm needed here, and I know I belong here. But I think I'm needed at home, too."

"So why not go?" I asked, rising quickly and walking to his side at the window.

"Go?" he asked, skepticism covering every inch of his face. "I can't just 'go', Brooklyn. We're in the Army now." His lips curled into a sad smile as he recited the famous line.

I shrugged. "You could always ask." I punched his shoulder jokingly, making sure to do it lightly. "We're special cases, remember?"

He shrugged, too. "Yeah, I guess." He made his way back to the door to my room. "Thanks for…everything, Brooklyn," he said. "It means a lot."

"I should be thanking you," I replied. "That Titan's Grip…can I get a dose of that more often?"

He raised his eyebrows suggestively, reminding me of the closeness of his body to mine. "I just might let you."

With that, he jetted out of sight.

20

THAT EVENING, I'D WOKEN UP EVERY COUPLE OF hours, greeted by nothing but the inky black space around me. On any other night, the dark comforted me as I slept, like some kind of weighted blanket I could pull up and around my shoulders, but it was different this time.

This time, I knew what was waiting for me in the morning.

I woke up for good an hour or so before the sun's yolk cracked on the horizon. Major McCoy had asked us to meet him in the lobby bright and early for yet another drill and exercise, created especially for the six of us.

The way he'd said it had made me shudder. I'd failed his first test of endurance miserably, and I could have sworn his eyes gleamed with malice when he announced the new one.

I put my Army sweats on and made sure my hair was worn off the collar, wrapped into a bun at the top of my head. I brushed my teeth and looked in the mirror, staring at an expression that looked entirely too much like startled prey: wide-eyed and terrified.

And after waiting on the edge of my bed for five minutes and making a half-hearted attempt to study my Plebe Bible, I made my way out of the dorm into the main lobby to see if anyone else was up and ready.

Isaac, Bree, and Liam were already waiting. Bree gave me a tired wave and a yawn. Isaac's head was resting on the palm of his hand, and the hood of his was sweatshirt up. I suspected he was snoozing, but he was turned away from me at an angle, so I couldn't tell. Liam sat straighter on the couch as I entered, and despite my nervousness, I stifled a laugh. A shoot of his hair was sticking up and out in the back, making him look boyishly cute, like an overgrown Dennis the Menace.

He looked at me quizzically. "What?"

I reached out and attempted to tame the wild curl, admittedly letting my hand linger a bit longer than necessary. "You're a mess first thing in the morning," I teased.

"Well not everyone can roll out of bed looking like a ballerina on center stage." He playfully tapped the top of my bun.

"Roll out bed looking ready to go?" I asked. "Ha!"

"Girls never look good just rolling out of bed," Bree agreed, leaning in between us. She gave her brother a stern look. "It takes time, Liam."

"Maybe for some girls," he said. Then he gave me a wink. "But not all of them."

I was saved from having to reply when Adrianna strode in, securing her ponytail and looking rushed, with Major McCoy and Jacob on her heels.

"Good to see that you're all up and ready to go," Major McCoy declared. He lightly tapped the side of

129

Isaac's head, jolting him awake. The sight of Isaac jumping out of his skin made us all laugh.

"This morning we're heading down to the Field House – Gillis Field House."

"Where they play volleyball?" Isaac asked sleepily. He immediately looked embarrassed. "I may have seen a practice or two," he explained. "In my spare time."

"Yes, it's where they play volleyball," Major McCoy answered. "But the basketball and track and field team practice there, too."

"Ugh, we're not running again, are we?" Jacob asked, a tinge of fear in his voice.

"Not today, no," Major McCoy said. "But you *do* have your inhaler, right?" Jacob nodded.

Major McCoy's voice got quieter as he leaned down a fraction of an inch. "Today we're going to a private area of the Field House, unknown to the majority of athletes and coaches. Today we're going to The Labyrinth."

"The Labyrinth?" I asked. "As in, a maze? Are you going to put cheese in the middle of it and see how many tries it takes to get us there?"

Major McCoy considered my joke. "Something like that."

Before we could ask any questions, he turned on his heel and opened the front door. "After you, Cadets." And like a short line of ants following their instincts, we scurried through the doorway.

WE WERE IN THE BASEMENT OF THE FIELD

house. Major McCoy had slipped behind the solid gray mat that loomed in front of us now, having excused himself to do a final inspection of The Labyrinth, wanting to ensure everything was ready for our challenge. The mat looked like those anchoring the ends of most gymnasiums, only it was a few feet taller and much, much wider. It had only one doorway in the center and was connected to the walls on each side. The room we were in seemed as expansive as the stadium above it, but I couldn't tell for sure because the barrier was blocking my view.

Jacob was hopping from one foot to another, trying to see over the wall, while Adrianna was studying it from the side, as if she was prepping for a final exam. The rest of us stood silently, waiting for directions.

We'd arrived here after weaving in and out of various rooms and practice gymnasiums, going down side staircases most would never notice. The workout areas, tracks, and gyms were huge, and everything was painted and stained in the school colors: black and gold. The upper levels radiated a level of pride I'd never seen on any of my college visitations.

The military. The athletics. The academics. We were given the best of all three things, wrapped in a West Point bow, presented only to the most gifted youth.

I thought of my dad's image from the video my mom had sent me, comparing his eager grin to my anxious stomach. He carried a level of pride and promise that I didn't feel, that I'd never experienced. The fact that I'd failed the first test so badly, that I was struggling to memorize everything I need to in my Plebe Bible, that I constantly felt like I didn't deserve to be here – it all made me feel like I was a kid sister playing dress up, pretending to be somebody great, when the only thing extraordinary about me was the level of 'ordinary' I carried.

"Okay, Cadets," Major McCoy commanded, rubbing his hands together as he emerged from behind the wall. "Looks like we're all ready to go." Jacob and Adrianna returned to the group as he continued.

"Behind me is The Labyrinth. It's made up of a series of walls and rooms. The purpose of those walls and rooms is to hide something that needs to be found. In this case, that's *you*. I'm going to take five of you back until you are hidden securely within an assigned area."

"Sir?" The question came from Adrianna. "There are six of us. You said you're only taking back five."

"That's right," Major McCoy continued. "One of you will be left out here while the others are tucked away in their individual spots. *That* cadet's job is to use this or her gifts to find the others. You'll have ten minutes to do it. When your time is up, it'll be someone else's turn."

"What will we win?" Jacob asked.

"I'd be more concerned with what you'll lose," Major McCoy said, watching to make sure his underlying threat was understood.

"What else is there besides finding the others?" I asked. "I mean, there's got to be something else involved, right?"

Major McCoy was quick to cover up his momentary grin. "Yes, there are a few more factors you'll have to consider."

He held our gaze for a moment. "Those who are hidden will experience something a bit odd: a slight vibration you'll feel throughout your body. Other Crest members have said it feels a bit like electricity pulsating in and around their frame. The pulse is used to keep you from leaving your hiding place. It, uh, *intensifies* if you try to open your door to escape."

"Does it hurt?" Bree asked.

"Depends," Major McCoy answered casually. "For most, it's simply annoying, but tolerable. As time passes, however, it's been known to increase in intensity."

A shudder of fear coursed through my body, and I wondered if that was how this pulse would feel.

Or if it'd be worse.

"The cadet finding the others," Major McCoy continued, "will be blindfolded. But they have the benefit of not being distracted by the pulse as they search. If you are found, you must not interfere with the remaining search. You must let the finder use his or her gifts to lead you to the others and out of the maze."

"So how are we found?" Adrianna asked. "Do we shout out?"

"You can yell if you want," Major McCoy said, "But they won't hear you. The walls you're hidden within are sound-proof."

"So in order to find them, we open every door we come to?" This time the question came from Liam.

"You won't be able to see the doors, Liam. You'll be blindfolded, remember?" Major McCoy smiled. "I'm afraid I really can't give you any more guidance than what I already have, Cadets. Otherwise, how will I be able to see how you use your gifts to help others?"

Major McCoy reached into his pocket and held out six straws. "Pick one," he ordered. We reached in at the same time, and each of us pulled one out. Mine had a number four written on it.

Bree nudged me with her elbow to show me her straw labeled with the number one. "Wanna trade?" She looked even paler than usual.

"Not a chance. Sorry." I shuffled to the doorway, where Major McCoy instructed Bree to wait while he guided us to the area behind the mat. Liam rushed over to his sister and said something in her ear. It must have been encouraging because she smiled back before we disappeared from her view.

We turned left, then right, then left again, followed by another left. It was, by and large, more of the same with each turn we took. The gray walls were so tall they almost met the ceiling, and they were always to the left and right of us, guiding us to unknown destinations.

One by one, we were dropped off: Jacob first, then Liam, who squeezed my hand in solidarity before the door shut on him. Then Adrianna and Isaac. And finally, me.

Major McCoy instructed me to do the same as he'd instructed the others: sit in the corner and wait. The ceiling of the cramped room hung low, and as soon as the door shut, I was surrounded by complete nothingness.

It was dark – darker than I'd ever experienced in my life. I felt what could have been the pulsing sensation running through my veins – but maybe it was adrenaline? Maybe I was actually claustrophobic but never even knew it?

Maybe something bad would happen here and I'd be stuck here to rot forever.

I screamed out loud, over and over. Not because I was scared – or at least, that's what I told myself. I screamed to test Major McCoy's theory that I would not be heard.

Minutes passed, I was sure of it. I'd scream out once in a while, but mostly I found that counting did the best job of soothing my soul while I waited.

And something else was happening, too. Something really weird. The hum I felt inside of me came in three distinct waves: stronger, then an abrupt relief, then a gradual strengthening all over again. Three times it occurred, and each time it made me feel like my hair should be standing on end.

Pressure began to build inside me so intensely that my body felt like a weakened dam – ready to break at any moment. It was more than adrenaline, more than a hurt. I remembered reading once that prisoners of war sometimes had to endure small drops of water being dripped on their foreheads for extended periods of time. I didn't bother them at first, but after a while, they lost their minds and felt as though each small drop was torture.

The hum was like that. Inconsequential at first, but spreading like oil, reverberating in every cell of my body, in every atom of my environment.

I couldn't stand it anymore. I had to get out.

I stood up and remembered the wall across from me in that small room – the wall with the door. Using every ounce of power I could muster, I channeled my energy by ramming my shoulder into it: once, twice, three times.

And suddenly a brilliant light blinded me as the door cracked open. At the exact same time, the pulse got so bad that it felt like I'd been struck by lightning. Pain tore through my body. My fingers pulled at my hair.

I couldn't even muster a scream, it hurt so badly. I heard footsteps come down the hall and used all my remaining strength to pull the door shut again.

The intense pain stopped immediately and the quiet hum took its place.

Again, light flooded the room as the door opened. This time, I didn't experience pain. The hum ended and I felt relief. Major McCoy stood in front of me.

"Take a moment to gather yourself," he advised. "I know the sudden light can be disorienting."

I stumbled out of the room and breathed deeply, as if that small room had been depleted of air as well as light.

"It's your turn to try and find the others, Brooklyn. Let's make our way to the front." He grabbed my elbow, and for a brief moment, I felt as if my heart had been jump-started by those defibrillators you see doctors use on TV. Like a lawn mower when its string is first pulled, it took a second for it to sputter back into its natural beat.

"Did you — I mean — is that *your* power?" I asked.

"I'm not sure what you're talking about, Brooklyn," Major McCoy answered, his tone sharp and clipped.

"The electricity. The- the – "

"No time to get into that," he said. "It's almost time for you to be blindfolded. You need to find the others. None of them have been rescued yet."

Crap. Blinded. Again.

Crap.

And the others…were they freaking out, too— the way I'd been as I waited? I realized that I had no idea who numbers five and six were, who'd have to wait the longest in the dark to be saved while that pulse and the darkness assaulted them.

I needed to be the one who could rescue them from that hell.

We'd reached the front of The Labyrinth. Major McCoy shook a black handkerchief loose from his pocket and folded it over my eyes.

"You ready, Brooklyn?" he asked.

As if I'd ever be ready.

21

MY HANDS WERE EXTENDED UNCERTAINLY IN front of me as I stumbled through the first minute or so of my turn in The Labyrinth. Once again, I was enveloped in total darkness, but this time, I didn't feel the pulse of electricity flowing through me, so could actually think clearly and logically about what I needed to do. My breath came quick and fast. It was beyond disturbing that it was the only sound I could hear in a space where six others were present.

I needed to find them, and fast. The blindfold and soundproof rooms ensured I had no way to find out where they were, though, unless my gift could work somehow.

My mind traveled back to the dark room, when I used every ounce of strength I'd had to ram the door open before Major McCoy had arrived.

So... there was a possibility I could use my gift to knock the doors down.

But how could I see them?

As if it were a sign from the heavens, the blindfold shifted slightly on the bridge of my nose. Was it loose?

I brought my hands to the cloth and pulled it out at the bottom.

I could see the floor.

I could see the floor.

I paused for a moment, listening intently for any sign of Major McCoy around me. I pulled the cloth up a bit more so I could see a bit, and turned slowly.

No sign of him.

I placed the blindfold back down over my eyes, but not all the way, leaving a space at the bottom that would allow me to see a break in the wall that would signal a door. I still walked with my hands in front of me, my head tilted slightly back so I could see where I was going. My pace had quickened with the assurance of solid ground beneath me.

I turned a corner, saw the first door, and backed up, steeling myself for the impact that was to come.

With all my might, I rammed into that space on the wall – maybe even a bit too hard, because the door swung open on the first try. A squeal of delight from Bree was my reward. She hugged me hard, and I could feel the wetness of her cheeks. She must have had a really hard time.

Buoyed by that success, I inched the blindfold up a tad further. Bree followed me from a distance as I rounded another corner, and then another, and found yet another break in the wall that indicated a door.

Once again, I gave myself a running start, and once again, I freed a grateful Crest member. This time, it was Jacob.

Those two followed me as I found Liam. It was hard for me to hide my smile when I'd seen his broaden widely under the loose fold of the handkerchief. He gave me a quick peck on the cheek. "Of course you did it, Brooklyn. I knew you would."

I could feel in my bones that time was almost up, and I still had Adrianna and Isaac to find. The others huddled close together behind me, and I weighed my options.

I knew we had to be close to the back of the maze. I'd started at the front and had gotten three of them so far, so I had to be quite a ways in. I tilted my head even further back to look up and down the long passage.

There was an exit at both ends, but something unidentifiable was pulling me to the right. Forgetting about the others and that I was supposed to be blindfolded, I sprinted to the end, through the opening, and turned left, then left again, and then right.

I hadn't even been searching for the hidden doorway that now stood impressively in front of me. I'd simply followed something my heart heard loud and clear, as if I were a captain of a wooden ship from long ago, being beckoned by a Siren. What stood behind the door was a Siren that beckoned me.

I rammed into the door, and Isaac stood, grinning from ear to ear.

"You felt me!" he proclaimed.

And in that moment, I realized I'd been seeking peace the whole time.

"WELL DONE, BROOKLYN."

Major McCoy had entered the area and was clapping slowly. "You got most of the other cadets in the ten minutes we gave you. *Most* of them."

Adrianna shuffled in behind him and quickly joined our group.

"I'm not surprised you were able to break through the doors," he said, as if still mulling the circumstances over in his brain. "But what *does* surprise me is the fact that you were able to find the doors in the first place."

My heart hammered in my chest.

"Jacob could find them," he commented. "And Isaac could find them, too, because of their gifts of sensing thoughts and feelings. They just couldn't find a way to get in and retrieve their comrades. But why did you succeed at finding them when Liam, Bree, and Adrianna could not?"

I didn't know how to answer. Suddenly the rules of the game were more pronounced then they'd been minutes earlier. He'd said we were to leave our blindfolds on, and I obviously didn't abide by his instructions.

"Is there a gift you have that I'm not aware of, Cadet Blackburn?"

I shook my head.

"Then what possible explanation do you have?"

"I – uh – my blindfold wasn't on that tight," I admitted. "I could see through it a little." I studied my shoelaces.

"I see," Major McCoy said simply. "Well, then, I guess there's nothing left to do here. We better make our way up to the courts and take care of this little problem." He turned swiftly and rounded a corner, then motioned for us to follow. "Come on, now," he instructed.

We followed in silence, back through the maze, through the doors that led to The Labyrinth, and up the stairs. I was wracking my brain to try and figure out why he didn't even yell at me for cheating after my admission. Did he understand that I was only trying to get them all away from the pulsing that had driven me mad?

We were weaving our way back through one of the practice gyms when Major McCoy held up a hand. "Wait here."

"I'm sorry, guys," I whispered hurriedly. "It's not fair that I won, and I'm – I'm sorry."

They weren't given a chance to respond. Major McCoy had returned swiftly with something that resembled two large grain sacks slung over his shoulder and a metal folding chair. He placed the folding chair in the center of the gym and walked to Adrianna, heaving the grain sacks at her feet.

They were actually heavy-duty ankle weights, the biggest I'd ever seen. He strapped them to her legs and asked her to jump. She was barely able to. "You need these to even the field a bit," he remarked. She didn't answer him – just gazed straight ahead.

He told us all to get on the end line and pulled his whistle out. Weighed down with embarrassment and about to cry, I suddenly yelled out, "Please. Please don't make us run. It was my mistake. Mine. Not theirs. I'm sorry."

"Oh, right," the major said dismissively. "*Your* mistake. You're right. I almost forgot, Brooklyn. *You* were the one who took the easy option in order to succeed, correct? You're the one who cheated?"

I nodded. As much as I didn't want to run, I didn't want the other Crest members to run because of me.

"Ah," he answered. "Well then, that chair's for you." He pointed to the solidary metal chair on the half-court line.

"Ex-excuse me?"

"The chair. It's for you. It's the cheater's chair." He said it as if he were describing something completely unremarkable. "Go on. Sit in it."

I walked on shaky legs to the middle of the court, wondering if this was some kind of old-fashioned, humiliating exercise like wearing a dunce cap in the corner of the classroom. And as I took a seat and listened to what Major McCoy had to say next, I wished it'd been that easy.

"You didn't just sign up to go on duty for your country, Cadet Blackburn. You signed up for *honor*, too. And West Point cadets don't cheat."

"Now sit back in your chair. Enjoy the break. Celebrate the win." He turned to the others. "And you five, get ready to run on her behalf for the mistake she made."

He blew a whistle, and I closed my eyes as the rest of the Crest members blew past me. Shame covered every inch of my body, and I couldn't look anywhere but my lap.

Down and back, they ran, for so many laps and for so long that I lost count of how many they'd done. I chewed my nails until they bled, rocked back and forth – asked him repeatedly if I could take their place. He said no. I began pleading with him to let me join, too. Again, he denied me and told me to sit and watch.

I prayed for a miracle to happen, for Major McCoy to take pity on my friends who had done the task right and let them stop running.

He didn't.

That is, until Bree started puking. I jumped from my chair to help her, but Major McCoy threatened to make them run even longer if I didn't sit back down.

"Sit down, Brooklyn! You've done enough!" The command had come from Adrianna this time. She spat the words out loudly, but wouldn't even look my way. My hands flew to my ears, then covered my head altogether. At this, Major McCoy let his whistle fall from his lips and told the rest of the Crest members they could stop.

"You," he declared, looking directly at me, his voice dripping with distaste and contempt. "Do me a favor and go back to your room without them, since you're only looking after yourself, anyway."

I couldn't wait to escape and lurched out of the double doors of the gym, finally able to run like I'd wanted to when they had done it for me. I heard Liam yell my name from behind me, but I ignored him and made myself sprint across campus until I started to feel a searing level of pain in my muscles and lungs.

Finally arriving at the barracks, I collapsed onto my bed and sobbed.

I didn't know who I was anymore. The old Brooklyn didn't fit in here, and the new Brooklyn didn't deserve to wear the same uniform as the heroes surrounding me.

22

I PRACTICALLY SPRINTED INTO THE CLASSROOM.

I wasn't afraid of being late to our first Tactics class - the only one we'd be taking with the "normal" cadets at West Point. And I definitely wasn't running because I was excited to get there.

I was running because I needed to see Isaac.

He was the only one that had been able to calm my sobs the last two days, the only one to bring peace to the chaos of my futile apologies.

One by one, the members had made their way into my room to tell me they forgave me.

Liam had come first, had laid his broad hands on my back as I cried.

"It's not your fault, Brooklyn," he'd told me over and over. "We know you. We know you weren't driven to win. You were driven to rescue. It's who you are, and it's not a bad thing."

The words were kind and true, but they didn't take away the sting of having all of them punished for something I had done. He'd left, defeated, giving me a fierce hug. "I wish there was a way I could heal your heart," he said. "But give me time and maybe I can learn how."

"I'm sorry I snapped at you," Adrianna had explained when she visited. "I was just exhausted and the whole reason we were running was unfair. But it wasn't you I was mad at – it was Major McCoy."

Bree and Jacob had come together. "We didn't even run as hard as we were supposed to be running," Bree confided to me. She elbowed Jacob in the ribs to speak up. "She's right," he added hastily. "I wasn't about to be punished for something I didn't even do. I coasted the whole time."

I remembered his beet red face as he was finally allowed to stop. My friends were sweet, but they weren't being honest when they insisted that my bad choice hadn't hurt them.

Isaac had come to me last. He'd opened his arms widely, and I knew he was inviting me into a Titan's Grip. Suddenly, I'd recognized it as the only thing that would help me, and I'd been right.

Being surrounded by Isaac was the same as being immersed in peace.

It was that peace I needed now.

I skidded to a stop and slid into the nearest, unoccupied table I could find in the classroom, leaving an empty chair next to me, then frantically searched the area around me.

No sign of him.

And no sign of the other Crest members, either.

I tried to slow my breathing and searched the doorway instead. Maybe he was just late. Yeah, that was all.

Any time now.

I did my best to slow my breathing and calm the hell down.

I'd woken up before dawn — 4:05 a.m., to be exact — and had been freaking out ever since.

The thing is, I couldn't even explain why I was so upset — couldn't pinpoint it, anyway.

It wasn't just what had happened after the last drill. *Everything* that had gone wrong at West Point — and anything that could go wrong, here and even in the world — was racing through my mind. It was a horror film on repeat, and I was a mess because of it.

It was scary as hell, being so afraid. And the thought of being stuck in that level of anxiety made me freak out even more.

That's why I needed Isaac.

I needed him to calm me down before I was taken to the psych ward. I searched the doorway again.

Liam entered and grinned at me. Suddenly, his eyes widened, and he sprinted to my side.

"What's wrong? What happened?"

I blinked up at him, then looked over his shoulder.

"Where's Isaac?"

He paused, but just for a beat. He shot a concerned look at Bree, who had materialized at his side. "He went home for a couple days."

My shoulders fell as I heard the words — as I truly digested their meaning — and I couldn't help it. My eyes teared up, too.

"Major McCoy said he could go," Liam continued. He sat in the empty seat next to me.

He looked at Bree, who had sat down in front of us, as if she could provide more clarification into why I was acting like a crazy person.

"He said Isaac being at West Point has messed with his family," he explained. "They left…" He glanced at his watch. "About three hours ago, at oh-four hundred. But Brooklyn?" he asked.

I wiped a tear away.

He grabbed my hand and craned his head down and to the side, so his gaze would meet mine, even though I was trying to look into my lap. "Why does it even matter where Isaac is? What happened to you?"

And for a second, even though I'd been lost in a panicked fog, I was now found in the calm of his eyes. The deep green drew me in.

He relaxed with me, then looked at the hand he'd just grabbed and gasped. I looked down, too, and saw blood on my fingertips.

I'd chewed my nails down to their beds. They were still bleeding, and suddenly I could feel their deep, resonating sting.

I clenched my hands into fists, hiding what I'd done, and I closed my eyes. Liam draped an arm over me.

"I don't know what's going on," I choked, my chin resting on my chest. "I just – I woke up before dawn and I –"

I shot up. "Wait. What time did Isaac leave?"

Liam paused, his eyebrow slightly furrowed. "Four o'clock this morning. Why?"

And for a moment, I didn't answer. I couldn't. I was too freaked out.

"I can't be away from him," I finally whispered, dropping into my seat again.

"Who?"

"Isaac." I turned toward Liam. "I need him."

And for a brief moment, his eyes changed. No longer just concerned, they were...I don't know. Sad, maybe?

"Should I get an officer, or someone else that can help her?" I heard Bree whisper.

Liam shook his head. "No," he whispered back. "We gotta keep a low profile, remember?"

But suddenly, as if he had a sudden and unexpected idea, he sat upright.

I threw him a questioning look, and he answered with a mischievous grin.

23

"I READ ABOUT THIS IN MY PSYCHOLOGY CLASS last year."

Liam leaned back and casually crossed his arms across his chest. "It's not a big deal at all. Sometimes, under traumatic circumstances, people objectify the source of their fears, and sometimes, they objectify the source of their happiness, too – their peace and calm."

"So..."

"So you've turned Isaac into something he isn't. You've decided you need him to be calm and stay here. But you don't."

"All this change," he said, motioning to the brick walls around us, "It's a lot to adapt to. And you've decided you've only coped because of Isaac. But you're wrong."

"I am?" My chest felt hollow.

"You are," Liam said, grinning again. My heart beat a little harder.

He leaned forward again, speaking quietly as more cadets entered the room. "You're stronger than you know." He smiled again.

His eyes. Oh, god, his eyes.

"And you're more beautiful than you'll ever admit," he added.

My heart was hammering my ribs now. I couldn't help it. I bit my lip, then brought my ragged fingers up to my face and started to hide behind them.

"Stop," he commanded, but it came out as a gentle whisper.

He reached out for my bloodied hand and laced his callused fingers in mine before lowering them below the table.

His timing was perfect. An officer had walked in, and with the commotion of everyone in front of us clambering to stand and salute as he entered the room, he was oblivious to the very public display of affection Liam had just shown.

"At ease," he commanded.

Everyone sat.

I felt strong and weak at the same time, unable to concentrate on anything while he lightly traced circles with his thumb. I shivered as the rough, callused surface of his thumb glided across my palm; it was heaven, coupled with the sensation of his soft touch.

But I needed him to stop.

Because I didn't need him. I didn't want him to like me this much, to make me like him. And when Liam did things like compliment me, or smile at me, or hold my hand... the only thing I could concentrate on was breathing normally.

"Cadet?" I finally heard. It was coming from the front of the room. "Cadet Blackburn?"

Liam dropped my hand.

I blinked. "Hmm?"

Stifled giggles and opened jaws surrounded me. I blinked again and saw the officer in charge stride toward me. He was almost completely bald and had beady black eyes. His voice was gruff and his language abrupt.

I sat straighter. "Yes, Sir."

The officer stopped in his tracks.

"Oh. So you *can* hear."

"Yes, Sir."

"Nothing is wrong with your hearing, New Cadet?"

"No, Sir," I answered.

"But something is wrong with your response time."

He studied me, unamused. He jutted a square chin out, as if he were offended that I was wasting his time.

"Er – Um." I couldn't find the words.

"I believe walking the area might help you improve your response time, Cadet," the officer remarked. "Midnight to three. Understand?"

My heart sank. Walking the area was a horrible punishment, and everyone knew it. It was relentless walking and standing at attention, guarding the barracks during what would normally be your free time. Cadets hated it because it was exhausting, especially in the middle of the night after a day's worth of PT had taken its toll.

"Yes, Sir," I replied. "I'll be there at midnight."

The officer appeared to be momentarily appeased, and he turned his back to me and made his way, once again, to the front of the class. All of the cadets in the classroom followed him with their stares.

Except for Adrianna.

She was sitting in the front row with some firsties, way ahead of us. She gave me a motherly, reproachful glare, then turned around, too.

But she couldn't be mad at me for *this*, I thought. I wasn't the one instigating this public display of affection...and besides, she was breaking Major McCoy's rules, too: we weren't supposed to hang out with the other cadets.

And she was a plebe...sitting with firsties. That would be unheard of, even if we were normal cadets.

But still, it wasn't as scandalous as Liam was behaving. He had reached for my hand again, under the table. I was sure my cheeks were reddening, and he turned slightly, smiled, and winked.

Damn him.

I couldn't focus all over again and passed the time praying Officer....Officer....Who? (DAMN YOU, LIAM!).... Praying Officer What's-His-Name wouldn't call on me.

Thankfully, he didn't.

But I was still lost when the screeching of chairs against the tiled floor assaulted my ears. Liam had dropped my hand and had stood with the rest of them. He grinned and jerked his head toward a table that was pushed up against the wall under the window. I followed him clumsily, searching the room for clues about what we were supposed to be doing.

There were numerous tables just like it, scattered around the room, and the other cadets had all paired off and were stationed at them.

The top of the table was a shallow box. In fact, it took me leaning over it to realize it wasn't a table at all, but a diorama, filled with miniature trees and a carefully sculpted terrain. Little army guys – like the ones Bryce and I used to play with when we were young – were in a pile in the corner.

I immediately brightened – whether it was at the thought of doing something hands-on and harmless, or the fond memory, I wasn't sure.

"What are we supposed to be doing?" I whispered to Liam.

He grinned. "Weren't you paying attention?"

I rolled my eyes. "I could always get a new partner."

"Hmmm…." Liam replied, feigning offense before letting his lips curve back up into a smile. "I don't know about that, Blackburn."

He leaned closer to me. I could feel his body heat, and felt the heat deep in the pit of my stomach, too. "I think we'd make a pretty great team."

What a line, I thought. But his eyes showed nothing but sincerity.

"A team?" I asked nervously. "Of two?"

I thought of the others in The Crest and stole a glance at Bree and Jacob, who were at another diorama across the room. Jacob was already playing with the little army men, and Bree was laughing at him. Adrianna had paired up with Austin Stovall, the nice firstie who had given us our initial tour.

And Isaac was gone.

He was gone.

And I was fine.

I grinned – freakishly wide, I was sure, but Liam laughed.

"Wow," he commented. "Welcome back to the land of the living."

"And you got me here," I replied.

For once, it was Liam who blushed.

"Isaac's gone, and I'm fine," I declared, as if it were front-page news. Liam was kind enough to smile back.

"Alright, Cadets!" I heard from across the room. "Now that you're all stationed by a model…"

"I know I am," Liam whispered.

"Shut. Up," I mouthed.

I was here to learn, not to flirt. Right.

"I want you to think tactically about how you and your fellow soldier would get out of a S.O.L. situation."

"S.O.L., Sir?" Jacob asked.

"Sh---Uh, 'crap' out of luck," Liam answered.

The officer looked at Liam with a humorous expression and corrected him, putting the intended cuss word in its place. The class laughed quietly.

"So, cussing isn't your thing," I commented to him in a whisper. His blush deepened. To his credit, he smiled back. "My grandparents hated it. I can't even bring myself to do it and look cool. Instead, I look like a preschooler using too big of a word in a completely incorrect way."

His unabashed innocence didn't repulse me at all. If anything, it added to his appeal. His pure mind seemed almost hilariously at odds with his dangerously good looks.

I stifled another giggle. The officer cleared his throat and shot me a stern glance.

"Your job is to create your own S.O.L situation, using the model and the men that have been provided for you. And use the four principles of tactical warfare I just taught to get yourself out of it."

The cadets in the room either stirred or froze, depending on their excitement level for the project.

I froze.

"I don't have a clue what to do," I admitted to Liam.

He swallowed a smile. "Darn. Neither do I."

"But you were paying attention," I insisted.

"Only to you," Liam countered.

And I wanted to be mad at him for it, but I couldn't.

"Guess we better just make it up as we go, then," I said, dejected. I peered into the diorama. There were two green army men and around twenty brown.

"So…twenty on two?" I remarked.

"Looks like it," Liam said.

We spent the next half hour configuring and reconfiguring the twenty opposing men in brown, stationing them in miniature trees, behind dilapidated buildings and on top of hills. When we were finally done with the setup, we had to do the rest: make our two guys S.O.L.

That meant putting them in the middle of an open field, lower than any of the surrounding hills. Every plastic weapon was pointed at them, and they were surrounded.

Our poor plastic men.

I looked at Liam. "Okay," I said. "We've created the S.O.L. situation. Now what are we going to do to get out of it?"

Liam's brow furrowed as he studied the two soldiers below him. "Hmmm….Not sure." He fiddled around with the army men for a couple of minutes, then gave up and let me have a turn.

"The only thing I can think of is…going back-to-back," I stated lamely. "Because they have the best view of the aggressors that way, and having someone behind you, poised and ready to shoot, is like having eyes in the back of your head. You know, if you trust them."

Liam was still looking at the diorama, but brightened at the suggestion. "You know what? I think you might be right. I think I remember him saying something about trusting your platoon during class."

"So back-to-back it is?" I asked.

Liam raised an eyebrow and threw a teasing grin my way. "I don't know, Blackburn. Do you have my back?"

"Yes," I laughed. "And do you have mine?"

His face was suddenly serious. "Always."

We turned our miniatures back-to-back so they were facing opposite directions, then collected our books at our desk and started to leave with the other cadets.

Out of the blue, Liam held his pointer finger up. "One sec," he said.

I waited patiently in the hall, just outside of the doorway, when he went back and changed something at our table. Officer-What's-His-Name joined him, seemed to ask a question, and then nodded his approval after Liam spoke.

"What'd he say?" I asked as Liam met me in the hall.

"He liked what we did," he answered. "He said it was the only solution that made sense, and we were the only ones who had thought of it."

"Really?" I asked. "That's awesome!" I paused. "Wait a minute. Did you change something, though?"

"Just a little modification," Liam said cryptically.

"Like what?"

"I'll show you when we have Tactics again," he assured.

But he never did get the chance.

24

FIGHT.

It was the last word General Richards had said to us. But as we entered into the second half of October, I couldn't even think about how it was the reason for all of my efforts at West Point. My mind was desperately doggy-paddling among the crushing, crashing waves of West Point academia. We were back with Major McCoy today, and with only five of us, he made sure we were paying attention. To everything.

First, we had marching drills to practice and remember. We had to memorize the Plebe Bible. Be tested over tactical skills. Learn about dates and wars. Explain their implications to present-day warfare.

On top of everything else, I'd had to walk the area last night, so I was three hours short on sleep.

Major McCoy must have sensed that I wasn't on my A-game, but he didn't say anything. Instead, he addressed what had happened three days earlier in the field house. "Let's pretend we're starting over, Brooklyn. I still highly regard you as a soldier, and you respect me as your commanding officer."

The words had brought me some level of comfort, but I was still barely staying afloat.

My brain just couldn't take any more.

I entered the cafeteria and made my way to the salad bar, then picked up a porcelain plate and stared at the food.

So many choices. Too many to remember. Too many to choose from.

I couldn't even focus on food. Things really *were* dire.

I felt two big hands rest on my shoulders and a whisper in my ear. "You too, huh?"

"Hmmm?" I asked, my mind still muddled.

Isaac leaned over me and grabbed a peach, then set it on his tray.

"Isaac!" I exclaimed. "When did you get back?"

He grinned. "Just now." He looked around him to make sure no one was listening. "Going home was a good idea. Mo was still loopy from Titan's Grip when I left. I think they'll be able to handle life for a little bit longer in my absence this time."

I sighed, relieved. "Good. Now you can stay here with me."

He returned my smile. "So you missed me, did you? Don't tell me that you can't live without my gift."

I considered it. "Well, I actually thought I couldn't. But now I know I can."

Isaac looked at me quizzically.

"I found out the hard way," I explained. "Almost had a nervous breakdown." I waved my hand as if it were a topic worthy of dismissal. "But I survived." I turned to him and grinned. "Your gift is nice and all," I told him. "But it's not necessary."

Isaac shook his head. "Ooooookay. Guess I missed a big story about that. But what other kind of craziness did I miss? You're acting all weird," He nodded to our table. "And Bree is, too. I think she's gonna go AWOL any time now."

I turned and looked. Sure enough, Bree was staring off into the distance and didn't even respond as Liam placed a plate of food in front of her.

"You two going to eat, or just hold up the line?" Major McCoy interrupted, slicing his way between us.

"Uh, yeah. We're going. Sorry, Sir," I stammered.

"That's the reason we're all going crazy," I whispered to Isaac as Major McCoy walked away. "He's torturing us, I swear – even beyond whatever it was he did to us in The Labyrinth. He's pushing us to exhaustion during PT and tactical and all of the intro-to-Army classes, too."

Isaac laughed. "I'd tell you 'I'm sorry' for having missed it, but I'd be lying."

"Jerk," I teased.

I reached behind him, plopped a quick spoonful of cottage cheese onto my plate, and threw a banana on there for good measure. I made my way over to another line and splashed some macaroni-and-cheese onto the tray as well, then headed to our table.

"There you are," Liam said, shifting forward in his seat as I approached the table. "What took so long?"

Isaac threw his plate down next to mine. "She's a typical woman, that's what. Couldn't make up her damn mind."

I backhanded him across the chest.

His chair flew backwards a few feet. Isaac winced and let out a wheeze.

160

"You okay?" I asked.

"I'm — I'm okay —" he choked, and I laughed. It was entirely possible I had hurt him, but it was obvious he was acting more injured than he actually was.

"You guys," Adrianna admonished. "Can you act a little more like soldiers, please? I mean..." she jerked her head to the other tables around us.

The other cadets were studying us, and a mixture of curiosity, distaste, and awe hung in the air. They were showcasing their impeccable manners.

We were not.

I cleared my throat, then looked into my lap.

"You three. Grab your belongings. Come with me." I only saw the shiny black tips of Major McCoy's shoes — didn't see who exactly he was referring to — but knew I was one of them.

I quietly pushed my chair back and forced myself to look up when I stood. Major McCoy's face was a deep shade of red. He pointed to a hallway at the other end of the cafeteria. I made a beeline to the destination, food and all.

The moment I stepped into the dim hallway, Major McCoy pushed past me to open a door. I entered the room, which was much like a lounge, with only enough space to accommodate one round table.

"Sit," he said as Liam and Isaac shuffled in behind me.

They sat, one on each side of me, placing their trays down quietly as well.

"Who the hell do you think you are?"

I didn't answer. He wasn't asking like he wanted a response. He was making a point.

"Don't you realize our entire country's future is at stake with your powers?"

I stole a glance at Isaac and Liam. They were both looking into their laps, so I did the same.

Major McCoy marched over to me.

"First, you did over a hundred pushups in front of a Regimental Commander. And now you've hit Isaac so hard it took the wind out of him. And you did it in front of the entire campus."

He took a deep breath and leaned down so his face was next to my own. His voice came out as a whisper. "Four thousand, five hundred, Brooklyn."

"Sir?" I was still looking into my lap.

"Four thousand, five hundred. That's how many cadets are out there. They are your brothers and sisters in arms, the best and brightest in our country. And you will risk getting them killed – every single one of them – if you keep using your gift in public."

My eyes flew to his face. He was serious.

"How could I hurt them?"

Major McCoy's face darkened. He marched to the door and jiggled the handle, making sure it was locked. He turned, and his gaze rested on me again, the intensity of his stare penetrating my very core.

"General Richards thinks there's a spy here, Brooklyn. If a spy tells the enemy you have a gift, you become a target. But so do the rest of the cadets."

"Why would they become targets?" My voice was shaking.

"Because we live in close quarters here," he answered, not missing a beat. "Close enough that if you wanted to fight one of us, you'd have to fight us all. You need to

162

keep your gift a secret so it doesn't warrant that kind of unwanted attention." He straightened. "No true soldier will start a fight. But if the fight comes to our front door and knocks, then we will answer. And people die during those conflicts, Brooklyn. Good people. I would have thought you'd think more critically about the repercussions your actions have on others after that episode this weekend."

"I didn't mean —" I stammered. "I mean, usually I can control it-"

"Your gift is different here, Brooklyn." Major McCoy interrupted. "The moment you decided to come, you relinquished the hold you had subconsciously placed on it. It's been simmering beneath the surface for years — I could see that from the moment I first looked at your file. Your power is untamed, and until you know how to harness it, you could cause real damage. You could hurt everyone here."

I swallowed my tears, which were threatening to spill over onto my cheeks. I didn't want to hurt anyone with my gift anymore, especially innocent people. I'd had enough of that.

Major McCoy moved to the door. Isaac and Liam looked up as another officer passed the doorway.

"O'Dell and Blackburn," he commanded, addressing Liam and me. We knew that tone — it was the one he used when other officers or non-Crest cadets were present. It was more formal. The unspoken expectation was that we adopt the same posture, so we stood at attention.

"Yes, Sir!"

"You will be training together this afternoon. Wear your PT clothes and meet me at the OMD Strength Development Center. And Jackson?"

Isaac stood at attention. "Yes, Sir."

"You will be training with Cadet Montoya. We're going to see how your tranquility affects her endurance."

"Yes, Sir."

Downcast, Isaac returned to his seat, and Liam and I followed.

25

THE STRENGTH AND DEVELOPMENT CENTER was located right by Miche Stadium.

I expected to see some athletes there as we entered, but was completely caught off guard when almost a hundred huge guys began exiting the building all at once. Suddenly I felt like I was trapped in a stampede, trying to go against the direction the human tidal wave kept moving. I was obviously unsuccessful.

Liam wrapped a protective arm around my waist and pulled me to the side.

I told myself I didn't like it, but my heart was pleading for me to reconsider.

The team of giants passed, and Liam squared my shoulders to face him. "You okay?" He shook his head and scoffed. "Football players. I'm just glad you're still standing. I almost lost you there."

"I'm not yours to lose," I reminded him, standing as tall as I could and brushing a nonexistent crumb off my t-shirt.

He recoiled, but only slightly before he smiled shyly and gently nudged my shoulder with his own.

"You're 100% right. You don't need protection. But still… I can't help but want to give it to you." He held the door open for me and motioned me inside. "We'd better go, Wonder Woman."

My heart beat stronger as we made our way through the door across the entryway, to the hallway, and finally, the weight room.

With ridiculous ease, Liam had repaired my injured ego and marked himself even more of a gentleman.

Maybe healing would be his gift. But believe me when I say he had plenty of talent without it.

"Cadet O'Dell. Cadet Blackburn."

The greeting was gruff enough to snap me back to reality.

Major McCoy was standing in front of us, looking less like an officer and more like a dorky PE teacher. His gray army tee was tucked a little too tightly into his black gym shorts, his socks were pulled up a little too high, and he wore a stopwatch around his neck. I would have laughed, but my attention was quickly diverted to the beautiful room behind him.

The weight room was definitely the biggest one I'd ever been in. The windows were humongous — floor to ceiling — and they offered an incredible view of the grounds. I could have stayed there for ages, watching all the cadets move from one building to another in formation, with the rolling hills and trees behind them. The room was almost too pretty to sweat in.

Almost.

Much faster than I would have preferred, Major McCoy asked Liam and me to follow him. He ducked his head to the left and right, looking around our shoulders, searching for any bystanders, although there were none. Still, Major McCoy rushed us through the massive room. We walked right past the big windows and passed under several painted patriotic words on the walls: words that were a reminder of the pride, pain, and sacrifice that came with being a soldier at West Point.

I was still looking around me – my head swiveling in all directions and my mouth open, in awe – when Major McCoy had us round a dusty corner, only to come to an abrupt halt at a mirrored wall.

There was nothing that stood out about it. In fact, it would have seemed like just another part of the gym if it weren't for the light layer of dust that lined all of the old equipment, which was stacked haphazardly in the corner. Major McCoy looked behind him to make sure no one was looking, placed his index finger to his lips, then pushed the mirrored panel near a seam, exactly halfway between the floor and the ceiling. The panel swung forward to reveal a secret – a hidden room.

And while it was much smaller than the rest of the workout area, it didn't feel cramped. It was located on the corner of the floor, so two of the room's sides were floor-to-ceiling windows, matching the larger area.

"Privacy windows," Major McCoy informed us, smiling as Liam and I took it all in: our own private training grounds. "You can see out, but no one can see in."

A pair of treadmills and two bench presses lined the wall, and a bunch of weights were stacked neatly on racks next to them. Jump ropes, weighted medicine balls, and pull-up bars were hung on the wall as well.

"What do you say we get to work?" Major McCoy asked.

And Liam and I – grinning – didn't even answer. We raced each other to the treadmills to warm up.

26

I WAS SITTING ON AN UPRIGHT WEIGHT BENCH,
lifting an iron bar up, then down, over and over again. The
heaviest weights we had in the workout center were
stacked up and secured on both sides of the bar, and it
still wasn't enough to challenge me, so I was doing a
hundred reps to push my muscles beyond anything I'd
ever done.

Just two feet away stood a group of West Point cadets,
who were clustered together just outside the privacy
window.

I'd already warmed up on the treadmill and maxed out
on squats and deadlifts. Liam had spotted me then and
was now on the stair-stepper, hooked up to heart rate and
oxygen monitors. He was pushing himself to the limit,
and for once, I was, too.

Even though it was my first time lifting weights with
legit effort, I had already shattered the national record for
nineteen-year-old girls.

For obvious reasons, I wouldn't be able to make it
public, but I didn't care. I liked being able to do superhuman
things in secret. It made me feel scandalous — rebellious,

even – to covertly do them under the nose of unknowing Army officers.

And for once, my muscles were tiring and sweat was dripping off of the tip of my nose as I heaved the bar up for the ninety-seventh time. My body was tired and was becoming weak.

And I couldn't be more thrilled.

There was a satisfaction in working this hard, in pushing your body to its utmost limit. I was experiencing it for the first time, and I didn't want the feeling to end. I relished the fact that, for once, my body needed me to quit, instead of my mind forcing it to stop so I could conform to natural standards.

"Come on, Brooklyn!" Major McCoy yelled, just inches away from my face. "Hit a hundred. Do. Not. Stop! Not now. You're too close!"

I held my breath and heat rushed to my face.

"Niiiiine-ty….eight," I grunted, panting.

"Two more! Come on!" He slapped the top of the other bench nearby.

I took a couple of gulps and tried one more, only to have the iron bar almost drop from my clenched fists. I let the bar slide to the ground, then stood up and kicked the bench. Then I collapsed on it, exhausted. After a few moments, I looked up to face the music with Major McCoy, to see if he was as disappointed as I was.

But I didn't see the officer. Instead, I was staring at a cadet I'd never met. I didn't know him, but he was glaring at me through the privacy window.

The group from before was gone, but this one solider remained. His light grey eyes continued to squint at me, and the hair on the back of my neck stood up.

"Just back up," Major McCoy instructed, his voice quiet, as if he were a hostage negotiator.

I did as I was told.

And the cadet on the other side mirrored me, stopped when I stopped.

"It's probably a coincidence," Major McCoy commented, in between our two bodies in what seemed like a weird standoff. "But stay here while I go check it out. Just to make sure."

He sprinted toward the door, then paused. "Liam, go ahead and get off that thing and do some lunges. Brooklyn, rest for a bit, and then join him."

He exited, and I backed away even further from the unknown cadet, who was still curiously studying the room like the privacy layer on the glass didn't exist.

Liam ripped the heart monitors off of his chest and climbed off of the stair-stepper, his broad chest rising and falling with his deep breaths. He closed his eyes and placed his hands on top of his head, his fingers laced together and elbows bent: the stance a long-distance runner takes after a race.

I waited at the window and finally saw Major McCoy speaking with the cadet who had been looking into the window. The officer's stance was authoritative, but the cadet didn't look scared.

"Hmmm."

"You okay there?" Liam asked from somewhere behind me.

I hadn't realized I'd spoken out loud.

He placed a hand on my shoulder, and I allowed myself a quick glance at him. His hair was dripping with sweat, and his gray ARMY shirt was drenched.

He'd never looked better.

"Who do you think it is?" he asked. He waved a hand to the expansive glass in front of us.

"I'm not sure," I replied. I studied the two men again. "Major McCoy is smiling," I pointed out. "And so is the cadet. So it's probably no big deal."

"Good," Liam agreed, lightly squeezing my shoulder.

I winced.

"Crap!" he exclaimed. "Sorry! I'm stupid, squeezing your shoulder after all those reps. I should leave you alone. Or get you some ice. Or stretch the muscle. Or something."

I arched a brow. "What's the doctor's orders?" I'd meant to be playful, but I grimaced as I brought my arms closer to my chest. "Ice. I'll definitely need ice. But I think I need to stretch first."

I tried maneuvering my arms in a few awkward poses, but no matter what I tried, I couldn't figure out how to stretch the muscle that went directly on top of my collarbone.

Liam laughed. "Need a little help?"

I looked at him quizzically.

"I know how to stretch it," he explained. "I had an arm injury last year in baseball. Here. Let me help you."

He strode confidently toward me, then stood directly in front of me, just inches away from my face. He placed his hands gently on my hips.

I froze, trying my hardest not to look into his eyes, and failing.

"Baseball, huh?" I stuttered, thankful I could speak at all.

"Yep," Liam replied. "I wasn't good, though. I'm pretty sure my coach was glad I got injured so he had an excuse to bench me."

"Yeah, right," I argued. "I'm sure you were perfect at that, too." His physique was way too athletic for his claim to be true.

He shook his head. "It's the truth. You'll find out someday, I'm sure. Now. I gotta back you up to the wall," he said matter-of-factly.

I nodded, unable to speak, and he gently walked me back. Then, lacing his fingers in mine, he lifted my arm so it was completely stretched out at shoulder height. He slowly turned my hand so the thumb pointed down, then placed his other hand on my shoulder. He pulled the opposite shoulder toward him, and gently pressed the other half of me towards the wall. I gasped with the tender pull of the muscle.

It was a good stretch, and I could feel it working. But it felt like we were caught up in a slow dance, as well. Our breath came quickly, and our faces were inches apart.

I tried to look somewhere – anywhere – but directly into his eyes. They were too kind, he was too close, and I was too unguarded.

"Do I stink?"

I giggled, caught off-guard with the blunt question. "What?"

He grinned. "You're looking a little uncomfortable. I'm wondering if you're about to pass out from my stench."

Right. His 'stench'. That's what was making me unable to breathe. It wasn't the way he looked, his close proximity, or the gentle way he was touching me.

"Well it does smell a little," I admitted. "But I'm pretty sure I stink, too," I whispered.

"Nah," Liam replied, his face still inches from mine. "You're Wonder Woman, Cadet Blackburn: learning how to effortlessly save lives and look good while doing it. Even if you did smell, I wouldn't notice because you look so… badass."

I rolled my eyes and laughed.

And heard someone in the doorway clear his throat.

Major McCoy was studying us, curiosity marking his face as he strode toward the space between us that had just appeared.

"It was a false alarm," he informed us – as if we cared anymore. "Did you guys get your lunges in?"

"Yes, Sir," we lied, our voices a little too loud and enthusiastic.

He glanced at Liam, then at me. "Okay then. Training is over for the day."

"Yes, Sir," we answered, and we started to leave.

"Cadet Blackburn?"

I turned slowly toward the officer.

"Make sure you adequately stretch those arms out."

I swallowed a smile before turning toward the door.

"Right away, Sir."

27

THE SECOND HAND ON MY WATCH CONTINUED
its incessant tick, its agonizing circular crawl. I'd gone to
the library to study Krav Maga (Israel's renowned
fighting system), but to be honest, it was the last thing
on my mind.

I was preoccupied with images of Liam, anticipating
seeing him as soon as this hour finally came to an end.

I hadn't been with him since our last electric
encounter in the Strength and Development Center.
During the little down time I'd had, Liam had his
individual training, and when I'd had my training, Liam
was scheduled for his downtime.

Part of me was relieved.

Without him, I'd been able to do more: I was more
focused on my training, on learning tactical warfare, our
military's history, and world affairs.

Three days ago, Bree and I had creamed the others in
a sharp-shooting competition. Despite not having a gift
yet, she was an excellent shot, and I wasn't bad, either.

And yesterday, after my individual training session
where I did one hundred fifteen bicep curls, Major McCoy

had told me he'd never seen a person better suited to be a soldier.

I was born for it, he'd said. And he was right.

The compliment made me beam with pride. I was excelling, and I loved it.

Today was another opportunity for me to showcase my strength.

I joined the other members of The Crest as we made our way to the building that housed the wrestling and martial arts teams. We were going there to receive instruction in combat skills, to do the fun stuff: actual punches and kicks, headlocks and wrestling maneuvers — and even self-defense. Major McCoy said it had the potential to be one of the hardest workouts we'd do.

That part appealed to me. Using my gift appealed to me.

But admittedly, using my gift to fight the other Crest members did not.

If I was fighting people with the same gift as me — or even a gift of being able to withstand punches or something — I'd be completely pumped. But I was nervous about unleashing my abilities. I mean, superhero strength was bound to get superhero results, right? And I was strong.

Like, really strong.

What if I hurt someone in The Crest with that power? I don't think I'd be able to handle it.

So I decided to do what I'd always done in competitions: try and win, but not give my full 100%. I wanted to learn from the experience, and maybe I would be able to use those skills in a real fight someday. But I'd need to resist the urge to show off and control myself during the match. Somehow I had to appear to try my hardest, but make sure I just barely won.

Because I didn't want to hurt anyone, but I did want to win. Especially against the boys.

"The boys" were Liam and Isaac. Although Jacob was the same age as me, he was small – middle school small. His quiet and unassuming demeanor – and horribly, probably even the fact that he suffered from asthma – made me feel like a bully whenever I thought of fighting him.

But fighting the other two, who were both well-built and decent athletes? Not gonna lie, it kind of made me feel like a pioneer in feminism.

I saw Isaac first and easily joined his side. Liam approached us soon after, looking so good my heart hurt.

I walked the entire way with them. Isaac on my left, balancing my excitement and anxiety out with his gift, and Liam on my right. I nodded to Isaac, a silent 'thank you' he'd come to understand.

Liam's presence was making my heart race again. Isaac threw me a curious glance, and I ignored it, hoping he'd think my heart was beating like that because of my nerves, not because of my hormones.

I forced my thoughts to the others in the group.

Bree and Jacob were walking together in front of us, their shoulders hunched over, their eyes searching the ground in front of their feet. They hung out a lot (seemed like moped around, to me), mostly because they didn't train as often with Major McCoy. I didn't know if they were being purposefully ignored or not, or if they would ever develop their gifts – *if* they even had one.

Adrianna was the only one who didn't hang out with us, and that was because she seemed to prefer to be by herself or with the firsties. Even today, she was nowhere to be found. She'd gotten shin splints from whatever training she had to endure in her afternoons, and Major McCoy thought it was best she take it easy.

We entered a smaller room in the athletic field house. The fluorescent lighting did little to add any light to the dark wrestling mats on the floor.

As soon as we arrived, Bree and Jacob had found a corner of the room. They weren't showing a ton of effort, laughing and stretching on the blue mats.

We had all worn our gray sweats, and I stripped down to the simple gray USMA tee and black shorts. Adrenaline had already started pumping its way through my veins, and I started to stretch and bounce around to warm up my muscles.

Liam joined me. "You think you're ready for this?" he asked, a bantering edge to his voice. I hadn't heard his teasing in ages, and it felt like home.

I softly elbowed him in the rib. "I know I'm ready."

He chuckled. "Somehow I believe you." He leaned in close enough for me to inhale his sweet, musky scent, momentarily distracting me from my goal. "I'm kind of excited to see what surprises you have in store for us." I turned around before he could notice my embarrassment.

"All right, Cadets." Major McCoy stood in the middle of the mats. "Circle up."

We joined him.

"Today's an introduction to combat training. Considering your future in the Army, it's imperative you pay close attention. You're going to make mistakes; I guarantee that. But you must learn from them, and quick. Mistakes made the second time around will not be tolerated."

The major asked us to pair off quickly. Liam and Bree faced each other (They were twins. I mean, who wouldn't get a chance to settle any deep-seeded dispute in the ring?), and Jacob found me before Isaac, who didn't seem to mind, happily sitting on the bench for the first round.

I bit my lip to try to control my emotions. Jacob looked genuinely glad to be paired with me, but he hadn't seen me use my gift yet.

"Um, Jacob?"

"Yep!" He was bouncing around like some tiny rabbit to warm up. If the circumstances had been different, I'd probably have giggled.

"Just so you know… It wouldn't be a horrible thing if you were to lose to me."

"HA!" He threw his head back like a maniacal, little-brother-tyrant would do. Then he bounced around a couple more times and threw some air punches, looking more like a cartoon than anything else.

"I'm serious, you know!" I proclaimed. "Yesterday I was hitting a punching bag. The force of my punch was so strong, the bag swung up to the ceiling and made a dent in it. Seriously. Up to the ceiling. It made… a… *dent*."

I made sure to enunciate the last two things clearly, but it was like Jacob couldn't hear me.

I shook my head and threw my hands up toward Major McCoy, who was already aiding Bree in a maneuver to get out of Liam's headlock. He had to swallow a smile at Jacob's 'showboating' as well. He joined my side.

"Just remember, you have to fight him, sometime, anyway. Might as well get it out of the way."

I took a deep breath as the officer turned his attention to Liam and Bree, who were both having fun circling each other. Bree, in particular, was smiling broadly. She laughed out loud as she kicked the side of Liam's outer thigh. Turning to the bench, I placed the padded black helmet on my head and securely cinched it under my chin. I pushed a blue mouthpiece over my teeth as well, glad I didn't have trouble breathing through my nose, because there was no way I could breathe through the hard, bulky plastic in my mouth.

With that, I turned to the circle drawn on the floor mat and met Jacob in the center.

After giving them a few tips on blocking their faces from incoming punches, Major McCoy left Bree and Liam's circle and joined us, standing between me and my foe: the asthmatic 5'4" kid with glasses.

I sighed again.

Major McCoy put a hand behind both of our heads and brought us in close, instructing me to put my clenched fists on top of Jacob's as we faced each other. "Don't go too crazy," he instructed me – I mean, us. "We're just sparring. Just start going at each other a little bit and feel each other out. Let's see what happens."

And with that, he stepped back.

Jacob hopped circles around me, once in a while throwing a punch in my general direction. I let him hit me, but blocked what little force there was behind them easily by keeping my clenched hands by my cheekbones.

I'd decided that this was how I could fight the kid. I'd let him hit me and simply block them, maybe throwing in a few light kicks here and there.

We continued this way for a couple of minutes, until a blaring whistle interrupted our rhythm.

Major McCoy was blue in the face, spitting out words.

"This is what you give me, Brooklyn?" he jibed. "This? We invest thousands of dollars into you. The Army relocates me away from my family and my base to train you, and this is the effort you give me. THIS!" The last word was more like a roar. He was seething.

He sprung up closer to me and stared down my face. "Cadet Blackburn, you will fight, and you will show the effort you are capable of showing. Do you understand?"

"Yes, Sir," I replied. Then, under my breath, so only he could hear, "A hundred percent?"

"Is. There. Any. Other. Kind?" His eyes bulged and a rivulet of sweat made its way down his temple.

"No, Sir."

I turned back to Jacob and let out a breath. "Sorry buddy."

But he just smiled. I felt so bad for him. He seriously had no idea just how strong I was. What if I hurt him?

But Major McCoy did know my strength. He'd trained me the past two weeks, where I'd shown him as much as I could. He knew what my full capabilities were. And now he demanded 100% of them. I only hoped he felt confident in helping Jacob heal.

I closed my eyes and brought my fist back, torqueing my body with it like I'd been told, so my back and glute muscles could exert the force behind my punch.

My body weight shifted from my back foot to the front and I released my arm.

And I landed on the floor. I shook my head as Isaac laughed uproariously from the bench. I shot him a look and he collected himself.

Okay, I told myself, shaking off the embarrassment. Gotta have the eyes open. As ugly as it might be.

So I stayed alert and did the same maneuver over again.

With the same results.

Jacob furtively dodged my punch, and even as I tried a leg swipe from the ground, he bounced around the movement.

Panicking, I leaped to my feet immediately and squared my shoulders to him once again. I punched left. He dodged it. I punched right. He dodged it again. I did a left, right, left, left combo and ended with a kick to the gut.

It was as if we were the opposing ends of magnets. Everywhere I punched, Jacob would bounce off in a different direction. When I aimed my kick toward his torso, he simply jumped back.

We did this for a while before I said my body demanded a break. In reality, it was my pride that needed the interruption. The silence was broken by Isaac, who was still giggling.

"You wanna try?" I asked, frustrated and out of breath.

"No ma'am," Isaac said, showcasing his relaxed, confident grin. He licked his bottom lip lightly, then bit it. "You look good out there and all, but this kid?" He jerked his head in Jacob's direction. "He fooled everybody into thinking he didn't have his gift yet."

His gift. Prophecy.

OF COURSE!

I spun around to meet Jacob's stare. "You knew what I was going to do?" I asked incredulously.

He shrugged. "Yeah."

"So you always know what's about to happen?"

"With other people, sometimes. But only like a couple seconds in advance. And they have to be close by, so I'm not very good. And I have no idea about my own choices or reactions. I guess that's why I still get asthma attacks sometimes."

He knelt to tie his shoe and looked back up at me, pushing his glasses up the bridge of his nose.

"Huh." That was all I really knew to say.

"At least he has a gift," Liam interjected smoothly as he sauntered up to my side. "I'm still waiting on mine."

I smiled. "You'll get it. And you too, Bree," I added, nodding to his sister. "It's just a harder gift to hone, since you have to be around only sick and injured people."

Major McCoy stepped in. "I've been thinking the same thing, Brooklyn. The trouble that pops up with that is the danger of exposing their gifts. Whoever they heal has to know about the gifts of The Crest, or they have to be so out of it they won't remember. Any other way and they couldn't remain secret weapons of the Army."

The way he said that was almost startling. Secret Weapon. I'd always pictured a secret weapon as being some kind of nuclear bomb - not a person, let alone a teenager.

"Oh well," he said dismissively. "That's a problem for another day. Let's switch partners. Jacob and Bree, face off. Liam and Brooklyn, do the same."

Liam grinned widely and made his way over to my mat. The other two didn't waste any time at all. Bree giggled loudly as she made unathletic attempts to hit Jacob and he laughed out loud as he easily thwarted all movements.

They were like kids out at recess.

Liam winked lightly as he brought his hands on top of mine. I pushed all teenage-girl thoughts and emotions to the back of my mind and reminded myself I was a soldier, a soldier who wanted to beat the guys at sparring, but not injure them. We stepped back a foot or so and circled each other lightly. I threw the first punch and made decent contact with his jaw.

And I'd like to say it felt great, but it didn't.

Unlike Jacob, Liam didn't have a gift that would counter mine. I was following through on my plan, making a concerted effort to hit him hard enough to challenge him, but not so hard I would injure him.

But it was agonizing. Boring. Not fun at all.

And worse yet, Liam appeared to be adhering to the same philosophy. I could tell he wasn't trying his hardest.

Needless to say, the whistle blew just a minute into our sparring.

"What the hell are you guys doing? Attending a dance?" Major McCoy's face was that bluish shade again. Mine, a deepened red.

"No, Sir!" Liam replied.

"Then why aren't you hitting her, cadet? I've trained you, and this playing around is a shame, even for you."

"Sir! Maybe she should truly hit me, Sir!"

I blinked quickly. Are you freaking kidding me? He wanted me to pound him?

"No!" I shouted. "Sir," I said, calming down and turning to the major. "If I hit him as hard as I'm capable, I'll hurt him. Badly."

Major McCoy straightened. "You're confident of that, Cadet?"

"Yes, Sir."

Great, that was what every teenage boy wanted to hear: that a girl would probably hospitalize him during a fight. There's no way that'd injure the ol' ego.

I swallowed thickly, trying to keep myself from looking Liam in the eye.

"Well, we can't have him hurt," Major McCoy said thoughtfully. "But we are NOT leaving here today with any more gifts unchallenged!" He turned to Liam. "Cadet, I've sparred with you myself. You are an able and talented fighter. And yet you are unwilling to fight Cadet Blackburn to the best of your ability?"

Liam stared him down. "She is strong, Sir, but she doesn't have the gift of prophecy like Cadet Jay, and she isn't fast like Cadet Montoya. If I hit her, Sir, she'll get hurt." His eyes were fierce, but his gaze was unwilling to meet my own, his demeanor more intimidating and intense than I'd ever seen.

Major McCoy backed off. "Very well, Cadet O'Dell."

He walked leisurely to my side.

"If you are unwilling to show your talent, I have no choice but to force your true gift out."

Jacob gasped as Major McCoy — never wavering from his stare toward Liam — grabbed my arm at the elbow and ripped my hand backwards.

My forearm made a horrible cracking sound, and Bree's hands flew to her ears. I couldn't even focus on the noise. My other senses took over: my eyes staring at my forearm – a gnarled, crooked branch, and the excruciating pain radiating from it.

It was a while before I even heard the agonizing scream coming from my own mouth.

Isaac jumped from his spot at the bench and lunged at Major McCoy, who stopped him effortlessly and put him in a choke hold. After a couple of seconds, he slumped to the ground, unconscious.

28

LIAM HAD SPRINTED TO MY SIDE - WAS kneeling behind me and holding my head in his hands.

Whatever strength I'd had, had left my body.

He brushed the hair out of my face and framed my jaw with his hand. "Brooklyn. Brooklyn! Hey, focus on me!" I did as I was told.

But my arm. My freaking arm. My fingertips were tingling, and the pain halfway between my elbow and hand was intense in its power and exact in its location, a horrible combination. I bit my lip to keep from screaming again, but couldn't stop my tears from falling or my breath from coming in deep gulps as my eyes wandered to the unnatural angle of my limb.

"YOU BASTARD!" Liam screamed.

His usual, military-appropriate demeanor was gone. All respect was drained from him. Bree was shrieking, too, and Jacob's breaths were getting shallower as he reached for his inhaler. Isaac was still unconscious on the floor.

"You know it's my job to push you, Cadet," Major McCoy yelled back. "I know Brooklyn. She's tough. And I know you have your gift inside of you." His eyes were penetrating. "You were the only one we've been monitoring since the day you were born," he said. "You were more deeply affected by your mother's death than your sister. You almost didn't make it after your birth. Physically speaking, everything said you should have been stronger at birth than your sister, but you weren't. And that's because healing people affected you the same way it affected your mother. Liam, she died from healing too many people, and you almost died from it as well."

"You have the power, Cadet O'Dell. Fix it," Major McCoy commanded calmly.

"I-I...I can't." Liam insisted. "You saw me try to heal Adrianna's shin-splints. I couldn't. I've tried to heal people over and over again, and I've never been able to. Just ask Bree." He looked to his sister, who nodded right away.

"He's right," she explained. "We've practiced every night, just like you told us to." She showed us the inside of her calf, which had a couple of superficial scratches on it I hadn't seen before. "See? He couldn't heal them."

Major McCoy scoffed. "Those wounds mean nothing." He turned back to Liam. "Brooklyn is your weakness, cadet. You're letting your feelings for her get in the way of refining your gift. But you've got to use it now, to help her."

His feelings for me. The words comforted my heart momentarily, but left my mind as soon as they entered. The pain in my arm trumped everything.

"I already told you, I can't. I don't even think I have a gift," Liam replied, defeated.

"Fine. Then Brooklyn loses the use of her arm. And her other one, too, if you refuse to try. I can take that one out as well." He looked at me menacingly.

"No! Don't!" Liam begged. "How do I do it? How do I heal her?"

Major McCoy stomped his way toward him, authoritative, yet quick. "How am I supposed to know, Cadet? I don't have your power!" The force of his voice made me jump slightly, and the pain from even that small movement made me cry out.

The major's expression softened. "Try concentrating, Cadet O'Dell. Just focus on your gift. That's what the others do."

Liam softly placed me on the mat so I was lying down, gingerly placing my arm over my torso.

"I should set it first, right?" he asked Major McCoy.

"I'll do it," the officer replied. And before I knew it, he'd grabbed my arm again, and as he'd jolted it into a different shape, I was blinded by a flash of light. All sounds were blocked out.

I was still screaming when my sense of hearing returned. I heard Major McCoy say, "All yours" and leave my side. I felt a soft hold on my arm and opened my eyes.

Liam.

"It's okay, Brooklyn," he whispered, his eyes pleading. "I'm not going to let him hurt you anymore, okay? I'm going to try my hardest. Promise. I'm going to try and make it go away."

My body shuddered and my jaw clenched tight.

Liam closed his eyes and wrapped his hands tighter around my arm, caressing the inside of it firmly with his thumbs and breathing in deeply. Three times he did this, and my arm still ached.

Then he bowed his head, as if in prayer. His fingers went as rigid, poised over my forearm. He looked as if he were going to play the piano. He pushed his fingertips into my skin, creating small indentations in it. I tried my hardest not to scream out. Even this slight pressure was killing me.

But then whispers came, identifiable as a language, but one I didn't know and spoken so softly that I wouldn't be able to understand what he was saying, anyway. The words poured gently out of his mouth like a soft waterfall. He moved his mouth along the skin of my arm, a soft butterfly caressing a jagged branch. Once in a while he'd pause and breathe in gently, and when he did this - the breathing in and out, in and out - the sensation was incredible, like a potent painkiller was being administered into an IV in that exact location.

The unseen medicine was warm, and when it reached my severed bone, it stayed in the location for a while. I had lost track of time and honestly had no clue if an hour or just a second had passed. But it didn't matter because what I was feeling – although alien to me – it wasn't pain.

The invisible drug moved beyond my arm to other parts of my body, stopping quite often to stitch together any tears or breaks in my body before moving on, even the smaller ones away from my major bone break.

I would imagine this sensation as being the same feeling long lost twins would have after being reunited when they were separated at birth. Not painful, not uncomfortable. Just complete somehow, in a way you never knew you needed to be complete before.

I heard Liam stop his murmurs and felt his fingers leave my arm, but not with the nerve endings on my skin. I could tell he wasn't touching me anymore because I felt the invisible medicine leave the inside of my body as he pulled away.

"You did it." I breathed, still lying down, and an exhausted, grateful smile stretched across my face.

"I did," Liam nodded, and he smiled his beautiful, kind, smile. He lay down next to me and brought a hand up over his forehead, closing his eyes. His other arm lay limply at his side. "I had to. I couldn't let him hurt you."

Isaac came between us.

I wondered when he had come to, but was too tired to ask. Major McCoy went to Liam's side. "I'm going to stay with you for a bit, Cadet. I want to see how you recover from this. Cadet Jackson, please help Cadet Blackburn to her barracks and let me know if she has any adverse reaction to the healing."

Isaac nodded but didn't salute him. He didn't even answer with the required, "Yes, Sir!"

Major McCoy let it slide as he helped Liam to one of the benches.

Isaac slipped his long arm around my waist and grabbed the hand I'd put on his shoulder. We started our walk in that pose, side by side as we exited the building. I wasn't hurt or anything.

Just in a dream.

"Maybe he loves me," I mumbled to anyone, referring to Liam, in a stupor from the invisible drug he had given me. But Isaac was the only one within earshot.

He waited a beat. "I think he does," he finally said, his jaw tightly clenched.

We made our way back to my barrack, where Isaac ordered me to sleep and I happily obeyed.

29

I WOKE UP A COUPLE OF HOURS LATER TO A knock at my door, still feeling exhausted, but not foggy. My stomach was twisting in hunger. Adrianna peeked her head in.

"You okay?" she asked, limping her way to my bed.

I cleared my throat. "Yeah, I am, actually." I yawned. "Just tired, is all."

I lifted my right arm to show her, flexing my hand into a fist and then flat again. "See? I said. "Not even a bruise."

"That's amazing," she replied. "Isaac said it was completely broken in half?"

"Yeah."

"And did it hurt?"

"Like hell," I answered honestly.

"Wow."

A brief moment passed before she spoke again. "I can't believe Major McCoy did that. I mean, I know the Army pushes every soldier to their physical limitations, and West Point is supposed to do it even more, but if Bree or Liam couldn't have healed you, what would've happened? You may have never been the same again."

"I know," I agreed, propping myself up on my elbows. "It was messed up. I mean, he broke my arm like it was nothing and threatened to break the other. And he made Isaac pass out when he got up to help me."

Adrianna shuddered.

"Even just putting Liam in the situation where either he heals me, or I'm permanently injured, kinda makes him a sadistic SOB," I continued. I stood up and walked to my desk. "And that weird pulsing in the Labyrinth? And making Jacob run all that time when we first got here and inducing an asthma attack? It's like he's getting a thrill out of making us suffer or something."

"All drill sergeants do," Adrianna said. "At least that's what my uncles told me. But you're right. It's like inducing pain is his gift."

I snorted. "No joke." Shaking my head, I put my hair back in a bun and started to change into my grey-on-whites, the uniform worn for all meals. I yawned again. "Is it time to eat yet? I'm starving."

Adrianna glanced at my clock. "Yep, it's six o'clock. Let me change real quick and I'll come with you."

The mess hall had thousands of students in it, but it was like no other cadets existed when I sat down at our table.

"How's Liam?" I demanded of Bree. His absence was obvious.

"He's okay," she replied. Her eyes were red and swollen. "I just came from seeing him at the hospital. He's just tired. And his arm is in a lot of pain."

"His arm?" I questioned.

"Yeah," Bree replied. "Remember how our mom died? Because she healed too many people? That's because the power comes with a downside; the healer takes on the pain of the person they heal."

I couldn't breathe or move. I was only feeling tired, and Liam – who had done nothing but fix me up – was lying in pain in the hospital. "His arm is broken?"

"No, not anymore, anyway. It just *feels* like it, I guess."

Remembering the horrific pain in my arm, my hands flew to my face. *He was hurting now because of me.*

"How long does it last?" I asked.

"They're not sure," she answered. "We'll just have to wait and see."

I'd been so hungry before, but suddenly I had no interest in food and just picked at the plate in front of me.

"You need to see him?" It was Isaac.

I nodded.

"Here," he said, scooting his chair back. "I'll go with you."

We cleaned up after ourselves and made our way out of the front doors of the building, walking in silence at sunset. Just a minute passed and I was feeling better.

"Thanks," I told Isaac, knowing he was using his gift to calm my anxiety.

He nodded and gave my shoulders a squeeze. "Any time."

We entered the hospital on the edge of campus just as the sun was sinking below the horizon.

The receptionist showed us to Liam's room. My heart stopped for a moment as I entered. Wires were hooked up everywhere to him, and machines and screens beeped incessantly.

"It's not as bad as it looks," Liam insisted. He was alert, just lying down, watching the small television that hung by the window.

"Really?" I asked. "Because it looks pretty freaking bad."

"Nah," he replied, scooting to the top of the bed to sit up. "I'm just a lab rat. They want to see how my vitals react to healing other people since..." His voice trailed off.

"Since you take on their pain?" I finished.

His ears burned a deep red. "Yeah."

"Liam," I began, finding a seat on the edge of his bed. "You shouldn't have-"

"I'm glad I did," he interrupted, the corners of his lip curving up into a smile. It broke my heart and, at the same time, strengthened its beat. He was so, so beautiful. Inside and out. "I have a gift, and it's one a lot of people need."

"At the expense of what?" I asked incredulously. "Who wants to walk around all the time sick or injured? Who's that crazy?"

A few seconds of silence passed.

"I guess I am," he finally replied. "I know it may not make sense to you, but it makes sense to me. Like I was born this way or something." He laid his head back and stared at the ceiling. "The thought of being sicker, or walking with a limp, or-"

"Living with the pain of a compound fracture in your arm?" I interjected.

His smile broadened. "Yeah, even that." He let out a small laugh and shook his head, but then met my gaze. "Brooklyn, it doesn't bug me. That helpless feeling I had when I didn't think I could do anything to take away your pain...that was worse. Way worse."

He grabbed my hand. "Brooklyn, I-"

"Hey guys!" Isaac strolled right into the room, making his way to the other side of Liam's bed. He sat down with a thud, and my hand slid out of Liam's. "Lucky for you, I remembered my manners." He feigned an accusatory glance in my direction. "And I got you the Pepsi you always like to have at dinner."

"Hey! I knew I liked having you around for a reason!" Liam took the soda and clinked it with Isaac's.

"Any for me?" I asked.

Isaac shook his head. "Nope." He took another long drink. "Soda's aren't good for the musculoskeletal system. I read that somewhere. We can't have anything interfering with your gift, Ms. Strength."

I reached over the bed and smacked him on the shoulder. "HEY!" Isaac said, rubbing it. "That hurt. Remind me to never make you mad."

"Consider that a warning." I stifled a laugh as Isaac handed me the drink he'd hidden behind his back.

He was still rubbing his shoulder as he turned his attention, once again, to Liam. "So what's the word, man? You have to stay overnight?"

"Yeah," Liam replied. "Just for monitoring and stuff." He turned his attention to me. "I really do feel a whole lot better already. I'm actually moving it pretty well now." He turned his arm, which was in a sling, in a huge circle at his side to prove his point. "It'll be all healed up by tomorrow, I bet."

I said nothing, just nodded and looked at the can of soda, choosing to hone in on the hissing sound coming from the opening.

"Well, that's probably a good thing," Isaac said, "Cuz Major McCoy said we're being tested again tomorrow."

Both Liam and I let out a groan. "Seriously?" I asked. "In what?"

"I'm not sure," Isaac replied. "All he said was – "

Without warning, the window behind Isaac's head shattered.

I didn't hear the glass hit the floor. My ears were still ringing from the deafening boom.

I could see the shards fly through the air, but I was spared from their impact. Liam and Isaac dove toward me, pushing me and themselves under the hospital bed where Liam had just been. Dust and smoke filled the entire area, and before we knew it, a couple nurses came in, untangling Liam from his web of wires, and hustling the three of us out of the room and toward the emergency exit.

We passed a doctor on the hallway phone. His cheek was bloodied and his sleeve was torn. My ears were still not working the way they should, but I could hear his muffled yelling to the person on the other end.

"We've been bombed! I repeat, We've. Been. Bombed!"

I'd dream those words all night.

30

I WAS ON MY SECOND DAY STRAIGHT OF BEING
alone in my barrack, healing from the superficial wounds
I'd received at the hospital.

The three of us were okay. We only had a few minor
scrapes from either the fall to the floor or the glass
shrapnel. Thankfully, none of the hospital staff had
serious injuries, either.

Major McCoy had shown up immediately to make
sure we weren't injured. After he assessed the situation, he
had sent Liam, Isaac, and me to our barracks with strict
instructions to isolate ourselves to protect the other
cadets on campus.

I was grateful for the time off. I slept a lot, catching up
on the lack of sleep I'd had this whole month of early
mornings. But as soon as I welcomed the sleep – as soon
as I succumbed to it – I would hear the doctor on the
phone again.

"We've been bombed."

And even in my sedated state, my mind would process
that sentence. I'd think about how close the bomb had to
be for the glass in the room to blow out the way it did. I'd

think about who the bomb's intended target was. And I'd think about General Richard's warning to all of us almost a month ago: that our academy was a target of a terrorist organization.

Terrorists.

I shuddered at the meaning of the word, at the very people who did barbaric things on my TV, an entire world away.

Throughout my sleep, I recalled how General Richards had made eye contact with me when he'd said a spy was relaying information about gifts.

And we were the most gifted people there: people who happened to be incredibly close to the bomb when it detonated.

There were too many arrows pointing to The Crest to be a coincidence, and my subconscious told me as much as I half-slept the days away. Fear, I knew, was what the terrorists wanted more than anything else. And for the first time in my life, I was truly experiencing it, my heart beating intensely in my chest to try to compensate for how powerless it felt. The worst kind of atrocities in the world were no longer filtered through a news story on the television. They were suddenly right in front of me, staring me down with evil eyes.

But what could I do?

They'd terrorize me, or they'd terrorize someone else, someone without a gift to use against them.

And I realized, no matter how scared I was or how unprepared I felt, I had to fight them.

I had no choice- I was born for this. I was given this gift to protect everyone else. My future wasn't up to me anymore.

Because no one else in the world had the ability to fight evil the way we could. No one else had gifts like me. Or Adrianna. Or Jacob or Isaac. Or Liam.

Liam.

My heart ached for him. The rest of us had to sacrifice at some level in order to hone our gifts for the Army, but Liam's sacrifice? His was physical. Every time the rest of us used our gifts, we got to experience the euphoria that comes from winning, from using every ounce of our God-given skill.

But Liam didn't. His gift brought about suffering, not victory.

While the bombing plagued my nightmares, the image of Liam attached to all of those wires in the hospital room plagued my heart. I hated seeing him in so much pain, and I despised the fact that his body would have to experience it almost every day if he were in The Crest.

Bree had tried to make me feel better about it.

"He's always been like that – always playing the hero," she was saying dismissively. She and Jacob sat at my desk, having finally received permission to visit from Major McCoy. Adrianna had peeked in earlier, but her visit was more like one you'd get with a nurse: full of questions, boxes that were checked as she took stock of my condition before moving on to her next patient, Isaac.

"He's just… like…" Bree looked to the ceiling as she considered how she should describe her brother. "He's kinda like a mixture of Dr. Phil and Dr. Travis."

Jacob snorted as I looked at both of them quizzically. "Who?"

"You know," she explained. "Dr. Phil is the psychiatrist? The guy who gives advice to everyone on that show? And Dr. Travis is that doctor on another talk show? Everyone has a crush on him, but he's all about healing people- their hearts, too?" She paused to see if she jogged my memory. My naiveté must have been obvious, because she rolled her eyes and laughed. "Well, anyway, that's how Liam is. Well, until you came around. He's seems to be only focused on you these days." She winked. My cheeks reddened.

"C'mon," she said, changing the topic and turning to Jacob. "We're going to be late."

"Where are you going?" I asked. They'd just arrived.

Jacob hopped up. "The three of us who weren't injured have a group session with Major McCoy at ten," he said. "He thinks Adrianna and I can work together with our gifts," he explained, "And I still have no idea how."

"And I have no idea why I'm even required to come," Bree added. She held her hands in front of her in exasperation. "It's obvious I don't have a gift like the rest of you."

"Then why aren't you leaving to go home?" Jacob asked, his tone so tactless it almost shocked me. "Why stick around?"

Bree shrugged and looked past his shoulder to the wall behind me. "I have my reasons."

And she did. I didn't know if she'd told Jacob, but Liam had said their dad was overseas at the moment, so she didn't have a home to return to. But part of me wondered if it was hard for her to be separated from her twin, as well.

Bree and Jacob waved a hasty goodbye to me. As soon as they left, I glanced around my barrack, to the

201

immaculate tiled floors and the white walls, the plain oak closet and desk. And for the first time, I found it desolate and sparse, more like a prison than a path to whatever it was I was called to do.

A light tapping on the open door stole my attention. My favorite guy stood in the middle of the threshold, his red hair messy, his grin wide, and his workout attire accentuating his athletic build.

"Hey there, Wonder Woman," he greeted. "Major McCoy is about to work with the others. Isaac is chatting with his family. So…I was wondering… do you want to hang out with me for awhile?" He paused and smiled shyly. "Like on a date?"

"Now?" I asked, thinking of my unkempt hair and lack of fine attire. Also, a date? I tried to make my heart stop doing cartwheels in my chest.

"Yes, now," he laughed. "A day-date."

"Oh. A day-date. Sure. I mean….can we? Can you? How's your arm?"

"Completely better!" he assured me, circling it around. It was free of any cast or sling. "I told you I'd be fine." He grinned, and his emerald eyes sparkled. The light cuts on his forehead from all the glass made me question whether or not that statement was true, but I nodded, anyway.

Beneath a forced smile, my heart ached. His selfless attitude just punctuated his perfection: in his looks, his mind, but especially, in his heart. I wished it made me happy, but it didn't.

Because honestly, I wasn't sure I was worthy of his level of selflessness. I mean, why should a man with no visible flaws sacrifice himself for my mediocrity?

"Is it safe, do you think?" I asked. "With the heightened security and everything?"

Liam's face became more solemn. "I know, with the attack and everything – being on alert after General Richards' warning, I almost didn't even ask. It's just –"

He paused for a moment and smiled slightly again. "For some reason, being barricaded by myself in a cement room on a guarded base doesn't bring me the same level of comfort of being alone with you. But I only want to go if you feel safe with me, too."

I smiled wider, touched at the sincerity in his tone. "Where do you want to go?"

"How 'bout on a walk? Should be nice scenery with you around. But I hear the autumn trees around here are gorgeous, too."

"Always so smooth, Cadet O'Dell," I laughed. "You and your lines."

"I just speak the truth," he said in a serious tone. "I just wish you could see yourself the way I do."

I paused with my reply, and the moment stretched between us was filled with so much of what we felt, but couldn't hold or touch. The invisible thread connecting us was suddenly like an overflowing hammock with the weight of intangible things I needed to tell him about me- things that I didn't even understand.

"Let's go," I said, hopping up and grabbing a hoodie.

Liam stepped to the side as I walked through the doorway first. "I know just the spot," he beamed.

31

LIAM WAS AHEAD OF ME AND TO THE RIGHT by about twenty paces, walking swiftly to our destination. We'd left the barracks a few minutes earlier, passing some of the buildings that had become familiar to us over the last month: Grant Hall, where we ate; Jefferson Library, where most of our independent, Crest-members-only courses took place, and of course, the Strength and Development Center where we trained. Once we had hit The Plain, we'd decided to walk separately in order to avoid alerting Major McCoy to what we were doing. We didn't know where he was meeting the rest of the cadets and didn't want him to stop us.

Liam kept throwing the occasional glance in my direction as I trailed behind him, and every time he did, my heart would beat a little stronger. I wasn't sure where he was leading me, but the anticipation of it all was overwhelming in the very best way.

At long last, we arrived at the edge of West Point property, next to the Hudson River. As I trekked up a small hill at the base of the famous waterway, I saw a stone archway and knew immediately where Liam had chosen to take me:

The Flirtation Walk. The place where we'd run our first day here, where Jacob had his asthma attack, and where Isaac had healed him. The place where I found out my strength had limitations.

It was also the place where cadets took their sweethearts, where public displays of affection were allowed.

Liam beamed and gestured to the path on the other side of the arch. "Ladies first."

"Flirtation Walk, eh?" I remarked. "You're such a ladies' man, O'Dell."

"Who said I was bringing you out to flirt?" he said. "It's a workout spot for us, remember?"

I laughed. "Okay, so what are we doing today? Another run? Lifting boulders? Throwing rocks?"

"Nah," he said sheepishly. "Something a little easier. Just... getting to know each other." His smile widened. "You still up for it?" He held a hand out, as if presenting the stone archway as a prize.

Grinning widely, I took a step forward. Liam placed his hand on the small of my back, guiding me through the opening. His touch was electric, and a tingling sensation coursed through my body in response. He let his hand linger there for a moment before finding my own, softly interlacing our fingers.

"Is this okay?" He slowly held up our hands. His expression was so gentle, so genuine, the potency almost broke me.

I nodded. It was perfect.

We were silent at first. I couldn't be sure what was going on in Liam's mind, but personally, I was just trying to relish how amazing the moment was.

Liam holding my hand, leading the way, made me feel safe in a way I hadn't ever felt before. The beauty surrounding us was stunning, making me feel like I was the star in some made-for-TV movie.

"Check it out," he said, pointing to the distance. "The Great West Point Chain."

We left the river for a moment and made our way up the paved path to a small monument. Enormous black chain links interlocked together to form a circle around multiple boulders piled up in the middle.

"Crazy that this is all that's left of something so big," I said after reading the plaque next to the monument.

"Right?" said Liam, reading the same plaque. "But draping a gigantic chain across the Hudson was brilliant. It kept the British out of the waterways. When you think about it, this chain is what allowed America to exist."

"...In spite of Benedict Arnold's best efforts," I pointed out.

"Can you believe West Point used to be called 'Fort Arnold'?" Liam asked. "Crazy. Let's hope we never get betrayed like that again."

We spent the rest of our morning and the early part of the afternoon hopping to and from the different monuments and learning a little more about our new home. Every now and then, Liam's hand would find mine, and when it did, the look on his face was so innocent and triumphant, my heart couldn't help but soar.

Quite often, other cadets would pass us on the path. Most were holding hands, and some were even making out by the trees rather than going for a walk. Some couples were made up of one cadet and a civilian – others were made up of two cadets, like us. Liam pointed out how many of the tree trunks had hearts and names carved into them and suggested we play a game to see if we could find the oldest one. So far the oldest we'd found was from 1943.

"Whoa," Liam said, tugging my arm after we'd found another etching. "Check it out."

He led me away from the trees to a large gray boulder perched above the path right next to the river. "Chain Battery," I said, reading the inscription aloud. "1778." I took a deep breath and whistled. "Unreal."

"Right?" Liam gestured to the organized piles of rocks nearby. "And look - the leftovers of the fort. It's nuts to think this has all stuck around after 250 years."

"Yes. It's cool it's made that kind of imprint," I acknowledged.

"Well, some things are built to be beautiful and strong," he said. "Like you."

I was still recovering from my slight embarrassment when he said, "Brooklyn, I - I feel like a big nerd."

I stifled a laugh as he sat on the ground in front of the river. He patted the ground next to him, inviting me to join him. "A nerd?" I asked, lowering myself to the ground. "Why?"

"I didn't bring you on a date today to study West Point history," Liam said, shaking his head. He turned to me. "I came here to find out more about you. I just get so nervous around you, it's like I forget how to speak. And think." He chuckled.

Nervous? Around me?

207

"There's not much to find out," I said honestly. "I feel like you kinda know everything already. I'm basically normal. I'm from Brooklyn. My mom's a feisty Italian nurse. My brother lives a relatively boring life – loves videogames and girls. And oh, yeah... my dad was a superhero and I inherited his powers."

He laughed. "Right, just your everyday, All-American girl here, folks."

"Basically."

I smiled. The afternoon sun was beginning to disappear behind the large peaks looming above us, chilling the air, but splashing beautiful warm hues across the surface of the water.

Liam scooted closer and leaned in. "You're anything but normal. You're the strongest and most gorgeous woman I've ever met. So tell me, Wonder Woman." He paused, as if harnessing his courage. "What makes you weak?"

I thought back to my life before, when I had struggled. With confidence, with classes, with everything. I thought back to my own betrayal and what I'd allowed a boy to do to my heart.

"Trust," I answered bluntly, honestly. "Trust makes me weak."

Liam searched my eyes, his face first masked with curiosity, then understanding. "I see," he said. "But is that a blanket statement, or could there be an exception?" He paused, his lips pursed together as if he were concentrating. "I mean, do you think you could actually trust *me*?" He squeezed my hand.

I answered honestly, my breath coming quicker. "I'm afraid trusting anyone would hurt me again- that it'd make me weak."

He took a moment to consider this. "Maybe trusting *anyone else* would hurt you. But my power is healing, Brooklyn." He traced the back of my hand lightly with his thumb, sending a jolt of electricity through my body. "What if trusting me could actually heal you and make you even stronger than you were before?"

My heart hammered in response.

He whispered, "Will you give it a shot and see?" His eyes wouldn't leave mine. "Will you give us a chance?"

I didn't even take the time to think of the answer- it just came, like it was meant to be on my lips all along.

"Yes."

Liam leaned in closer to me, then brought his hand up to rest softly on my cheek. He cupped my jaw lightly and lifted my face to his. We stayed like this for a brief moment, with my heart beating faster as I gazed into the deep green of his eyes. Slowly, he leaned down, and his lips finally brushed against mine, fitting sweetly in the contours, as if they were home.

32

I HAD SPENT MY EARLY SATURDAY MORNING
scrubbing my barrack, making sure everything would be
in order for the SAMI, which stood for Saturday Morning
Inspection. Everything at West Point had an abbreviation,
and the more I used the nicknames, the more I knew I was
becoming intimate with the place, allowing it to have a
piece of my heart. SAMIs were notorious for having high
standards, so after two officers left my room with no
complaints, I allowed myself to have a moment of pride
in keeping my barrack organized and clean.

I headed down to the laundry room to retrieve the
workout clothes I'd worn yesterday during my time with
Liam. I was folding them neatly and putting them back in
the cupboard, reliving the sweet moments when Liam
held and kissed me deeply, when Major McCoy knocked
at my door.

"Cadet," he greeted gruffly.

"Yes, Sir."

"I'm gathering the group. Meet in Room 103 in
Jefferson Hall. Fifteen minutes. Dress warm."

"Y-Yes, Sir." Dress warm? It was unusually hot today — over seventy degrees.

Something was up.

I had just pulled my hair back and was lacing up my combat boots when Liam knocked on my door. "You ready?"

I practically leapt to him. "Yes."

He gave me a light peck on the lips and brought my hand up for a kiss, too, before reluctantly letting go and making some space between us once we entered the hallway and met up with the others.

As we made our way across campus to the library, Jefferson Hall, we couldn't help but notice the heightened security.

"Check 'em out," Bree said, nodding curtly to the MPs (military police) who were patrolling the roads in front of the campus buildings. "I hear they're even stationed around the perimeter of West Point — the acreage, too — hiding among the trees and everything."

I wondered if any of them were the same MPs we saw respond to the bombing when we'd stumbled out onto the hospital lawn on Wednesday. On that evening, they had their shields up and weapons ready.

Today, it was different. While they weren't staring down the sight of the guns, their eyes were alert, searching through the throngs of students for any suspicious activity.

Stationed all around us…seen and unseen.

The whole thing seemed incredibly odd to me. Sure, there'd been an attack on base, but did it warrant this level of hyper-vigilance? At what point was living in a state of fear giving the attackers exactly what they wanted?

We walked into a small room in the basement, one of those often used by professors to lead study groups. We sat next to each other at a long table. Major McCoy stood at the front of the room.

"Good morning, Cadets," he greeted without emotion.

"Sir," Liam said amidst our murmurs.

Major McCoy closed the door before returning to his spot, then began pacing while he spoke. "The individualized training the six of you have undergone this past month is not only impressive – it's amazing. When I work with each one of you, I can tell you are pushing your normal human attributes as well as your gifts."

"I wish we could begin our group training, learning how to use your gifts together in order to take down an enemy. Unfortunately, those lessons will have to wait." He took a seat at the front of the class. "Intel told us a week ago that a terrorist organization may have a vested interest in you, and the bombing at the hospital just outside Liam's room seems to support that theory."

He paused for a moment, studying his hands. "The government received another tip last night, Cadets. They were told a different attack on the grounds is being planned for the weekend."

"Son of a –."

The sound came from Jacob, but from the look on the others' faces, any one of them could have said it.

Major McCoy pressed on. "While the government wants to keep you safe and continue your specialized training, they also don't want your presence to risk the lives of the other cadets. So this weekend, we have to put all of you into hiding. Together, but separate."

"What do you mean by that?" Isaac asked.

"You will be protected," Major McCoy replied. "But you'll be taken off the main campus to an undisclosed location."

"Away from West Point?" Bree asked.

"Not entirely, just removed from the campus. We'll keep you on the grounds, though," Major McCoy answered. "You have protection here that's not available off the base."

Adrianna raised her hand. "You said you were hiding us 'together, but separate.' What does that mean?"

"It means we'll be separating you for the entire weekend."

"Wait- what?" Liam exclaimed, looking protectively at Bree and me. "I understand why we have to be hidden on the grounds, but why would you want us separated? And why would we agree to it?"

"It's not your decision, Cadet O'Dell," Major McCoy replied. "You are assets to the U.S. Military – the entire Crest division is. Should something go wrong, we can't risk losing all of our assets."

"So you're like…diversifying your portfolio? Making sure at least some of us will be safe if one or two go belly-up?" Adrianna asked crudely.

"Something like that."

A stretch of silence followed as a dark realization sank in: we were seen as a commodity. A valuable one, but *still* a commodity nonetheless. It made us feel sub-human – not super-human - which they had called us all along.

He stood up again and taped an aerial-view picture to the white board at the front of the classroom. "This," he said, pointing to the poster, "is a picture of the West Point grounds in its entirety. All 16,000 acres."

I spotted the campus immediately and could even identify some of the buildings. But the rest of the poster was a green canopy of trees.

"All of this is West Point's land?" I asked.

"Yes. We use it during The Beast for our basic training, and throughout their education at West Point, cadets use the grounds to test their survival and tactical skills. We do our best to simulate a war environment."

"In a way, we'll be doing this with you. Since the government is demanding we isolate each one of you, we thought we might as well take advantage of the distance between you guys and *really* test your individual skills. Don't worry," he added in response to our scared expressions. "We won't be launching any attacks or using any weaponry. Instead, we want to see how you use your gifts to survive- separately, with no dependence on one another."

He stood and walked over to Liam. "Are you healed up, Cadet?"

"Yes, Sir."

"And you?" he asked Isaac and me.

"Yes, Sir," we answered.

He turned to Adrianna. "And I take it your shin splints have healed sufficiently?"

She nodded. "Yes, Sir."

"Then we're all healthy," he said, clasping his hands together in front of his torso. "And if we're all healthy, then there's no reason you can't do well as we send you out onto the grounds."

He straightened, his tone serious. "General Richards wasn't kidding when he said the terrorists were zeroing on West Point as a target. And I think the incident on Wednesday should remove any further doubt from our minds."

I raised my hand. "Sir. Does the Army know who did it?"

I looked to my left and right, wondering if the other members of The Crest had the same question. Their eyes were set upon Major McCoy, their ears ready to hear the answer.

He straightened and looked each of us in the eye. "We cannot be certain exactly who did it, but we believe we've narrowed down the group."

"The group?" Isaac asked. "They think a group of people *here* is responsible?"

"I'm sure they're looking into that," Major McCoy replied. "But I was talking about a specific terrorist organization, a group who is soliciting the help of an individual. No guests were in the vicinity of the hospital when the bomb went off, so an individual already here at West Point must have detonated it. Remember, General Richards believes there's a spy here. And the attack verified that whoever it is, is willing to act out on the hateful rhetoric of the group. Truly, training now is more important than ever."

He stood up again and walked to the picture. "At noon, our Black Hawks will transport you to Fort Buckner." He pointed to a vague area of the green canopy. "The six of you will be dropped off at different places on the grounds. Your job is simple: Survive for forty-eight hours, using your gifts only – not the gifts of others."

"Will we have any materials given to us to help us? Or do we have to live off whatever we can find out there?"

The question came from Bree, but it easily could have come from me.

Major McCoy studied her, as if he were amused. "None of you is getting a huge survival kit. You'll each be given something to help, but it'll be up to you to make it enough."

"So just hunker down in a cave and use a sling-shot to kill a bird," Isaac joked. "Easy, peasy."

"I wouldn't take it lightly," Major McCoy retorted. "The woods can be dangerous in their own right. There are obstacles there none of you city kids have probably ever seen before. And there may be other difficulties that come up as well."

"Will we be safe out there?" Jacob asked. "Like we are here?"

His questions landed heavily on my heart. My mouth went dry, and raw fear – panic – set in at the thought of being completely alone out there. Not because of what secrets lie behind the trees, but because we'd just been attacked. It all seemed too primal – the prey being let loose in the wilderness, kept separately and given little, made vulnerable to the predator.

"You will be safe," Major McCoy assured. "You have no idea just how sophisticated our national security is, and since the bombing, we've implemented that high level of protection around all of the grounds, including the grounds away from campus."

I nodded. My mind believed him, but my heart was not so easily persuaded.

Adrianna raised her hand. "You said we wouldn't be given huge survival kits. But can you tell us what we will be given?"

"Not until you're dropped off," Major McCoy answered. "Thinking quickly on your feet is a mandatory skill for anyone in The Crest. It's about time you guys were tested in this area."

My brain was working overtime. Isolated from all other cadets. Then separated from the rest of The Crest. Surviving on our own was the test, and considering we had a giant target on our backs, it was a sick one.

I wasn't sure I bought any of it.

"You have three hours until we depart," Major McCoy commented. "I suggest you go upstairs and brush up on how to survive in the wilderness."

The chairs screeched loudly as we scooted them away from the tables and stood to leave. As we left the classroom and made our way to the main area of the library, Liam whispered to me and Bree, "This is crazy. I'm not doing it. We're targets of this terrorist group, and we're safer together."

"I agree. Something's off," I replied.

"Yeah, and you all have powers, and I don't," Bree interjected. "There's no way I should be out there alone."

Liam hugged his sister. "Let's make sure we find each other out there, okay? We can still stay separate from the other cadets, but I'm not leaving either one of you alone. We should wait out the weekend together."

"So that'll be our goal," I summarized. "Find each other, then wait: consequences be damned."

217

Bree nodded. "I agree. If they punish us, we'll tell them we didn't feel safe without one another. Simple as that. Should I tell the other three?" She asked.

"I think so," said Liam. "They shouldn't be alone, either."

Bree left to find them.

Liam's hand found mine, and the committed look in his eyes gripped my heart. "As soon as we get dropped off, we find each other, promise? I don't like the thought of being away from you. I mean, I know we have superpowers. But I've seen way too many movies to see how badly it can end when you're by yourself. Superpowers are never enough."

33

I SAW NOTHING AND HEARD NOTHING –
nothing over the roar of military transport, anyway.

The black blindfold had been expertly tied at the back
of my head, tricking my mind into thinking I was alone. I
knew that wasn't true, though. All six of us were headed
into the woods.

The staccato whirling of the helicopter rotor drowned
out everything I tried to hear. The only thing I could feel
was the swaying of the Black Hawk as it turned different
directions, and the hand of a soldier on my elbow, ready
to guide me off the helicopter onto the ground as soon as
the aircraft landed deep within the wooded acres of West
Point.

A sergeant had given me a survivor's handbook to
review in the library, and I'd studied it as hard as I possibly
could, wanting to be as prepared as possible for any
hardships that may come my way. I ate more than usual at
lunch, not knowing what my eating situation would be for
the next two days. Right before we boarded the Black
Hawks, we were given small packs and told each one had

different contents, purposefully unique to its owner. We weren't allowed to open them until we were dropped off.

I wondered what mine held, if it were the things I'd read about that could help me in the wilderness. Matches? A compass? A magnifying glass? I thought of the rugged terrain of the Catskill Mountains - the cold autumn air that hung over it - and shuddered, hoping I could live through whatever the next forty-eight hours would bring.

The firm tug on my elbow made me lean in the direction I was being pulled.

"THIS IS YOUR SPOT!"

It was yelled concisely and monotonously into my ear, but I had to strain as if it were a muffled whisper.

I blindly let the mystery person grab my other elbow, too, and lead me off the helicopter. From the movement of the aircraft, I was sure I'd been the first dropped off. Stepping onto land, my knees locked momentarily. It was vastly different from the moving platform I'd been on a second earlier. I walked with staggered steps, pulled along by my unidentified leader. The rotors were still moving rapidly, and my uniform clung to my body as the wind from the apparatus rocked against it.

"YOU CAN TAKE YOUR BLINDFOLD OFF NOW!"

I followed the directions of my guide.

I blinked rapidly after removing it, needing to give my eyes a chance to adjust to the bright light of the afternoon. A thick, black forest surrounded the clearing we stood in. The circle of tall trees loomed over me, the top the jagged evergreens leaning in to blot out the blue of the sky, reminding me of a sharp-toothed snare snapping down to trap its prey. The first sergeant who had given us our original tour – Austin Stovall – stood in front of me.

"WE'RE LEAVING NOW!"

And that was all he said as he thrust the pack into my hands and got back on the helicopter.

My heart raced in anticipation as I watched the machine I'd only seen in the movies rise and leave with the other cadets in tow. I stood there, breathing heavily and trying to calm my racing pulse for a full few minutes, listening to the sound of the helicopter as it moved beyond the trees surrounding me and faded out, got stronger, then faded again, probably dropping off the other members of The Crest at their assigned locations.

At long last, the thick buzzing sound slowly disappeared altogether, and it took that happening for me to move on to the task at hand:

Surviving.

I took a deep breath and closed my eyes. "I'm not alone," I said aloud as I released the air. "I'm not alone." I repeated the mantra a few more times, and the more I said it, the more I could picture the other Crest members hidden in the brush around me.

Isaac and Adrianna had agreed it was best we find each other, too. Adrianna's only reservation was that we didn't have a plan laid out in order to meet up, but considering weren't given any details of everyone's drop off locations, we decided to wing it and simply do our best.

Only Jacob hesitated when it came to making sure we found each other. Mumbling something about needing to follow the rules and never having any time alone, he sulked for a bit, then finally – albeit reluctantly – nodded his assent.

Not only did I picture the other Crest members around me, but Major McCoy's statement about heightened security on the entire grounds also stuck in my mind. It wasn't hard to imagine soldiers in the trees around me: hidden in the shadows so I could safely perform the tasks at hand. It was enough to push my fears of the unknown to the back of my mind, but not enough to completely eradicate them. Despite my best effort, I couldn't stop searching the hills around me for a potential attack.

It wasn't winter yet – only October – so the deciduous trees were still full, their leaves a stunning mix of bright yellow, dark red, orange, and purple. Their colors were made even more vivid against the dark grey backdrop of clouds, reminding me that the sunny day was giving way to stormy afternoon and evening. Evergreens skimmed certain areas – yet another color hovering over the rest, and each hue jumped from the scene in front of me, tattooing themselves in my mind. It was breathtaking.

The sun was out now, but thick rainclouds dusted the horizon. Under normal circumstances I probably wouldn't have even noticed, but suddenly the clouds were intimidating in their size and color. My head spun from left to right as my eyes searched to find a place to sit for a second and formulate a plan. It didn't take long to find a tall evergreen with a broad base that'd serve well as a canopy. I sat in a bed of pine needles and opened my pack, dumping its contents onto the soft, prickled pillow below.

Two things.

Out of the top one hundred things I'd read about, I'd been gifted only two: a blue tarp and a book of matches, which had already been opened. I snapped the cardboard flap up and saw only six left, spaced out in front of a brown-gray backing: lonely soldiers who had lost friends in battle.

Still, it was better than nothing.

The tarp, I remembered, could be used for a few things, but I could only remember three: a roof, a blanket, and a bucket.

The survival handbook had said the most important thing to find is water, so if I didn't have a fresh source, I considered myself lucky that rain was on the horizon, and I knew I'd better plan on using it as a bucket.

Any minute now, it was going to rain. I could smell it coming. The electricity in the air was thick, and the wind was rustling through the leaves, picking up speed from just moments before.

I started to unfold the tarp. Initially, I was going to create a makeshift cylinder to collect the water. But the thought occurred to me that, with the right tree and by angling the thick canvas just so, I could simultaneously drape the tarp over some low branches to fashion a temporary shelter and indent just a corner of the fabric to collect rain water.

Two birds, one stone.

It didn't take long to find the right tree: another evergreen with lower branches than the first. After implementing my plan, I stepped back to take a look, brushing the hair out of my eyes as the wind whipped any free strands into my face.

And I have to admit, I was impressed. The tree created a natural cocoon for me to sit in, and I'd threaded the ends between heavy branches and tied the corners — putting all the oomph from my muscles into making it secure.

It was secure, all right; an immediate gust of wind proved it.

While I'd been busy with the tarp, the clouds had crept in, and now they blanketed the sun. The warmth from midday was gone and suddenly my fatigues did little to combat the chill in the air. Already, pricks of rain were starting to pelt my face. I needed to get to my shelter and try to stay warm.

Warm.

I need fire, I thought suddenly. And for fire, I'd need logs – dry logs.

I looked up at the tree that was the foundation of my cocoon. Pushing aside the thick branches, I began to climb, knowing I'd have to reach the innermost branches to get the driest wood that had yet to be pelted by the rain, which was falling harder by the second. I climbed higher – to the middle of the tree, and was surprised at how silent and still everything was inside of it. I almost fell off when a small animal scampered nearby, but not before I used my gift to snap off two large branches. I held them under one arm and used the other to swing myself down – like rungs of a ladder – to the already dampened land below.

I ducked into my tent and giggled as I broke the branch up into logs.

Who needs saws? I thought, allowing myself this touch of arrogance.

224

The clouds released their fury as I dashed inside my tarp, and I took a few minutes to simply relish the fact that I was dry and the tarp was holding up well against nature's assault.

But then the rain became sleet, the air so thick with a temperature drop, I almost felt suffocated.

I hugged my body tight and nestled into a corner, but even in that position my muscles trembled relentlessly.

I was going to have to start a fire.

Reaching into the cargo pocket of my fatigues, I grasped the almost-empty book of matches, thankful I was given such a gift.

Had the others been as lucky?

The thought momentarily took me to their location on the grounds, and suddenly I wanted more than anything to check in on them and make sure they were okay. It occurred to me that I was the lucky one who had been dropped off first, so I had more time to prepare for this sudden change in weather.

Who had been dropped off last?

I shook the thought from my head, knowing that if I didn't start a fire soon, I'd be as bad off as the others.

If they were bad off.

I hated not knowing.

My heart rate increased as panic set in, and I was frustrated with myself. Worrying about everyone was something Adrianna did, not me.

It'd been awhile, but I mumbled a hurried prayer, asking they be kept safe. Then I pushed back images of them and the other Crest members and made a mental checklist of what I needed for the fire. I needed to concentrate on my survival if I was going to make it the full forty-eight hours.

I moved the logs I'd snapped off to the corner of the cocoon, where there was an opening off to the side and up the center of the tree where smoke could escape. I arranged them into a small peaked mountain and thought of the next step: adding kindling.

I cussed loudly, because I was screwed.

A log couldn't catch fire without kindling, and any small twigs or branches that would have been usable in starting a fire were drenched now. One hand pinched the book of matches while the other searched the ground around me – the tiny area that was under the tarp – for anything that was untouched by the moisture outside and the stifling humidity in the air. But it was all damp.

All of it.

My tremors deepened from the icy air around me, and I knew I had to try to light even the damp kindling on fire. If the cold weather stuck, I wasn't sure I could survive the night without fire of some kind. So, from my meager pile, I pulled out the driest leaf I could find, and set it on top of a cone made of pine needles.

Taking a deep breath in, I tore a match stick from the book and pressed it between the cardboard flap and the grainy, charcoaled strip, then ripped it across.

The satisfying pop of the match lighting up made my hopes burn brighter, too.

Quickly – but not so quick the flame would go out – I held the match stick to the leaf. Desperately I drew a line back and forth along the edge of the leaf with the flame, knowing that it had the power within it to shine brightly and ignite the kindling around it. It — this tiny thing — had great power within it to help me survive.

But despite its promise, the flame never took hold, burning the tips of my fingers instead of the intended target.

I swore again as it fell, smoking to the ground.

That left five.

It was colder still; the sleet was hammering the roof of my tarp. I blew hot air into my hands and rubbed them together, trying to warm them, but also trying to release the tension of the moment. And, taking a deep breath, I ripped another match from its home and tried again. It brightened my entire cocooned world, then disappeared in an instant with an unexpected gust of wind.

It was like seeing an old friend die. Frustrated tears forged an angry path down my cheeks.

I had only four left. I had to protect them.

Tucking the remaining matches into my breast pocket, I wrapped my arms around my legs and rocked gently, back and forth, wondering what I could do. My eyes searched for anything that was flammable, but came up with nothing. I grabbed my hair in frustration, tugging at the ponytail, plucking at the stretchy fabric of the holder.

Fabric.

The answer was simple. So simple. The only dry things I had that were also flammable enough to start a fire were my clothes.

I couldn't lose my fatigues, though; I needed to stay warm to stay alive. And even if I didn't have any other option, what would I do afterwards? Scamper around in the forest naked until the Army came to pick me up?

I don't think so.

But I had other fabric — fabric that wasn't as necessary and easily seen.

I ripped off my top and pulled my sports bra off, then as quickly as I could, I draped my shirt over my body again. I held it tight around me before buttoning it, layering one side over the other, needing to warm up even after that brief jaunt with the cold. I did the same with my pants in order to get my underwear, and then assessed what I had in front of me.

What I had was a small heap of life-saving lingerie draped over the logs in the middle of my cocoon.

I lit the third match, and the flame burned brightly on my small pile. I tucked the three that were left into my pocket for safe keeping, kissing the outer walls of the book that protected it first.

Just like I thought it would, the flame grew brighter, and it only took seconds for everything to go up in flames.

I added a couple more logs on the pyre and started to put the rest into a neat pile on the edge of my home.

"Brooklyn!" I heard, and wielding a log, I snapped my head around.

"Calm down!" ordered Isaac. "It's just me." And I did- out of relief or the byproduct of his gift, I didn't know.

I threw the log behind me and rushed to hug him, but the cold air and rain made me pull him inside my shelter, instead.

"How'd you find me?" I asked, unable to control my grin.

Isaac smiled back. "I felt you."

34

"FELT ME?"

"I don't mean-" Isaac stuttered. "You know, my feelers were out, I wasn't actually feeling, you know – with my hands, or whatever..." His eyes landed on the spot where my sports bra was. He took a breath and looked away. "Can we just pretend I didn't say that?"

I let out a nervous laugh. "Deal."

"So did you decide to have some kind of feminist convention?" he asked, a smile tugging at the corners of his mouth.

"Huh?" I questioned.

He nodded to the fire. "You're burning your bra."

It wasn't hidden at all, lying limply at the edge of the pyre. I kicked it into it with the tip of my boot as Isaac let out an uproarious laugh. "Go ahead, make fun of me," I commented sarcastically, trying not to be embarrassed. "I needed kindling."

"Ah," he responded, after finally calming down. He arched a brow. "Resourceful."

An awkward silence passed, and it occurred to me I had just been naked. Naked. And who knew how far away

Isaac was when I had been retrieving my improvised version of kindling? I shook the thought away as soon as it came, though. My body had probably mostly been masked by the tarp.

I cleared my throat. "So how far away were you dropped off?"

"Not far. Probably a mile or so. I was the third one to get off, and as soon as I did, I put my feelers out to see if I could sense anyone." He paused for a moment and searched my face. He licked his lips. "Turns out, I felt you."

Something was definitely up.

I wracked my brain for something – anything – that could distract from the current subject.

"What was in your pack?" I asked, my eyes spotting my own. It was a good change in topic; survival should always get the foremost attention, right?

"I got lucky," he said. "My pack was jam-packed."

"What?!?" I exclaimed. "I only got two things!"

He smiled and threw his pack toward my feet. "I got an empty canteen. But it's huge: gallon sized. And MREs – ten of them."

MREs stood for Meals Ready to Eat.

"Shut up."

"You shut up," he joked. "I'm serious."

I snatched them up like I was some crazed shopper on Black Friday and hugged them to my chest.

"Uh, will you share?" I asked, already knowing he probably would.

"Uh, will you?" he countered, mimicking my tone and my words while motioning to my cocoon and fire.

"Sure thing," I agreed, tearing open the first MRE and throwing one of the others at him. He caught it easily, then filled the canteen with the rain water the tarp had collected and sat down next to me to eat.

It wasn't a tasty meal, but was a welcome one under the circumstances. Even though I'd eaten a huge amount of food earlier that morning, I was famished after the stress and work brought about by the day.

Isaac and I didn't talk much while we ate, but after the food and after adding a log to the fire, we sat side by side, waiting for the outside world to grow dark. The rain disappated, then disappeared altogether.

"So," Isaac began. "We're spending the night together." His eyes gleamed as he playfully assessed my reaction. "And even with just saying that, you're turning all red." He elbowed me softly, a playful tease.

I shook my head and looked to the ground. "You know how to embarrass me," I scolded.

"I'm not trying to embarrass you," he replied, his palms facing up like he was offering something substantial. "Just trying...to...you know..."

I had to make him stop, act more like 'just a friend' than ever.

"And this is probably the first time you've been lost for words," I retorted.

He shook his head slowly, his eyes wide. "No. It's happened before. You have a way of doing that to me," he said, and as he said it, a new seriousness masked his face. His eyes were incredibly solemn, so opposite of his personality, it made me feel even more awkward. "You have this impression on me, Brooklyn, like a pull. It's hard to explain. It's like I needed to be close to you ever since we met at the banquet in the city."

The city.

The food. Our families. The fancy atmosphere.

"Seems like a lifetime ago," I said, almost depressed about it. I focused on that topic, rather than his feelings for me. Those were some unchartered waters, and I still had no desire to navigate them. If they were explored, I was afraid I'd lose him as a friend, and I didn't want to. I needed him, needed his power.

"Yeah. It does seem like a long time ago." He nodded morosely and clasped his hands together, letting them dangle between his knees. "It was a lot easier to think of myself as the kid of a hero than it is to be a hero-in-training."

I quietly agreed. Seconds ticked by. Isaac broke the silence. "Do you think you would have come? Had you known how hard it would be?"

I considered his words and all the events that had happened in this life, in this different world. They flashed through my mind like a montage: Saying goodbye to everything I knew. Marching everywhere. Learning to do ordinary tasks – like polishing shoes with a toothbrush – to compulsive perfection. Early morning PT. Late night studying. My broken arm. Liam's sacrifice. Isaac's pull. The bomb. Today. Here.

"Yeah," I replied honestly, yet sadly. "I would still come."

I stared out into the cold nothingness outside of our nest. "Part of me wishes I didn't have this gift inside of me, that I could have stayed at home and stayed safe."

He nodded, his thoughts returning home to his family, I was sure.

"But this thing we were born with…it's like having a part of our dads inside of us, you know? And in that way, it's like they never died. Instead, it's like they've been reincarnated inside of us, like they're still kicking terrorist ass, just in a different body." I let a smile escape. "And when I think of it like that, I'm not so scared…because the dad I've always dreamed about was larger than life and could conquer any of this." I gestured to the darkness in front of us. "So maybe we can conquer it, too."

Isaac put his arm around my shoulders, bringing me close to his heart and squeezing my arm tenderly. "Thanks," he said. "I needed that. Maybe that's why I can't stay away from you." He paused. "Maybe it's because I draw on your strength."

There he went again.

"My strength?" I asked, pulling my body back slightly. I needed to separate our bodies – draw an invisible boundary so I could study his face. "I mean, of course it's my gift in the physical sense, but definitely not in the emotional sense like you're talking about."

"C'mon, Brooklyn," he admonished, like I was a child trying to tell a lie. "You've got that strength inside of you, too. Who else could handle their arm being broken like you did? Why else would I feel like I needed to be around you when I was weak?"

His question shocked me. "You feel the need to be around me? Really?" I shook my head. "That's crazy. Because when you were gone – like far away – I thought I was going to lose my mind. I literally almost went insane with anxiety and fear."

233

"Really?"

"Yeah, when you went home, I completely freaked out. Liam had to help me snap out of it."

Isaac's grin faded, but just for a moment. "So, you feel the need to be around me, even when I'm not using my gift. And I feel the same way about you." His eyes pleaded with mine. I knew what he wanted me to say, but I couldn't do it. I took a deep breath. Isaac was doing a hell of a job making sure we talked about this.

"I can't even think that way, Isaac," I said, making myself look at him instead of my boots. "Not now. This crap we're caught in? Terrorists after us? Using our gifts to protect the country?" I shook my head slightly. "We already have too much on our plates…too much to even think about anything else." I clipped the end of my sentence, not wanting to give him the thought that what I'd said was even debatable.

Isaac sat back, considering the weight of my words. He grew distant, more silent. Part of me wanted to tell him I was sorry, but I didn't trust my heart with whatever my voice might say, so I cleaned up the twigs and leaves in our cocoon to combat the silence.

"Hello? Hello there?"

The voice was coming from the right, behind a thick pocket of shrubs about twenty feet away.

I knew that voice anywhere.

The flames flickered, making the orange glow they emitted dance off his face as he emerged from the darkness. Every perfect angle of his face was enhanced, his gaze smoldering as he walked toward me, a relieved smile spreading across his face.

God, he was perfect.

And he was walking toward me.

"Hey there," Liam said smoothly as he entered the cocoon.

I jumped to my feet and enveloped him in a hug.

His hands rested on my hips as he returned my embrace, and electricity coursed through my veins. His face rested near the nook of my neck for a moment, and I could feel him breathe in deeply. I did the same, and relished in the goodness of his woodsy scent.

I cleared my throat as I stepped back, nervously pushing a strand of hair behind my ear.

Soldier.

I was a soldier.

"Where were you dropped off?" I asked. "How long did it take you to find me?"

"Us. How did you find us."

I was almost startled by the intrusion. Seeing Liam had made me forget about almost everything, including the other boy, the one who was sitting right next to me.

The one who had just put himself out there by basically saying he liked me.

The one I had just turned down.

His eyes- usually so full of mischief and joy – were masked in sadness as they met my gaze.

My mouth opened for a moment, filled with a million things I should say, but couldn't. I knew I'd hurt him, but nothing I could say could erase the memory he had of me running into Liam's arms.

I was still faltering over words as Isaac's eyes left mine, and the sadness left his gaze, too, as he stood to embrace his other best friend at West Point.

"Hey, man!" he said, with an odd mix of sincere joy and sadness. "You better answer the lady's questions."

Liam greeted him back, then sat down heavily next to me, throwing his pack on the ground at our feet. "I was the second one to be dropped off, not too far from here. After the first person got off, I felt the sun's rays at my back, so I knew we were headed east. I just decided to walk west until I could find whoever it was they dropped off first." His eyes darted back and forth between Isaac and me. "Which one was it?"

"Me," I answered. "Isaac found me because I was feeling a little…"

"Wound up?" Liam asked, and the way he said it almost made me feel scandalous.

"I don't know about 'wound up'," I answered, blushing again. "But I was definitely excited. I mean, it's not every day I start my own fire in the woods. I was pretty proud of myself."

Isaac cleared his throat. "Yep. Brooklyn was being all…all female… with her emotions going crazy, so I had to come rescue her."

I slapped him on the arm, meaning to do it just hard enough to make him stop degrading women, but once again, I forgot just how strong I'd become. He winced and held onto it tightly.

"Sorry," I said, and I meant it. "But I wasn't going crazy. I was kicking butt at surviving."

Liam chuckled and I turned toward him. He put his hands up in mock surrender. "Uh uh. I'm not saying a thing. I don't want be at the receiving end of your temper."

I shook my head in mock annoyance. "You all haven't seen anything yet," I teased. "You guys just keep being all sexist, and it could be a different story."

We all laughed, and then Isaac yawned loudly. "What'd you get in your pack, Liam?"

Liam threw it toward him. "Not much, but stuff that'll probably come in handy: just a pocketknife and a water purifier."

"Have you eaten?" Isaac was already reaching for his MREs, had thrown one to Liam just as he began to shake his head.

Liam gave Isaac a huge smile, tore it open, filled the heater bag that came with it with water, and plunked in the food. I was sure he didn't even wait for it to warm up all of the way before he ate ravenously.

"This isn't so bad," I commented as Liam finished his meal. "It's kinda like we got a break from West Point and are camping for the weekend."

"Now it's nice," Liam retorted. "Now that we all have food in our bodies, water to drink, and a warm shelter. Earlier, when I was on my own, hungry and trying to find you, getting all mad cuz I had to wait through the storm, worrying about you..." His eyes peered into the darkness. "It wasn't so fun. Not then."

"I wonder how the other three are doing," I said. Liam had made a good point. Tonight was nice because we had each other, had the benefit of using something from all of our packs. What if the other three weren't so lucky?

"It's too late to tell," Isaac said. "And I can feel both of you worrying about it. Let's get some sleep, then pack up and move out tomorrow to try and find them. Sound good?"

237

Having a plan did make me feel better, and no doubt Isaac was using his gift to help us out as well.

As the world around us dimmed, it grew colder, too. But the three of us stayed warm, together in our makeshift home that was just big enough to fit our bodies.

Liam added one more log to the fire as Isaac and I curled up on opposite areas of the cocoon, trying to get comfortable enough to sleep. Liam found a spot in between us, but before bedding down, he leaned in so close I could feel his breath on my ear.

"Night, Brooklyn," he said, making damn sure I couldn't take my eyes off of him. "I can't wait to see how beautiful you are first thing in the morning." He kissed my forehead, and before I could reply – before I could even breathe – he laid down to rest, too.

It didn't take long, but my heart rate finally slowed down so I could succumb to the sleep I so desperately needed.

35

I WAS IN THE MIDDLE OF THE BEST SLEEP I'D
ever had, even warmer than I was when I had first fallen
asleep in the cocoon. I recognized the rugged scent
blanketing me immediately: Liam.

Somehow, through the darkest part of the night, we
had found each other, and between Isaac using his gift
to placate my worries about the others, and being in
Liam's arms for the first time, I was sleeping better
than I had in years.

"Pssst." I heard the sound clearly, but I tried
desperately to ignore the pest who was ruining my perfect
moment.

"Psssssssssst," I heard again.

Grudgingly, I opened my eyes.

Isaac was just a few inches from my face.

"I gotta go," he said with more urgency than I'd
expected, than I'd ever heard come from his lips.
"Somebody's freaking the hell out up there." He nodded
up the hillside. "I can feel it, and I need to go help."

I bolted upright. "I'll come, too."

Isaac gently pushed me back down, back in Liam's arms. "I don't think so," he said. "I don't think it's anything bad. I don't feel anger or hostility, or anything like that. I feel panic. I think it'll be better if I put my feelers out to see where they are, then come find you two tomorrow once it's light."

I was in a fog, too tired to argue, back in my best-sleep stupor. Isaac must have been using his gift. I nodded my agreement and lay back down.

The sun was well above the horizon when I woke next, flooding me with even more warmth than the night had provided. The fire had burned down to smoldering embers, and I was still in Liam's arms. I stayed, nestled next to him, fully awake but dreading the moment this level of comfort would end.

There were other things in my life that had brought me this much peace: sleeping in until I naturally woke up on Saturdays, the smell of Sunday pancakes at my house, and watching reruns with my brother while vegging out on the couch. But those things were part of a completely different life, one that was a fond memory.

In his letter to me, Bryce had told me about what was going on back home, about a new love interest he had, a college visit, a party with his friends, how he had seen something at the mall that had reminded him of me.

And it was all well and good. A small part of me hungered for those stories; it was why I'd read the letter over and over again. I wanted to pluck them up and pin them onto my brain so I could pretend they were my experiences.

But a much larger part of my brain had no interest whatsoever in pursuing the same things Bryce talked about. I knew most of my friends were like him, but for some reason, as soon as I donned a uniform, it was as if I had aged...not just days or months, but years. The world became much bigger to me somehow, the consequences of seemingly insignificant actions much more of a reality than ever before.

I still didn't know if it was a change I liked.

Liam stirred beside me. There was a short stubble on his face, which just barely softened the square angle of his jaw. As I turned over to study him more, the bare skin on my back brushed against the rough material of my fatigues.

I was braless.

I jumped from my spot immediately onto my feet. With Liam on the other side of the thin layer of cloth, I'd suddenly felt like I was lying next to him naked.

Liam bolted upright as well, swiveling his head in order to find the source of the sudden chaos in our cocoon.

His fatigues were unbuttoned, and a tee shirt snugly fitting around his torso was in full view. I pried my eyes off his body as his eyes landed on me. A beautiful, amused smile spread across his face.

"What are you doing?"

I wished I could answer him honestly, but even I didn't know how to explain the awkward position my body had landed in. One hand was on my hip, and the other was over my head. Worse, I was only standing on one foot. It was like those moments where you trip over nothing on the ground, so you pretend to go for a short little jog to cover up your clumsiness. That's what I did, but in my attempt to cover up my embarrassment, I looked even more like a dork.

"Uh, yoga. It's a good way to start the day. It's relaxing, and it's good to stretch first thing in the morning."

Right. Namaste. And all that.

"So this is you…relaxed?" Liam said, not even trying to hide his laughter.

"No," I said, trying to calm my nerves and letting out a chuckle. "This is me, trying to relax while you think I'm crazy."

He laughed out loud. "You are crazy. Definitely." He stood and took two long strides to meet me. Softly, he brushed the back of his hand against my cheek as I stared into his eyes. "But I'm crazy, too. About you." He smiled, and dear lord, even his teeth looked perfect first thing in the morning.

At that moment, I was incredibly thankful for Liam's sweet nature. It meant the whole awkward ah-crap-I-don't-have-a-bra-on-so-might-as-well-do-yoga saga was done. But I was anticipating what he might do next, as well.

I was cursing the fact that I wasn't given mouthwash in my pack when Liam straightened abruptly. "Where's Isaac?"

"Huh?" I asked. And then I remembered. "Oh yeah," I explained. "He woke up in the middle of the night and said he felt someone panicking."

"Panicking?" Liam looked like he was on the verge of doing it himself.

"*Isaac* wasn't panicking," I clarified. "But he felt someone freaking out. He didn't act like it was a dangerous situation or anything. He said it wasn't anger.

Just fear. He seemed confident he would find whoever it was, and then he said he'd meet up with us today."

I could practically see the gears turning in Liam's mind. "Which way did he go?"

"I think he said he was going to head up the hillside."

"Why don't we head that direction, too, so we can find him earlier? Just in case he has to stay with whoever it was who was panicking? Maybe they're hurt or something."

I looked around the cocoon and noticed just a few things that needed picking up. Isaac had left us MREs, and we would need to disassemble the shelter and take the tarp with us.

"Good idea," I agreed. "Just give me a second to wake up."

"I thought that's what the yoga was for," Liam said, and his eyes danced. I'm sure I blushed, but I tried to hide a smile as I did my best to ignore his charm. I walked out of our shelter into the morning.

I only went a few feet before stopping; I didn't want to get lost.

It was louder than I was expecting, this world just outside of the West Point campus, as if we weren't even guests in the habitat surrounding us. A screech of some kind – I wasn't sure if it was a bird or a small mammal – belted out from my left. Nothing answered its call, so it screamed out again. Insects chirped all around me, having their own little conversation that I was eavesdropping upon. The light breeze was an invisible current in the long grass, and when it moved, the stems would rustle their leaf-and-seed heads together, back and forth, accompanying the other noises with their soft percussion background.

It really was gorgeous here.

"Want some breakfast?" Liam called from the cocoon.

"Yes," I said, probably a little too enthusiastically.

I had just reached the opening of our shelter when we heard the blast of a gunshot reverberating off of the peaceful mountains that fenced us in.

～⚬～

OUR MRES WERE EATEN QUICKLY AND QUIETLY.

"Who do you think shot the gun? And what were they shooting at?" Liam asked.

"Not sure," I answered matter-of-factly. "It could have been one of us, if someone had gotten a gun in their pack to hunt prey with. Or…" I let the word, and all the uncertainty that it implied, linger.

"We could be the prey," Liam finished.

I nodded.

The bombing at the hospital – and the threats that had been made against us – were fresh in both of our minds.

The Army had said we'd be safe during this excursion, but how did we really know we were? Out here, there were no man-made walls to protect us, no MPs making routine walk-throughs as we scuttled from one safe spot to another. I'd initially taken comfort in the fact that we weren't alone, had imagined soldiers stationed amongst the trees in case we needed help. Now, it occurred to me that the trees weren't only capable of hiding protectors.

They could hide predators, too.

I scooted closer to the back of our shelter so my back was against the tarp… as if it'd be strong enough to stop a bullet, as if the bright blue of the tarp didn't actually make us an easier target amongst the more natural colors dotting the landscape.

We were like a flashing neon light on a dark night – a bright signal attracting attention.

Attract attention.

That's it.

That was one of the other uses of tarps I'd read about. The bright blue material can be used to get the attention of any search planes or rescuers.

Which made it useless for us, because the Army knew where we were – we didn't need to be rescued. But it did give me an idea.

Maybe the others were trying to signal for us, too. Maybe the gun shot was an 'S.O.S.' cry. Maybe they were flashing signals to us with the reflection of the sun's rays off of a mirror. Or maybe we would leave here and hear them shouting out our names. I pushed myself up and launched myself out of the protective tarp, turning back sharply to the base of the tree where we had slept.

"What are you doing?" Liam yelled after me.

"Climbing," I answered simply.

He may have had a reply, but I didn't hear it. I was scaling the tree way too fast.

At last I reached the top of the tall evergreen. I perched myself there – like an owl – and tried to make my eyes just as wide and thorough as they searched through the trees.

I had scanned the mountains in front of me back and forth- left to right – three times, when I saw it: a thin stream of smoke, shimmying its way up the trunks of a few trees, only to disappear once it reached the skyline.

It was a couple of miles away, due north and up the hillside, exactly where Isaac said he was heading this morning.

I scampered down the tree to alert Liam and gather our things.

36

WE'D BEEN WALKING FOR A COUPLE OF HOURS.
Before we left, Liam had insisted on taking the full canteen and the heavier pack, the one containing the MREs. I'd finally given in and let him. We only made it half an hour with me carrying the thin tarp before I stopped him and demanded we switch, holding out the tarp for him to grab in one hand, and holding my other hand to ask for the heavy objects. He didn't know I carried the precious matches close to my heart.

"Listen, I'm man enough to admit you could probably carry this pack better than I could," he said after my protests. His eyes studied my face. "But I'm also man enough to never let you carry a heavy load alone. My heart wouldn't be able to take it."

"Your heart needs to play catch-up to the twenty-first century," I'd quipped, and I snatched the pack and canteen out of his hands.

He'd laughed his gorgeous laugh and shook his head. "You amaze me," he said, simply and sincerely.

We'd been walking in silence ever since. The terrain was rugged and demanded all of our attention.

I wasn't sure where our destination was, exactly - only the general direction of where I'd seen the smoke. I had figured that as long as we tried our hardest to walk in a straight line, we'd be able to find whoever had started the fire as soon as we got closer to it.

But I was starting to doubt that strategy. We'd been walking a long time, calling out every now and then to the other members of The Crest with no luck.

I dropped my pack. The canteen was hooked to it, too, and it made a loud thud as it hit the ground.

"I'm going up," I told Liam, pointing to the large evergreen we were about to pass. "I gotta see what's going on, get a clear visual of where we are. I feel like we're just blindly trying to find the others."

He nodded his agreement. "Be careful, k?" he asked, his overprotective nature taking precedence over everything. "I'll stay here and guard the goods." He motioned to my pack on the ground and his own on his back.

I scampered up the tree relatively easily, admittedly getting slightly reckless as I swung from branch to branch just a little way off the ground. The branches were strong there and were spaced far enough apart that I could go from one to another quickly, almost artistically. It was a good thing my palms had hardened into giant callouses with all of the weight training I'd been doing; the branches were rough, but they didn't cut my hands. In fact, I felt like I was gymnast on the uneven bars.

I was having fun, and I grinned as I finally got myself as close to the top of the tree as I could. I rested a hand on my forehead to shade my eyes from the intensity of the noon sun. Repeating what I'd done earlier, I squinted and searched the area ahead, back and forth, looking for any sign of the smoke trail I'd seen earlier. Nothing.

Frustrated and ready to give up, I turned the other direction so I could make my way down the tree. And then I saw it: the thin stream of smoke steadily making its way to the sky.

We'd overshot our target. I dashed down the tree.

"We gotta go this way," I told Liam, jerking my head in the direction I'd just looked. "It's not too far, but it's uphill. Real steep. Maybe a half-hour walk."

His eyes lit up. "Great." He heaved his pack back onto his shoulders, then froze. "You said it's not that far away?"

"Nope," I shook my head. "But like I said, it's really steep — almost vertical at some spots. Still, it shouldn't take long."

"Hmm." His jaw flexed, and he wiped some sweat off his forehead as he studied the horizon. He took a swig from his canteen before handing it — and our packs — over to me to carry.

"What?" I swung the packs over my shoulder.

He forced a smile. "I'm sorry," he apologized. "I'm not trying to worry you. It's just — we've been thinking whoever is up there is one of us, right?"

"Uh, yeah?"

"Then why haven't they answered when we've called out?"

My breath caught in my throat. Of course. "The gunshot."

Liam nodded. "What if someone else is out here? Who's to say that same person who tried to hurt us in the hospital isn't hoping to hurt us out here, too?"

We stood in silence, our feet frozen with fear and indecision.

"What do you think, Wonder Woman?" Liam asked. "You're the natural- the real soldier here." He smiled slightly. "I'm just the one who promised to have your back."

"We're not in tactics class, O'Dell," I replied, knocking him lightly with my elbow. "You're off the hook."

His face was masked in seriousness. "Not a chance, Blackburn."

I tried not to blush and failed.

"Let's go, then," I decided out loud. I tucked a strand of hair behind my ear. "Just no calling out to them, okay? And make sure we can get a visual before we get too close."

He nodded his agreement, and we trekked our way to the top of the incline.

37

FOR THE NEXT TEN MINUTES, WE CONCENTRATED
on simply making our way up the steep hill, which was much harder than we'd initially assessed. The hillside had lots of dangers lying in wait, even beyond its sharp slope. Jagged rocks and gnarled branches seemed to grab at my legs like the zombie corpses did in my brother's video games. Needing to focus on avoiding these obstacles, and also unsure of what was to come — not knowing whether to be excited or anxious — I focused on my breathing and the sound of crunching twigs, leaves, and pine needles underfoot as we pressed onward.

The predictable pattern was broken with a sudden grunt. I snapped my head around in time to see Liam trip over an exposed root and hit the ground. I reached for him, but was too late. Careening backwards and gaining speed as he rolled down the rocky hill, he somehow found a way to call out to me: a desperate, panicked sound I knew I'd never forget.

"LIAM!"

I sprinted after him, swallowing my own fear and sliding down the incline myself, losing our packs and spraying sticks and sharp stones in all directions. Through the shower of debris, I could still hear him — still hear my name — even as he was slipping away.

But there was only silence when a boulder crunched against his ribs.

He went limp, having passed out, no longer reaching for something to stop him from sliding down the side of the mountain.

I had gained some ground, though, when the rock had slowed his momentum.

I closed the gap between us as his body continued to slide, down and fast, toward the cliff with the ravine that loomed menacingly below.

I made a last-ditch, desperate jump toward him just as he reached the edge, just as his body was rolling limply over the precipice.

With one hand, I grabbed the skinny trunk of a young tree. With the other, I clutched onto Liam's wrist as he fell like a rag doll over the cliff.

With a guttural cry of a girl I didn't know, I held on, then swung him up and over.

His body landed next to mine. I saw his belly swell with an inhaled breath and let a relieved one out myself.

"Liam. Crap. Are you okay?"

He didn't answer. He was still out.

I spun around and looked at the bottom of the ravine, expecting to feel grateful I'd reached Liam before he'd landed there.

But I couldn't rest, or even be thankful just yet.

Because far below, lying forgotten at the bottom of the abyss, almost unseen because of the camouflaged fatigues, was another broken body.

※

"ISAAC," I WHISPERED.

And then I screamed it.

I saw him twitch at the sound, as if I were a nuisance waking him from a deep slumber.

He was okay.

I wasn't sure how okay he was....but he was okay enough to be moving, even if it was just a little bit.

"Isaac!" I yelled again. "Isaac! Tell me if you can hear me!"

His head turned my direction. His eyes were glossed over, as if he were waking up from a dream in the middle of the night. He weakly held a thumbs up for me to see before dropping his head and arm to the ground below, and Liam stirred behind me.

I cupped his head in my hands and placed it gingerly on my lap. I assessed the damage done to his body – the bruises and cuts and scrapes – and said a quick prayer of thanksgiving it wasn't worse.

His fatigues were torn on the side, where the boulder had hit him. I picked the torn fabric up by the edges and looked at his side.

It wasn't pretty. A deep, angry gash had slashed through his flawless pale skin. I could see meat and bone.

"Mmmmf." His head moved slightly.

"Don't move," I insisted.

But he didn't listen. Drawing on some kind of hidden strength, he propped himself up on his elbows and checked his wound out himself.

"Umpfff," he groaned, touching the wound slightly. He laid back down, closed his eyes, and swallowed thickly. "Either I need stitches, or I need the miraculous ability to heal myself." He managed a grin. "Oh, wait…"

I let a smile escape, too, before studying his face. "Are you okay?"

He jutted out his chin. "I'm okay, Blackburn. I'm just sorry I almost took you with me." He drew a shaky breath. "Who were you yelling at?"

"Isaac," I replied. "He's at the bottom of the ravine."

Liam bolted upright, then grimaced with the pain. I ordered him to lie down, then left his side to peer over the edge again. Isaac was still there, sitting up now, with his head in his hands.

I looked to my left. About fifty feet away, there was a way down. It was still steep, but at least it was a way down.

"He'll be okay," I promised Liam, though I knew little to back the assertion. "I'll go down and get him." Liam opened his mouth but closed it quickly, as if he wanted to say something, but decided against it. He nodded his consent.

"You'll be fine," he said, as if he were convincing himself of the fact. "You're Wonder Woman. But be careful. Even Wonder Woman has her kryptonite."

I arched a brow. "That's Superman," I corrected.

He cracked a smile again, in spite of it all. "Whatever. You get my point."

"Actually, I don't," I teased. "I mean…come to think of it, I don't think Wonder Woman has a weakness."

254

"I'm pretty sure it was men," Liam said.

My jaw dropped.

"What?" Liam asked.

"Not true!" I argued. "She fought men and won all the time!"

"Yes," Liam explained. "But once they restrained her, she was powerless."

My cheeks grew hot. "That's got to be the most sexist – the most ridiculous thing I have ever heard. Wonder Woman is the greatest of all women but could be restrained by any man? Are you serious?"

He nodded. "I heard the creator was sexist."

"You heard right." I wanted to stomp off. "What an ass."

He chuckled, then swallowed the sound when I shot him an angry look. He coughed awkwardly. "Ahem. You might want to, um, go help Isaac."

I took a deep breath to clear my head. "Right."

I left him behind me and made my way over to the path I'd spotted earlier.

It took a while for me to reach the bottom, but with some controlled slipping and sliding and strategic holds, I finally reached him.

"There she is," Isaac announced, still sitting on the ground. "Here to rescue me in all my glory." He waved a hand up and down and in front of his body.

"You okay?" I asked. I leaned closer to check out his pupils. Enlarged – he was definitely concussed.

"Probably fine," he answered, slowly shaking his head. "I can't walk, or even stand. My ankle's broken, I think. And I have the worst headache ever."

"I'll get you out of here," I promised. I turned to check out his ankle. I wasn't sure if it was broken or not, but it was definitely swollen and bruised. I turned back to face him.

"I gotta swing you over my shoulders."

"Of course you do," Isaac slurred, after only pausing for a beat. "Because you couldn't have possibly emasculated me enough last night when Liam showed up. I mean, do you have a dress I could put on, too?"

At first my cheeks darkened, and I felt the urge to apologize. I didn't want him to feel even worse than he had the night before.

But I stopped myself.

Don't apologize for your strength. And don't apologize for your feelings, I silently admonished. *You have gifts, too, and you have every right to flaunt them.*

Take that, Wonder Woman creator.

"You're cranky when you're concussed," I replied instead, and I heaved him over my shoulders like a shepherd would a sheep.

38

I WAS AS CAREFUL AS I COULD POSSIBLY BE,
lying Isaac down next to Liam. Even still, he bit his lip and
mumbled an obscenity.

"What happened?"

Liam had directed his question to Isaac, but I replied
instead.

"He's concussed," I explained. When it came to first
aid, head problems were always a priority. "And I think he
may have broken his ankle, too."

Liam scooted closer in order to examine Isaac more
closely. He peered into his pupils.

I cleared my throat. Liam shot me a stare. "I already did
that," I told him confidently. "And I told you, he has a
concussion."

Liam nodded sheepishly and made his way to Isaac's
ankle. "But you're not sure if it's broken?" he asked.
"Doc?" His tone had a teasing edge to it.

"I'm not the doctor here," I answered. "I'm the
Wonder Woman." I grinned.

Liam did, too.

He got to his feet and quickly – almost too quickly – plopped down on the other side of Isaac to take a closer look at his injuries.

"Seriously?" I asked.

Liam just looked at me.

"What?" they chorused.

I kept my eyes locked on Liam. "You're better? Already?"

He cleared his throat and glanced down to remove Isaac's boot. "I heal fast. Remember?"

Of course. When he'd healed my arm, he only had an overnight stay at the hospital. The injury would have taken weeks to heal with me.

He swept his fatigues to the side so I could see his abdomen. Already, the wound was closed and scabbed. In fact, it looked like the scab was falling off, and the edges of the wound had the swollen, red tinge of a newly-healed lesion. I reached out and brushed it with my fingers.

He flinched.

"Sorry," Liam apologized. "I heal fast, but it still hurts. You know?"

"Actually, I don't," I said, realizing I had never assessed his pain level when he was in the hospital with his –er, my – compound fracture. "You never told me exactly how much pain you were in before."

Liam swallowed thickly. "It hurts," he repeated. "But it heals fast, too. Gotta take the good with the bad, I guess. It's worth the pain if everyone else is healed, especially if my wound heals quickly, too."

And it was healing. In the short time our conversation had taken place, the scab had cracked some more. "Wow," I acknowledged. "Impressive."

Both the healing and the abs.

"What happened to you?" Isaac asked Liam, his face still stoic.

"I fell," Liam answered simply. "Hit a rock. Almost plummeted over the edge and ended up down by you. But Blackburn here," he said, nodding to me, "she saved me at the last minute."

"Nice," Isaac commented. "Guess we can keep you around." He grinned, and I realized it was the first time I'd seen his smile since our awkward moment the night before. It was nice to see.

"So how'd you end up down there?" I asked. "Did you trip when it was still dark or something?"

Isaac's grinned vanished. He shook his head and looked down. "Nope. Nothing like that."

And just like that, the atmosphere changed.

"What happened, Isaac?" Liam questioned. I was grateful he could speak. Suddenly, I was too afraid to.

"I was attacked last night," Isaac whispered. His chin was at his chest. "Y'all...I left because I felt like someone needed me. Whoever it was, was panicking." His eyes glanced up the hill. "They still are."

"But anyway, last night, I had my feelers out, you know, and was just walking along here, when someone shoved me."

I swore. "Oh, Isaac." I rushed to his side. "Do you know who did it?"

He shook his head and his eyes glazed over. "Nah. No clue. It's just-" He paused.

Liam and I exchanged a look.

"Whoever it was," Isaac carefully explained, "He didn't have an ounce of peace in his body."

259

39

"YOU'VE GOTTA GO WITH ME," I INSISTED. "I need your gift in order to find whoever it is who's panicking."

"And like I said, my gift is useless if I can't fully concentrate," Isaac replied. "And I can't concentrate when I'm being heaved around like a sack of potatoes by you." He crossed his arms in defiance.

We'd been trying to solve the problem of how to move forward and move quickly. Carrying Isaac seemed like the way to go, in my opinion, because if Liam healed him, it'd incapacitate him and he'd have to stay behind.

Isaac wasn't about to let that happen, though. "Why don't you lovebirds go on without me?" His voice trailed off at the end, as if it were a dramatic ending to a pouty child's soliloquy. Liam's ears reddened in embarrassment, but I rolled my eyes. I mean, I did feel bad about Isaac feeling left out, but this dramatic side to him was almost too much to take. I much preferred the easy-going Isaac.

"BECAUSE I NEED YOUR GIFT," I declared. How many times would I have to spell it out for him?

"Tell you what," Liam interrupted. He left my side and sat next to Isaac. "I'll heal you. You go with Brooklyn and find whoever it is who needs help, and I'll wait right here and let my ankle and concussion heal until you guys return."

I opened my mouth to protest, but Liam held up a hand. "It's the only thing that makes sense, Brooklyn. I'm still not a hundred percent from my run-in with the boulder, so it'd be hard for me to make the hike, anyway. And you have to have Isaac with you in order to find whoever it is who's in trouble. But we need Isaac fully healed." He slapped Isaac's knee slightly, as if he were a father encouraging his son to play a good game.

I wanted badly to argue with him. So, so badly.

The short amount of time I'd had to spend alone out here wasn't easy. And it was even harder when I'd been alone with Isaac. I mean, that's what unwanted emotions do: they make everything harder. But when Liam showed up, things got easier, almost enjoyable. I didn't want him to leave and ruin the good vibes.

But he was right, and I knew it. I had to leave him behind.

I nodded my consent.

Liam jumped at his chance. Without hesitating, he placed his hands on Isaac – one on his head, and the other on his ankle, and he closed his beautiful eyes.

I didn't know where the feeling of serenity was coming from. Maybe it was Liam's magical incantations - whispered so softly - they were almost silent. Or maybe Isaac was using his gift. Or maybe it was something else: a peace I would never understand, the kind that comes with sacrifice.

Either way, it was there. It was present, and it was palpable.

When Liam was done, his words fell silent and his chin drooped.

"Do you feel sick?" I asked.

His face paled, and he nodded.

I rushed up to catch him just as his eyelids began to close. I lifted him easily and carried him a few yards away, placing him gingerly underneath an evergreen tree, where there was adequate coverage and camouflage, and where there were plenty of pine needles to soften the ground.

I took just a moment to let my eyes linger on his perfection, then brought my lips to his cheek. I inhaled deeply and uttered, "Be safe, please. I'll come back for you before you know it."

His eyes were still closed, but the corners of his mouth turned up slightly.

It took every ounce of strength I had to turn on my heel and leave his enclosure instead of jump right into his arms.

Isaac was stretching as I emerged, even doing small hops, as if he were warming up for a basketball game or something.

"Thought I should get loose," he informed me. "But your boy Liam's got some gift. Damn! I feel alright!"

He grinned broadly, and I grinned back. It was good to have the real Isaac back with me.

"Well, let's go then, shall we?" I proposed.

"After you, Miss," Isaac said, waving out a hand. I surged past him and led the way to the path, excited to complete our mission.

I couldn't wait to return to the man we were leaving behind.

40

PROPELLED FORWARD BY THE THOUGHT OF
returning to Liam, I worked my body harder than ever as
we trekked through the woods. My heart rate was up and
so was my breathing, until I inhaled a lungful of smoke
and coughed, stopping dead in my tracks from the
intrusion. Isaac stopped, too.

"Up there," he instructed. I searched up the hillside
and saw a rocky outcropping about ten feet almost
directly above us. Sure enough, a thick stream of black
smoke was making its way out of the top.

"Whoever it is," Isaac continued, "they're scared as
hell."

"Better move," I added.

It'd only taken us an hour to get to our destination, but
we'd have to rock climb to finish the trek.

"I'll go first," I told Isaac. "Then I'll reach down and
help you up."

He nodded, putting his pride on hold. "We need to
hurry."

The fact that he was speaking such short, clipped
sentences was making me worry. Isaac didn't miss any

opportunity to tease me or spew a sexist joke. This had to be bad.

Not bothering to drop my pack, I reached up to find a hand hold on the natural rock wall in front of me. It didn't have a lot of them, but I found two narrow holds and was able to lift my body weight where my feet could find small indentations to rest. I did this a few times until I finally reached the top. I swung myself up and over.

There was a small cave directly in front of me, but I wasn't brave enough to go in there without Isaac. I dropped to my belly and scooted to the edge.

"You'll have to start the climb yourself," I told Isaac. "But I should be able to lift you up the rest of the way."

He nodded quickly and got to work. He had paid attention to the holds I'd used when climbing and grabbed the same, then reached his right hand up for mine. I grabbed it easily, then bent my arm as if I were doing a bicep curl, lifting Isaac up to the edge, then pulling him up the rest of the way with my other hand.

He shook his head. "Not sure if I'll ever get used to you doing all the heavy-lifting," he said. "But thanks."

He sprinted toward the cave. I followed.

Inside, Isaac knelt immediately over a body, one that only took me a second to register.

It was Jacob.

I couldn't help but cough again with the thick smoke inside the cave. I could only imagine what kind of assault it had done on Jacob's asthmatic lungs.

"Is he okay?" I asked, kneeling down in an effort to avoid the smoke.

Isaac had his ear to Jacob's chest. "I think so," he said. "But he's wheezing bad." He let out a cough of his own.

"Do me a favor and put that fire out," he ordered. "The hole in the top of the cave isn't big enough to let it out, and I can't relax him or myself if I'm choking."

"What do I use?" I asked, panicking. The fire was big and billowing, and I knew we didn't have enough water to put it out. And I was afraid it'd melt the tarp if I tried to suffocate the fire by lying the tough fabric over it.

"Never mind," Isaac said, scooping Jacob up in his arms. He ran with him outside the cave and lay him down on the hard rock. Isaac put his hand on Jacob's chest and closed his eyes.

Immediately I felt my own heart rate slow. I slumped to the ground and closed my eyes, too. I didn't know why; I knew I didn't share his gift, but I thought maybe Jacob would do better if I relaxed, too.

I tried to tune out the sound of Jacob's raspy wheeze, but when he coughed, I jumped to my feet.

With asthmatics, when it came to closed airwaves, coughs were good until they opened fully again.

Isaac kept one hand on Jacob's chest and motioned for me to sit down with the other. "Hang on a sec, Brooklyn," he ordered, his eyes still closed. "A lot of damage has been done to his airways. They're still constricted." He breathed slow, deep breaths while I sat down again. It seemed like forever, but finally, I saw Jacob sit up. Isaac was giving him some water from a bottle I hadn't seen before.

Jacob struggled to slow his breathing down. "I found…the cave…and it was s-so…cold…"

"Don't talk," Isaac commanded. "We can figure out what happened next. You started the fire to stay warm.

The smoke messed with your breathing. Did you bring your inhaler with you?"

Jacob shook his head slowly. "The…chamber…in… it…with the… medicine…it…i-it… was…empty…"

Isaac jumped to his feet and ducked into the cave.

I made my way to Jacob and held his head in my lap. "You're okay now," I told him, and he trembled and nodded as if he were a child. "Isaac's here, so you'll be able to breathe, and I'm sure we can set up a better camp for you to stay warm tonight."

Isaac emerged from the cave, holding a pack that looked the same as the ones we were given.

"Did you find the inhaler?" I questioned.

"Yeah," Isaac replied, throwing the emptied tube in our direction. "They must have switched it out." He swore loudly.

"What'd he have in the bag?" I asked.

"A few flame blocks," he said, holding something compact. "They hold a flame for a long time, without using twigs or logs for fuel." He threw me a teasing stare. "Which is a good thing, since we can't get any more kindling from you," he said.

"Hahaha," I replied through my blush. I'd almost forgotten about my burned undergarments.

"What's he talking about?" Jacob asked.

"Nothing," I said, too soon for the answer to be honest.

Jacob looked Isaac's direction. "I'll tell you when she leaves," the traitor promised.

"Jerk," I mumbled, and Isaac's eyes gleamed mischievously. "Do you think it's okay to leave now?" I asked, changing the subject to more pressing matters.

"Probably," he said. "We still have about four hours of daylight and other Crest members to find." He nodded toward the cliff we'd climbed in order to get to the cave. "Check it out. We have a better vantage point here." He waved a long arm to the scene in front of him, and for the first time, I really took notice. We were higher up than we'd been at any time – even when I'd climbed the trees before – almost to the top of the mountain.

"I need to stay with Jacob to make sure he can breathe," Isaac continued, "so that means you probably have to go back for Liam on your own."

"Anything in Jacob's pack that will help me with that task?" I asked, once again in full soldier mode.

"Only a radio," Isaac replied, holding up a small black device with an antenna.

"Uh, yeah," Jacob replied, still breathing heavily, but not as badly as before. He propped himself up on his elbows. "But it doesn't... work. I tried... all night...."

"Hmm," Isaac said, looking at it a bit closer.

"Here, I'll show you," Jacob insisted. Isaac placed it in his hands. Jacob flipped the switch on, and a screeching static filled the air. He turned the knobs and held down buttons. He even turned the antenna in all directions. The screeching continued. "See?" he asked, turning it off after his demonstration.

"Yeah," Isaac replied. "It doesn't make sense for you to have one out here, anyway. I wonder why they even gave it to you."

"I better leave soon to go get Liam," I interrupted. My thoughts had wandered away from the boring radio conversation. I studied the sun's position in the sky. "I better get out of here soon. I'll break branches so I can find my way back after I get him. You know, like Hansel and Gretel."

"Look for Adrianna and Bree while you're out there," Isaac advised. "They might be needing us, too."

41

I PAUSED, TAKING GREAT CARE TO BREAK
another three branches on the tree in front of me.

That's how I was keeping track of where I'd been; breaking three branches in a row would be an obvious sign I had passed that way before. I also warned Isaac he'd have to answer me when I returned. I was planning on playing the Marco Polo game (where you answer 'Polo' when somebody calls out 'Marco'), no matter how silly it seemed. I wanted to ensure I could easily find him again after I retrieved Liam.

I reached for the last branch and grasped it firmly with two hands. But before I had a chance to snap it in half, I heard something snap behind me.

I whipped around.

Nothing.

"Marco?" I whispered. Evidently I reverted to this kind of childish game in times of crisis.

But oddly, I found comfort in it. "Marco???" I called, voicing it this time.

"POLO!" a feminine voice answered, and the response was close.

"WHO IS IT?" I asked the trees, which obstructed all views in front of me.

In seconds, the reply was crunching footsteps, which quickened in pace as I watched a petite figure with ivory skin and deep red hair materialize in front of me.

"Bree!" I yelled, starting to run toward her and waving my hands over my head.

Relief spread across her face as she gave me a quick hug.

"Here, give me your pack," I demanded. She had no problem complying.

"Do you have water?" she asked as I hoisted it onto my back, and for the first time I noticed just how cracked and pale her lips were.

I retrieved Isaac's canteen and thrust it at her. "Drink," I ordered, thankful we had such a gift. Again, she did as she was told, only stopping to gulp air before she continued her deep swigs.

Minutes passed, but finally, she stopped and lay with her back to the ground, eyes up at the sky.

"Oh, I'm so glad you found me," she said, her eyes closed. "I don't think I would have made it through another night."

"Where did you stay?" I asked.

She shrugged. "I was the last one dropped off. It started raining before I could find anything. I just slept under a tree."

"With nothing else?" I asked.

"I had a blanket," she said. "And a first-aid kit. But that's it. It was freaking cold. And I woke up wet. I walked all day in the sun so I could dry off."

My eyes studied hers. "Without food or water?"

She nodded. "I couldn't find any water. I saw some berries, but I was afraid they were poisonous."

I swore. "Let's get you to our camp," I prodded. "You need to relax and eat something. And keep drinking water."

"How did you find stuff for a camp? And food? And water?" She sat up.

"It's not just me," I said. "Isaac and Jacob are up there, and Liam will be there soon, too, so we're able to use stuff from all of our packs. Isaac got MREs, and I had a tarp so we could collect some water. Jacob has a flame block so we'll be able to stay warm tonight, too."

Tears spilled over onto her chiseled cheeks. She quickly tried to brush them away.

"I'm sorry," she apologized. "I just..." She broke down, sobbing so loudly I feared something else was wrong.

"Shhh," I said, more to comfort than to hush. I kneeled down next to her. "Bree, you're safe now. You don't have to worry."

"I know I'm safe," she explained, wiping her cheeks with her hand. "But I'm only safe because you found me. You all have your gifts, and I don't. I don't have anything. I'm freaking useless, out here and at the campus." She wiped her nose with her sleeve. "I wish I could just go home, that Major McCoy and General Richards would realize I don't have a gift like you guys do.

"What makes you think you don't?" I asked. "What about your great eyesight? Your ability to shoot accurately?"

Bree rolled her eyes. "I may be a decent shot, Brooklyn, but I'm not super-human. And you know it." She kicked a stick with her foot, and it left a track of freshly uncovered dirt from where it had scraped the ground. "I've never had any amazing talents, not like the rest of you."

"I mean, even when we were little, before he could heal anything, Liam would always try to take care of me when I was sick or got hurt," Bree continued. "And he was super sensitive whenever anyone else got hurt- like, he internalized their pain."

She brushed away another tear. "All of the rest of you have been talented in your areas, too. I've just always been normal. I like to sing and stuff, but c'mon, what am I going to do? Sing at terrorists when they come for me? Play my flute at them?"

I couldn't help it. I laughed.

"Like the Pied Piper," I joked. You'll just lead them all away from us and we won't even have to fight."

She laughed, too. "If only little kid stories were true."

"Hey," I interjected. "Just a month ago, we thought superheroes were fiction."

She smiled. "Then I guess there's hope for me yet: the female Pied Piper. Now who wants to be the first to see how well I'd fare against terrorists?"

There was a very real fear underlying her attempt at the joke, and for the first time I thought about what it must be like to be a target of terrorists without having any way to protect yourself.

"I've tested out that theory, you know," she said sadly. "After Liam showed his giftedness, Major McCoy insisted I sing and play my flute for him once, just to make sure those things didn't have some kind of secret power. But they didn't. I sounded like I always did. I think Major McCoy was disappointed. They'd had twins in The Crest before us, and they both got their gifts at the same time. But not us. Not me."

"Maybe you guys are different," I assured her. "I mean, just because The Crest's only set of twins each got their powers at the same time doesn't mean you can't be different. Right?"

The sun was sinking lower in the sky. I had to get her back to camp – and quick – so I could retrieve Liam before dark. I offered her a hand up and she accepted. "Come on," I said. "Let's make our way back."

Returning to camp took a lot more time than it had to get here. I was a little bit worried that Bree was dehydrated and wanted to make sure we kept a slow pace so she didn't exert herself more than necessary.

After the first four trees I saw with three broken branches, I began to yell, "Marco!" and was answered by Isaac.

Before I knew it, we were at the base of the cave, with only the rock wall as an obstacle to our camp. I was anxious to drop Bree off into Isaac's capable hands so I could bring Liam back before it got dark.

Little did I know, it wouldn't happen.

42

Twelve Hours Later

THE GROUNDS AT WEST POINT HAD SEEMED SO vibrant this morning. Waking up next to Liam in our cocoon, I'd noticed the beauty in it. The life. Now, that beauty was masked by tones of black and navy and grey. Only a few things stood out among the shadows of three a.m., and that was thanks to the weak light emitted from a small sliver of a moon. Darkness masked the rest..

I'd searched for Liam until dusk and couldn't find him anywhere. Either I had done a horrible job marking my way back to him, or he had moved.

Or he'd been forced to move.

Ever since then, I'd been perched on the precipice in front of our cave, searching the blackness for something I knew I wouldn't be able to see.

Another gun shot rang out. And again, a shriek sliced through the air. I hugged my knees to my chest and glanced over my shoulder.

But they were still in the cave, still safe.

Bree and Jacob were sleeping, thanks to Isaac's gift. But Isaac returned my frightened stare with his own.

And Adrianna? And Liam?

They were missing, lost amongst the trees and the shadows and the shots and the shrieks.

I bit my lip and tasted blood, welcoming the pain. It allowed me to focus on something other than swallowing back my tears.

Two more hours until dawn.

Mid-Morning

I was more than slightly annoyed.

I'd wanted to hunt for Liam on my own, or at the very least, with Isaac. We could have used his "feelers" when guessing which way to go, and he was athletic enough to keep up.

But he'd stayed behind to make sure Jacob didn't suffer another asthma attack, and Bree had insisted she come with me.

"I know you like him, Brooklyn," she'd said. "But he's *my* brother. *My* twin. I need to go."

And because I let her play the 'twin-trumps-all' card, we were moving at a snail's pace and had been for two hours.

With no signs of him. Or anyone, for that matter.

And I was freaking out.

I heard her stumble behind me. This time I didn't even try to feign patience. I crossed my arms. "Really, Bree? You're telling me you couldn't see that log, either?"

Her face darkened. "Some of us have other gifts, Brooklyn. Like knowing when to shut our mouth."

I opened it, wanting to tell her exactly what I thought of her and her selfishness – how her 'need' to find Liam was impeding the actual act.

But the words never came.

Footsteps thundered behind me, so quickly I didn't even have time to ready myself for whoever it was who was aiming right for me. I turned around sharply and swung my fists blindly, wanting to attack the assailant the same way they'd attacked my heart and mind all night.

43

"HEY, WATCH IT!"

Adrianna had deftly moved from my flying fist and now gazed at me, looking a little confused and a lot annoyed.

"Sorry," I told her. "I thought you were..." I let the sentence trail off because I didn't know how to finish it.

"The guy from last night?" she finished.

Bree and I nodded.

"Have you seen them?" I asked.

"Not at all," Adrianna replied. "I don't know whether to be thankful about it or not." She perked up. "But what about us? The Crest? Do you know where the others are?"

"Isaac and Jacob are in a cave just north of here," I said. "But —"

"We can't find Liam, Adrianna," Bree blurted. She nervously bit at her thumbnail. "Brooklyn left him injured out in the middle of nowhere yesterday, and now we can't find him."

I couldn't add my thoughts. I was reeling too much from the blow of Bree's accusation.

"He's safe," Adrianna cooed, grabbing Bree's hand. "He was with me all night, up until a couple of hours ago."

"Liam's with you?" Bree's eyes leapt to the trees behind Adrianna's shoulder.

My heart wouldn't stop dancing. I closed my eyes and muttered the prayer I'd held onto all evening.

"No," Adrianna explained, pulling me back to the present. "He stayed back in our cave."

Um. *Our* cave?

"Why?" I demanded, ready to fight all over again. I wanted Liam. Here. With us.

"I left to find one of you!" She turned to Bree. "I found Liam yesterday, after following your voices from when you were playing Marco Polo. He told me you had gone north. He was completely out of it – in a lot of pain and moaning and stuff, so he wasn't in any shape to go exploring. I was able to get him back to my campsite, but he still can't move. We think he took too much on yesterday so it's slowing down the process." She turned to me. "We could really use your help."

"How far away are you?" I asked the question after clearing my throat, which was suddenly constricted.

Because she and Liam had spent the night together. All night.

Together.

Liam and Adrianna had probably lied as close as we had the night before, in order to stay warm.

It was Survival 101, and I knew that. And dammit, I wished I didn't care. But Adrianna, despite having to camp out with no amenities, still looked insanely gorgeous, like the beauty queen I'd thought she was that first night at the Waldorf Astoria.

And Liam – the boy who made my heart beat out of rhythm, who sacrificed his own health so I could be healed – he'd woken up to *her* today.

"Brooklyn. BROOKLYN!"

Bree's demanding voice snapped me out of the swamp of self-pity I was mucking around in.

"Huh?"

She laughed and looked to Adrianna, who smiled her movie star smile at me.

The jealous part of me wanted to wipe it off her face. The sane part of me let her speak.

"I just told you where our camp was." She swung around and pointed to the direction she'd come from. "I only had to jog about thirty minutes to get here. I was given a map of the grounds in my pack. Liam figured out that it included all of our drop-off points. He said one of the dots - representing me, I guess – was located next to the spot where you'd left him. So I used that little tidbit of information when I set out for you guys this morning."

"And speaking of setting out," she continued, turning towards Bree, "No offense, but I don't think you should go with us. It'd take too long."

Bree started to protest.

"You're outvoted," I said, agreeing with Adrianna. "Liam is the only one who's alone. And he needs us. NOW"

Reluctantly, Bree agreed.

Adrianna shifted her attention back to me. "Maybe we should take Bree back to the camp? And then you and I can go back and get Liam and bring him there, too? I'd ask

Isaac to go, but he should really stay with Jacob just in case
—"

"Just in case he has trouble breathing again," I finished.

Adrianna nodded.

"Yeah, sure, uh, we can go."

"Let's do it, then." She turned to hike up the side of the mountain with Bree. I fell in step behind them.

44

WE WALKED IN SILENCE: BREE, BECAUSE SHE

was having to work hard on the incline; me, because the last thing I wanted to do was the 'girl talk' thing with Adrianna; and Adrianna, because she was in her natural leadership mode, focused and intent.

Finally, we got to the natural rock wall. Adrianna waited at the bottom while I gave Bree a piggy back in order to get her up to the others.

"That was fun, but scary!" Bree giggled. "I still can't believe it doesn't even faze you to do stuff like that."

I shrugged. "It just felt like I had a backpack on," I replied honestly.

"That's awesome." She grinned again, then plopped herself down by Jacob.

Isaac started to get up to greet me, but I held a hand up. "I'm leaving again," I told him. "Adrianna's waiting for me. Liam is still recovering from his - I guess *your* injury, so I'm going with her to get him."

"I could —"

"You've gotta stay here for Jacob, in case he has another attack," I told him.

I could tell Isaac was silently wracking his brain for a reason to go with me, but I knew he wouldn't be able to find one.

"You ready to go?" Adrianna yelled from where she was waiting below. "Or do you need to eat?"

I shook my head and yelled back. "I'm fine. I don't think we have time."

Isaac threw the canteen down to the ground by Adrianna, and she took a few drinks while I made my way down the side of the mountain to where she was waiting. I'd grabbed the blue tarp, thinking it could help with transporting our patient.

"Okay," Adrianna said after she finished drinking, when I landed softly at her side. "Let's do it. Are you okay with running?"

I had to work to contain my relief at the suggestion. Running meant no talking. "Sure," I said as nonchalantly as possible, and we started a leisurely jog.

It was good to have my muscles endure some of the pain and pressure my heart felt. I was frustrated that I was even reacting this way to Liam and Adrianna being together the night before, and was grateful for the excuse to physically exert that frustration.

I trekked on: left, right, left, right, long strides, deep breaths, relishing the sameness of the act, enjoying how hard it was for me to do.

I allowed tears to sting my eyes, temporarily giving myself permission to be hurt about Liam and his close proximity to Adrianna the night before.

Why did I even care?

Far ahead of me, Adrianna stopped and turned, searching through the trees to spot me. She did, then waved impatiently to me to hurry up.

Just as I was about to reach her, she held back a thick branch with tons of heavy needle-leaves cloaking its slender limbs: a prickly door to a hidden place. Then, as suddenly as I registered she had gone into whatever it was behind that branch, the door closed behind her.

Sweating and out of breath, I finally reached the same tree. I let the needles poke into my arm as I opened the door as well, then let them scrape me as it swung shut as I released the tightened limb.

It took a moment for my eyes to adjust to the darkness, but my heart rate never did, as I saw Liam pale and trembling on the floor, blood trickling down his cheek from a bloody source at his temple.

45

"LIAM."

I sprinted to his side. Adrianna was already holding his head in her hands, applying pressure to the wound with a small bit of cloth.

"Liam," I said again, grabbing his hand.

"What happened?" I demanded from Adrianna.

She looked as if she'd been slapped. "I have no clue, Brooklyn. I was with you, remember?"

Liam blinked rapidly. A trail of blood was trickling down the edge of his left eye, and it was beginning to bruise and swell. He greeted me with a weak smile. "Hey there. I was wondering why I was suddenly feeling better."

My heart surged with so much affection for this man, it almost hurt. A tear escaped and I tried to wipe it away before he noticed. He was so pale. And so, so weak. What had happened to him the last twenty-four hours?

"Did you fall again, Liam?" Adrianna asked.

"Again?" I questioned.

Adrianna nodded. "He fell twice yesterday. Once before I arrived- after you left - and another time trying to put a log on the fire."

"I'm right here, you know," Liam said, his tone a mixture of seriousness and humor. "You don't have to talk about me like I'm not."

"Sorry," I said, turning to him instead. "I didn't mean to talk around you – it's just – you look so…"

"Sick?" Liam clarified.

I nodded. "Why aren't you healing quickly like before?"

He shrugged his shoulders. "I think it's because I was injured and still healing when I took Isaac's injury on. I'm still not feeling great," he admitted, his green eyes wide. "But seriously, I feel a hundred percent better now that you're here." Once again, he smiled his sweet smile, and once again, a piece of my heart broke with it. He turned his attention to Adrianna.

"I didn't fall," he explained somberly. "I was attacked."

"Attacked?!" we barked simultaneously.

My head snapped toward the opening of the cave. No one was there.

Liam nodded. "I scooted toward the door over there to see if I could spot anyone else." He turned to Adrianna. "It'd been an hour since you'd left, and I wanted to see if I could see Bree or Jacob's drop-off points by comparing the map with our view of the grounds, like you did. So I took it with me to go have a look. It took me awhile to stand and hobble my way over to the door, but as soon as I made it to the opening, someone hit me over the head with something hard. I blacked out. When I woke up, I was all bloody and couldn't find the map."

"They took it?" Adrianna asked. The color was draining from her face.

Liam didn't answer. He simply closed his eyes and nodded, swallowing thickly.

"You left the map here?" I exclaimed, turning to Adrianna. "Why would you do that?"

"So it wouldn't get stolen. I figured it was safer tucked in here than out there with me." She gestured to the opening of the cave before waving her hand dismissively. "It doesn't matter, anyway. What's done is done."

Adrianna beckoned me to sit behind Liam and take his head in my hands. She jumped up and began pacing.

"Isaac, Bree, and Jacob are all at Jacob's drop off point," Adrianna thought aloud. "And Brooklyn and I were on our way back to you when you were attacked. So we know for sure none of us could have taken the map."

She stopped pacing and looked at me. "There's someone else here." She got even paler. "They have a gun." Her gaze went to the Catskills, beyond the walls of vegetation covering their cave. "And now they know where the others are."

46

I WAS ACTUALLY BREAKING A SWEAT.

Not because it was hard to tow Liam in my makeshift sled (the folded tarp I'd brought along), but because I was trying to catch up with Adrianna, even though I knew it was probably impossible. It reminded me of our first morning at West Point, when I had realized my gift was useless when it came to speed, but that Adrianna's body was made for it.

Ugh. Her perfect body. Her perfect face. Her perfect everything. Her gift was just another thing to tack on to her impressive resume.

She'd left just minutes before us. Liam and I would have slowed her down, and she needed to get to the others before he did: whoever it was who stole the map.

I knew Adrianna would get there soon, but it didn't stop me from wanting to be there, too. Bree had no powers. Jacob was weak from his asthma attack. And who knew how long Isaac could keep a situation calm? If someone really was trying to get to us, at some point, a fight would happen.

And I was the fighter.

I needed to be there when it did.

We were only a few minutes away, but time stretched as endlessly as the blue sky above.

I lengthened my strides, determined to go even faster.

"Mmphf."

I stopped for a second to look back at Liam, to see why he was moaning. He held an elbow and was masking a pained expression on his face with a brave grin.

"What's wrong?" I asked, taking a deep gulp of air in an attempt to slow my breathing.

He shook his head and relinquished the hold on his elbow. "Nothing. It's fine."

"Something's wrong." I kneeled next to him and tentatively reached out for his arm. "Come on," I demanded.

He rolled his eyes to the sky and held it out, as if he was annoyed.

I gasped. "What the hell happened?" It was swollen twice its normal size and was already an angry purple color.

Liam jerked it back toward him, cradling it as if it were a baby I'd just insulted. "It'll be fine," he defended, again forcing a smile. "It just accidentally hit a tree trunk on that last incline."

I brought my hands to my head and tugged at the roots of my hair in frustration. "Crap," I said through clenched teeth. "I must have been going too fast and not paying attention."

He brought his elbow back toward his body, as if he was trying to cover it up so I didn't notice it anymore.

"I'm sorry," I told him, and I was. My mind was preoccupied with the others – even with my stupid insecurities and Adrianna. Liam had done so much for me. The least I could do for him was pay attention to where I was going.

He forced a quiet laugh. "It's fine, Brooklyn. Seriously." He dismissed my concern with a wave of his uninjured arm.

I sighed, and once again, picked up the front of the tarp and started my march up the hill. This time, I went slower.

"Liam?"

"Yeah?"

"Your wounds aren't healing quickly because you've taken on too much out here, but you're getting hurt more easily, too, aren't you?"

I didn't want to ask because I dreaded the answer. But I had to know.

He didn't respond, so I stopped pulling for a second and turned around.

He shrugged. "I mean, maybe. Rotten luck?"

"Bull."

His eyes met mine, more intense than his kind soul usually let them be. His jaw clenched, and the muscle above it tightened into a knot, making his jaw more square, more like a grown man than a teenager.

"I guess my gifts are probably more like my mom's than we'd thought," he began. "Major McCoy told me that after healing someone, she would recover eventually, but sometimes it would take days, even weeks. Besides taking on their pain," he continued, "she became more susceptible to injury and illness, so she was forced to lay low. When I recovered so quickly from my arm injury-"

"*My* arm injury," I corrected.

He smiled shyly and arched a brow. "Fine, *your* arm injury. Anyway, when I got better so fast, Major McCoy thought maybe the gift was stronger in me than it was in my mom. But I guess it's not. And after healing Isaac, it's even worse. I've never been so accident prone in my life." He paused and looked into his lap. "It sucks. I feel like I'd break a hip if I jumped rope."

"Then stop," I commanded. "Stop being a...a..."

"A what?" he asked, his eyes amused.

"A hero," I answered honestly. "You don't have to do this, Liam. Pretend, if you have to – pretend like you don't have your gift anymore." I closed the gap between us in a quick stride and knelt down next to him, my eyes demanding that his look into them. "You shouldn't be doing this to yourself."

An insect buzzed around his ear and I lifted a hand to shoo it away. The movement was sudden, but Liam captured my fingers in his and tenderly brought my hand to his cheek, his eyes refusing to stop searching mine. The stubble of his rugged, day-old beard was like sandpaper on my hand, yet it had never known such comfort.

"I can't stop this, Brooklyn."

Stop what? I thought. What was happening to my heart, what electricity was generating between us? Or stop using his gift?

"It's something that's always been inside of me," he continued, "just waiting to come out. And now that it has, I feel more like myself than I ever have."

He was perfect. And that was his only flaw.

"I know what I am and what I want." He paused and let his movie-star smile spread across his face. "And I can't stop it from happening any more than you can."

"What are we talking about, here? Your gift? Or...or something else?"

His green eyes widened. "Both." And slowly, gingerly, he traced the line of his jaw with my hand and brought it slowly to his lips.

A low hum in the sky interrupted the moment. Both of our heads snapped up to spot the source.

"A chopper," Liam said, going on sound alone. The trees masked a visual. His jaw clenched. "It's weird, though. It hasn't been forty-eight hours. They shouldn't be coming for us yet."

"We've got to get to Jacob's cave," I said, jumping up and readying myself to pull him again.

I sprinted as hard as I could, pulling Liam behind me. Thankfully, there were no bushes or trees or boulders standing directly in my path for him to bump into.

The two minutes it took to reach the rock wall were the longest of my life, punctuated by the sound of the helicopter rotors getting louder.

I yelled up to the landing where we'd left Isaac and the others. "Hey guys! Guys! Are you there?"

Isaac peered over the edge and let out a sigh of relief.

"Thank God you're okay." He nodded toward the sound of the helicopter motor. "You think that's for us?"

"It has to be," I answered.

"But why?" Liam asked. "Unless –"

"Unless something big has come up and we have to be rescued," Isaac interrupted.

We stood there for just a second as the sound of the aircraft got louder, unable to decide what we should do next.

"Let's get Liam up here, then get Jacob, Bree, and him to the cave," Isaac said, breaking the silence. "You and I can guard the front. If the chopper is Army, great. If it's not, then at least we can try to keep them away from the other three."

"I don't think so," Liam interjected. "I'm not some kind of sad case here, you guys."

"Wait," I said, holding my hand up to Liam. I looked back up at Isaac. "You said only you and I would guard the opening to the cave."

He nodded.

"But where's Adrianna?"

Isaac arched a brow. "She isn't here."

In the blink of an eye, a shadow blanketed where we were standing, and the incredibly loud sound of the helicopter was overwhelmed by the sound of its automatic guns firing at the trees behind us.

47

I FELL ON TOP OF LIAM.

I didn't even think twice.

He was weak and vulnerable, and I knew I had to protect him, keep him from getting hurt. But as soon as I landed on him, with the first sign of strength I had seen from him all day, with a clenched jaw, he rolled on top of me, shielding me from any spray of bullets that could have come our way.

My gift was strength. I could have easily pushed him off and done what I should have done, which is escape his protection to do something – anything – to help the situation. But I stayed there, trapped under him, knowing he was simply doing what he was born to do, too:

Save people.

So I let him do the protecting. And despite it going against my very nature, it was the most natural thing I could do.

The bullets sprayed, and the sound of the motor dimmed slightly, and again, got louder. My heart beat wildly and my eyes locked with his. Liam removed his arm, which had been protecting my head within its nook, held himself above me, and brought a hand to my cheek.

He framed my face softly with his hand, as if it were a valuable painting. If he'd have spoken, I knew his tone would have been determined and desperate, but he remained poised above me, letting his eyes speak with the passion his voice didn't have the time to say.

With one last intense look, he closed his eyes, rested his forehead on mine, and spoke the only words spoken during the whole attack.

"You're okay. You're safe."

He opened his eyes again, and with a grimace lifted himself off of me, then grabbed my hand and lifted me to his chest. The bullets had stopped; now only the familiar sound of the rotors on the helicopter assaulted my ears. Trying to forget about the moment I'd just experienced with Liam, I made my eyes follow the sound. The chopper was on the ground about thirty feet away.

Major McCoy jumped out first and held out his arm, signaling us to stay put. Five or so other soldiers poured out of the aircraft and assaulted the tree line, going after whatever it was they'd been shooting at.

Seconds later, they emerged with a body.

WE DIDN'T GET A CHANCE TO SEE WHO IT WAS, but our worst fears were alleviated when Adrianna ran out of the tree line herself, with a pale First Sergeant Austin Stovall trailing her.

"He – he – he…" Adrianna's breaths were coming in gulps, not because she was tired from running, she was freaking out.

"Calm down," I demanded. "You're safe now. And we are, too; we're all here. All those soldiers came to get us, and Major McCoy, too."

She turned around to see the officer, and instead saw First Sergeant Stovall, the one who had given us the tour on our first day, the one who had been with us when we were dropped off.

To me, he was just a memory of a particular soldier at West Point who had given us a tour. But obviously, he was much more to Adrianna.

As soon as she saw him, she ran to him. He closed his arms around her, and closed his eyes, too, as if savoring the fact that she was okay. The moment was beautiful and ended all too soon, as First Sergeant Stovall held her at arms' length and simply looked into her wide, scared eyes, commanding her to leave him and come back to us.

She refused, and he yelled at me to help. It felt like I was watching a movie in slow motion as I tore her away from him kicking and screaming. Her shrieks resounded in my mind long after we switched scenes.

48

AS SOON AS WE GOT TO THE HOSPITAL, MY
focus was locked on Adrianna. She was hollow,
disengaged.

And she was scaring the heck out of me.

Removing herself from the rest of the group, she had
been staring blankly out of one of the large picture
windows of the hospital room and was sitting as quietly
as she could.

But her silence did nothing to mask the fact that
Adrianna was losing it. She was repeatedly pulling out her
eyelashes, letting them fall like feathers to the ground. She
didn't answer when we told her to stop, so I wrapped my
arms around her, holding hers down at her sides.

Major McCoy suggested I do it until the Army Psych
Department arrived, and I was more than willing to
oblige.

Liam was snoozing in the room next door, recovering
from his numerous bumps and bruises. We'd had a full
military escort back to campus, but most of those soldiers
had left.

The major reentered the room, ordering us to be "at ease." He quickly checked Adrianna's pupils, and asked me to move to the couch. I hesitated to step back, afraid Adrianna's bizarre behavior would return, but she returned to her seat by the window and her blank stare returned, so I joined Major McCoy and Isaac, Bree, and Jacob on the couches.

The major leaned over – his elbows on his thighs – and placed his hands together. His fingertips were matched up and drumming slowly.

"Okay," he said simply. "Where to begin…"

"How about with the body?" Jacob asked. "The one you guys carried out before you rescued us?" His bottom lip quivered. "Who was it? Were you guys the ones who killed him? Or did…" He jerked his head toward Adrianna.

Major McCoy straightened, nodding slightly. "Fair questions, Jacob. I can tell you how he died, but I can't tell you who he was. Not just yet. We know he was part of the international terrorist organization that was targeting the West Point cadets, specifically the members of The Crest. And he took his own life, rather than be captured and interrogated. I suspect that's one of the reasons Cadet Montoya is having such a hard time. She witnessed the act."

Poor Adrianna. I wanted to sprint to her and wrap her in a hug.

"And how did he get on the grounds?" The question came from Isaac.

"We're still trying to figure that out," Major McCoy answered, his palms facing up, as if he were asking the question himself. "But we're certain he got in with help from someone on the inside – that spy General Richards had spoken of."

"That man… was he the one who was shooting the gun and hurting people last night?" I asked.

"He was the one shooting the gun," the major explained. "But he wasn't hurting anyone. He was alone." Seeing the confused looks on our faces, he continued. "He was shooting his gun into the air and screaming afterwards because he wanted to coax you out from your shelters. It was a trap – an easier way for him to catch you."

"How do you know this?" I asked. He'd been dead before there was a chance to ask such questions.

"We were monitoring him."

"Wait- WHAT?!?!?" Bree jumped to her feet. "The whole time? You knew he was out there with us the whole time? You knew a murderer was after us out there in the woods, and you did nothing to save us?"

"Sit down, Cadet!"

Bree stared at him.

"I said, 'Sit. Down.'"

She finally did, but not without an icy glare hurled his direction.

"Intel informed us this particular terrorist had received orders to kidnap members of The Crest. Not to kill," Major McCoy explained. "And with a kidnapper on your hands, the only viable option is to capture the enemy as they commit the crime. Just like any trial, we have to have evidence when we convict them. Without him actually capturing any of you, we'd only be able to accuse him of terrorist acts – we'd have no solid proof. We'd probably only get a trespassing violation to stick."

"So, yes, we put you in the woods on purpose. We made it seem like you'd be alone on purpose. But you weren't. There were Army rangers and infantry units dispersed all around, with strict orders to monitor each and every one of you, but not interfere with your operation."

"So we were bait," Isaac stated.

Major McCoy considered it for only a moment. "In essence, yes."

"But why not group us all together, then?" Jacob asked. "Why separate us in the beginning?"

Major McCoy's stare bored into Jacob. "Do you remember that conversation we had before you came to the woods about a diversified portfolio, Cadet Jay?"

Jacob nodded. "You put all of your assets into different investments."

"So if the price of one plummets...or tanks altogether..." Isaac added.

"You still have other assets to use." Bree had finished the thought.

I was too pissed to add one of my own.

"Well, lucky for you..." I spat a moment later. "Your assets are alive and well. And you still control all of them."

"And most have risen in value," he combated. His eyes gleamed with a kind of pride I couldn't understand, given the circumstances. "You certainly have proven your worth, Brooklyn. You did an excellent job saving Liam and Isaac, and rescuing Bree, too."

The way he said it didn't feel like a compliment. It felt like we were a commodity. Like cattle.

At that moment, I hated the Army.

"If you wanted us to remain separated, then why did you give Adrianna a map of everyone's dropoff locations? And why are you all proud of Brooklyn for saving the others?" Bree asked.

"Ah, very astute of you, Bree," Major McCoy replied. "While we wanted to divide our assets as much as possible, there was also a risk that you would hide so well, you wouldn't lure the enemy out. Brooklyn's central placement in the woods and the map given to Adrianna were meant to entice them to leave- *only* them. After all, we knew their gifts of strength and endurance would fare the best against a potential attacker."

I glared at the major, my hands balled into fists.

"Take all the time you need to digest that information," Major McCoy instructed as he rose from his seat. "You'll get a short respite. But eventually, training will resume as it was prior to this weekend's events. Now that we have Adrianna's testimony...we should be able to hold those monsters accountable and put this mess behind us."

"Did he hurt Adrianna in any way?" Bree asked, looking across the room at our friend.

The major fell silent.

"We deserve to know," she prodded.

Adrianna answered for him.

"He wanted to get Isaac," she explained. "He said Isaac's peace needed to be the first to go for their plan to be successful."

Her eyes were still focused on something outside the window. She spoke to us as if she were detached from the place we sat somehow. "Since none of us came with the fake shots and screams, he thought he'd get me to scream instead – so Isaac could feel me panicking, you see."

She looked into her lap, and her voice cracked. "He told me all the things he was going to do to me – all of the ways he was going to hurt me."

She turned from the window. "He wanted to scare me. He wanted Isaac to feel me panic and come running."

She looked at me with a clouded gaze. "But I didn't panic. I escaped. Not with my body – with my mind."

Adrianna looked to the window again. "I see now how they do that – the victims." She rocked slightly. "It's easier to handle if you escape." Without pausing a beat, she pointed to something outside the big windows of the library and added, "Look. Buses."

I followed her gaze. She was right. There were at least ten buses lined up, bumper to bumper, on the road that ran in front of The Plain. A large crowd had gathered behind them on the field. Hundreds of cadets were scattered around the grassy area, greeting those getting off of the buses with hugs and handshakes.

"It's Family Weekend," Major McCoy explained. "But I advised yours to abstain. I thought it'd be easier for all of us."

A smile broadened across my face. "Well, they didn't listen."

My heart leapt from my chest as I saw my mom and Bryce get off the first bus in line. My mom shook her long, black hair loose. It cascaded over the shoulders of the bright yellow blouse she was wearing. She checked her lipstick in the small mirror she always carried around in her purse.

Bryce looked out of place with his backwards cap and khaki shorts, curiously studying the buildings that surrounded him.

But nonetheless, they strode confidently – happily – across the lot toward where we were.

I couldn't wait to race down the stairs and see them.

But that want… it became a need in a fraction of a second:

When a string of explosions erupted among the buses, just feet away from where my family stood.

49

I SPRINTED DOWN THE STAIRS OF THE HOSPITAL,
skipping three or four at a time, the rest of The Crest
close behind.

My brother.

My mom.

My dad.

Those bastards. THOSE BASTARDS.

My heart was pleading for it not to happen.

Not again. Please, God. Not again.

Not ever again.

I lowered my head and let my shoulder lead, ready to
bulldoze through the emergency door on the side of the
building and rescue my mom and brother, when suddenly
I was jerked back by the collar on my fatigues.

Major McCoy raised an index finger to his lips. "Calm
yourself, Cadet. You're no good to them dead."

I blinked. And breathed. And the tears came. And I
was about to lose it – lose control, lose everything.

"I can't – I need to stop – how do we save –"

"We plan," the major answered. "Now get to the floor,
Cadet."

I collapsed into a heap on the ground and brought my hands to my face.

Isaac joined me and laid a hand on my shoulder. "Breathe deep," he advised.

And sooner than I could have possibly imagined, a peace I couldn't explain grew deep within my heart and spread to the rest of my body.

"Thanks," I said, still feeling his calming influence work on my strong emotions. "I mean it."

He smiled slightly. "I'm here for ya, Brooklyn."

I smiled weakly in return.

Preparing myself for whatever it was on the other side of the window, I strode toward Major McCoy. He was talking animatedly to First Sergeant Stovall, who had suddenly materialized at his side. The first sergeant had his arm wrapped protectively around Adrianna, who still looked shaken, but not the fragile being I'd seen next to the window minutes earlier.

"Major McCoy," I addressed formally. "I'm good now. I promise."

He studied me for a moment, then nodded toward Isaac. "Good work, Cadet Jackson." He leaned toward me. "He just got done with Adrianna." He glanced sheepishly at his shoes. "And Stovall's presence seems to help her, too."

The firstie blushed, but only slightly, and he remained firmly planted next to Adrianna.

Major McCoy motioned me toward the window.

I held a breath and studied what was on the other side.

Plumes of smoke raced up to the sky, somewhat inhibiting our view. There were bodies of dead or injured men and women lying on the ground between us and the buses. I held my breath as I forced myself to look for a bright yellow shirt.

And I breathed a quick sigh of relief when I didn't find it.

"They were taken to The Plain," Adrianna informed me. "With everyone else."

It was then I noticed the other cadets. Hundreds of them — maybe even thousands — were all lined up in neat little rows, lying on their bellies with their hands poised behind their head.

"They were standing at attention on the field," First Sergeant Stovall explained. "That's how we wait for our families when they arrive."

He turned to Major McCoy. "They must have known that, for them to know where to infiltrate our campus and when."

I couldn't even see the grassy plain anymore. Smoke was billowing from buses, and in between that and the rows of cadets lying on the ground, I saw teems of civilians. They seemed to be everywhere: men, women, and children. Some were huddled closely together, sitting and standing around in small groups. Others were lying on their stomachs in the same perfect rows as the cadets.

"Where'd all the helicopters come from?" I asked, spotting the large aircrafts on the perimeter. They formed an informal barrier against the rest of the campus. They weren't military-grade — they looked more like the fancy private helicopters we saw on TV.

"They came all at once," First Sergeant Stovall explained. "To drop them off."

Them.

The men were touting assault rifles, using them to prod the innocent people who were cowering in their presence. They were dressed in all black and their faces were blanketed with ski masks. Although I couldn't hear them, they appeared to be shouting demands at everyone. They were dumping contents of purses and bags on the ground, searching them thoroughly, but not pocketing anything – not even wallets or cash.

"What are they looking for?" I asked. They were on a military base. It was full of officers and other soldiers- maybe even classified information.

Why come here to harass civilians and comb through their purses? They didn't need to do that on a base. They could do that in any city.

Suddenly, the door to the ground-floor hallway was shoved open, and Major McCoy jumped in front of us. He drew a pistol and aimed it expertly at the intruders, who stopped dead in their tracks.

50

"CADET HARLOWE," MAJOR MCCOY BREATHED, pocketing his pistol. "Cadet O'Dell."

Liam rushed past his escort, right to me and Bree and Isaac.

"You're okay," he breathed, and he said it as if it were an order, not an observation. He gave Isaac a handshake and a hug, tousled his twin's hair, and locked eyes with me, squeezing my hand.

"Are you better?" I asked. He'd needed to recover just an hour ago.

"I'm good now," Liam assured me. "I'm exactly where I need to be."

Regimental Commander Tessa Harlowe filtered in right behind him, the firstie who'd given us hell on R-Day, but saluted the twins on their birthday.

She let out a sigh of relief. "Major McCoy. First Sergeant," she said, addressing both her classmate and the officer. "Cadets."

They were words you'd hear any day of the week on this base, but there was more emotion packed into them than I'd ever heard. It seemed more like a plea and a prayer than a formal greeting.

She turned and ushered in two civilians who were eager to get in front of her.

"I ran into Cadet O'Dell in the hallway," she announced as they entered the small room. And these two are my parents." She directed them over to the opposite wall. They followed her direction, looking like field mice seeking asylum from a predator.

"Any intel, Major?" she asked Major McCoy.

He shook his head. "No, Cadet Harlowe. I've been out in the woods with these cadets for the last forty-eight hours. I have no idea who these men are or what they want."

Tessa pursed her lips, as if she were choosing her words wisely. "Rumor has it there was a casualty in the woods today."

"That's affirmative. But I can't confirm that the two events are linked."

"Oh, I think you can, Major," Regimental Commander Harlowe stated. She turned to face us. "Because they're looking for them." She pointed to us.

Us.

The dozens of masked men touting assault rifles and flying in on fancy helicopters were looking for us.

"I need to go," Tessa told Major McCoy, before we could even sound off on what she'd just said. "I have a regiment to look after."

She turned toward her parents. "Stay here," she ordered. "And if those men come here, hide under the stairwell." She paused before reaching the door. "I love you."

Her mom began to wail. Major McCoy shot Isaac a look. The wailing stopped.

"Regimental Commander," I called out, surprising even myself.

She met my gaze.

"You don't have to go back," I told her, though there were a thousand other things I wanted to say.

She pursed her lips together. "I'm an officer in the U.S. Army, Cadet Blackburn. Where my regiment goes, I go."

And before she exited, she added, "And you would do the same."

51

THE DOOR DIDN'T EVEN CLOSE ALL THE WAY
before something from the hell outside wormed its way
into our safe haven.

The blood-curdling scream assaulted my ears, and my
eyes immediately leapt to its source.

You couldn't miss it. You couldn't miss her.

The bright yellow blouse stood out in the crowd.

My mom was being dragged along the road by the
collar of her shirt. Bryce was forced to follow her. His
hands were tied behind his back, with another masked
man guarding him and making him march forward. The
one who was dragging my mom along like a sack of
garbage had her purse tucked into the nook of his arm,
and he was brandishing the plastic photo sleeve from my
mom's wallet in front of the crowd with his free hand. He
turned suddenly, and I could see it was my picture he was
holding.

Their bodies got smaller and smaller as they inched
their way up the road. They didn't stop until they came to
the front of the most imposing, formidable building on
campus.

And my heart sank.

Thayer's Hall was a fortress, something that appeared to be snatched from a scene from centuries ago and placed in this modern world. Its outer walls were thick and tall and entirely made of stone.

It seemed impenetrable.

The masked man holding my picture dropped my mom's collar and pointed his rifle at her. He circled around and raised his boot, kicking her square in the back, over and over again, as she attempted to stumble into the opening. She finally succeeded crossing the heavy, double oak doors that marked the entrance. Bryce was forced to follow her as well.

The doors closed behind the entire group, and though I couldn't hear the thud of the oak door meeting stone, I could feel the definitive sound in my heart.

52

THAYER'S HALL WAS BASICALLY A MEDIEVAL castle: beautiful, dramatic, and intimidating.

At the moment, it loomed over me, and as I crept along its outer walls and skirted the turrets that anchored its corners, I was sure I had gone back in time.

A sharp coppery scent was ripe in the air. Though the terrorists cleared the road of all the bodies, the bloody streaks left behind when dragging them left an imprint on the road – and on my mind. I struggled to choke back coughs and breathe normally as the plumes of smoke attacked me.

I was in a war zone. *A war zone.*

And the only family I had left had been kidnapped by the barbarians who created it.

I had to save them.

Liam and Jacob were with me, too. Major McCoy had insisted they come.

I needed Jacob's power of prophecy to see what the terrorists were going to do. Major McCoy also instructed him to hone in on their thoughts and see who they were working for and what they wanted with The Crest members. He'd taken the orders without objecting.

And Liam was sent with me just in case we were too late, in case my family had been hurt in any way.

I choked back the fear of possibility with the smoke.

The rest of The Crest was with Major McCoy. He and First Sergeant Stovall had quickly laid out a plan to get to Building 586, where all the ammunition and weaponry was stored. Once there, they planned on strategically scaling buildings and taking aim at the terrorists, sniper-style. If they could find other soldiers, they'd grab grenades and other detonating devices as well for them to use in their attack.

Since Bree was such a good shot, she was going to scale buildings and take aim, too. Isaac was going to keep the families and cadets calm during the commotion – and the terrorists, too, since their behavior seemed to be getting more and more erratic. And Adrianna was going to sprint in and relocate as many women and children to a safe space as possible.

They assured us they would send help to Thayer's Hall as soon as they could, in the form of America's best and brightest: The Long Gray Line of West Point cadets. I was petrified, but also prepared.

After all, we were all meant to be training for war at West Point.

Instead, the war had come to us.

53

WE'D BEEN AROUND THE ENTIRE BUILDING, and there was no way to sneak inside.

The walls were too thick. Even if you possessed my kind of strength, they wouldn't budge.

I bit my lip in annoyance. We were wasting time.

"We've got to go in the main doors," I declared. "The ones they forced my mom and brother to go through."

Liam and Jacob exchanged glances.

"Are you sure?" Jacob asked. "I mean, I know we need to help your family, Brooklyn, but what if those men are waiting to ambush us, just inside those doors?"

"Can you hear them?" I prodded.

Jacob paused for a moment and shook his head.

"Then I'm guessing they're not right inside. And if they are," I added stubbornly, "Then I'll just fight them ahead of schedule."

"Brooklyn," Liam began.

"No, Liam," I interrupted. "I completely understand if you two don't want to go with me. I get it. You are more than welcome to stay behind and keep watch for me. Truly."

The people I loved most in this world were inside that building, and their lives were in danger. Jacob and Liam's lives didn't need to be in danger, too.

I needed to take a page from the Army playbook and divide my assets, not put them all in the same building with dangerous murderers on the loose.

Unfortunately, the gorgeous asset standing in front of me wouldn't listen.

"Where you go, I go, Cadet Blackburn," Liam said simply. His eyes bore into mine with an intensity I'd never felt before.

I turned away from it before it'd weaken my resolve.

"Yeah, you need us," added Jacob.

"Okay then," I said, and I crept up to the main entrance, with Liam and Jacob close behind.

54

THE HEAVY DOOR TO THE ENTRANCE HAD
closed with a whisper, and our feet barely tapped the
white marble floors.

But even still, every sound was amplified.

The enormous lobby – with its thirty-foot ceilings,
mahogany arches, antique furniture and chandeliers – was
completely empty.

I ducked behind a tall bookshelf and signaled the
others to join me.

"Everyone must have evacuated," Jacob whispered as
they arrived. "Maybe when this all started?"

Liam nodded. "You're right," he whispered back.
"Everything's a mess. Whoever had been here left in a
hurry."

There weren't that many of them, but the few seats
and desks that occupied the lobby had papers and books
strewn across them. Pens and pencils were left resting on
top of open books, and purses were lying limply by the
armchairs lined up by the window.

An abandoned cell phone rang out, haunting the hall.

When no one responded to it, I was confident we were alone.

"We've gotta go further in," I commanded as quietly as I could. Jacob's skin paled.

"It'll be fine," I insisted. "It's not like it's an S.O.L. situation like it was in Tactics class."

"I don't know about that," Liam argued smoothly. "It's definitely an S.O.L. situation. It's just reversed."

I looked at him quizzically.

"Well, we saw two men take them in, and there's three of us," he boasted. "Hopefully we can surround them. And knowing you, Wonder Woman, if they do anything to try and hurt us, they're the ones who are going to be S.O.L."

I locked eyes with him, remembering how I'd fallen for him during that class. And I couldn't find the words to express what I was feeling in my heart.

"You got my back?" I asked after a moment. It was the question he'd asked me, one week and a lifetime ago.

He returned my grin. "You know I do, Blackburn. And I know that you've got mine."

ADRENALINE SHOT THROUGH MY VEINS AS WE crept through the lobby.

"Jacob, see if you can —"

"I can hear them!" he interrupted, looking into the hall across from the entrance. He looked at me. "And I can hear your mom and brother, too."

317

"What are they thinking?" Liam demanded.

Jacob turned to me. "Your brother's trying to think of a way to escape."

My heart leapt.

"We gotta get there, Brooklyn. And quick."

"Go," I commanded Jacob, and the smallest of us led the way.

55

FINDING OUR WAY WOULD HAVE BEEN impossible without Jacob. Because of his gift, we didn't have to hesitate at all as we crossed two balconies overlooking deserted hallways, shot down two flights of stairs, and took three lefts and a right.

It was a direct route to a dusty, abandoned corner in the basement of the facility. We hovered in the doorway, remaining in the shadows.

For now.

At one time, the expansive area in front of us must have been a conference room. Circular tables were strewn about, and there was a small platform at the far end of the room that might have once been used as an informal stage. Dim beams of light streamed in through the dirty basement windows, and the few fluorescent bulbs that worked, flickered from neglect and disuse.

I spotted my mom and brother. My mouth went dry, and my throat constricted.

They were tied to old arm chairs in the middle of the room – blindfolded and guarded by the two men who had dragged them here. The men's masks were gone, lying in a heap on the floor next to the chairs.

My brother's head hung limply to the side. Blood was trickling down his temple.

My mom, in spite of it all, appeared straight-backed and confident. She had that look she always got when she was ticked off, seeming larger than her 5'2" frame.

A muffled static noise and frantic shouting poured out from the men's walkie-talkies that were hooked onto their belts. For a brief moment, they exchanged a distressed look. Heated dialogue volleyed between them for a moment before they turned their focus to my mom.

"Angela Blackburn," one of the men purred. He twisted the knob on top of the walkie-talkie, effectively quieting the shouts and the static coming from its speakers.

The man had a thick accent, but I couldn't place it. His greasy black hair was slicked back into a ponytail, and his brown eyes were slits on his ashen skin.

"You marry bad man," he accused. "And you have bad children." He leaned closer to her face, and she did nothing to hide the disgust and contempt I knew she must be feeling. "Maybe you — maybe you are bad, too. Maybe you deserve a lesson. Unless you tell us where bad child is?"

My mom pressed her lips firmly together, obviously resolute in her silence.

The greasy-haired man nodded to the other man who stood by Bryce. He had a dark, wiry beard and eyes that were set far apart, appearing too big for his face. He grinned maliciously, his thick lips framing missing and rotted teeth.

The man pulled a knife out from the holder at his waist. It made a slicing sound as it strained against the metal sheath.

My breath caught in my throat. I reached for Liam.

"Go to hell," my mom snarled.

And the two men laughed. The hairy one reached for her, tearing the blindfold from her face. He pulled her head back by the roots of her hair, his wild eyes inches away from her own.

"You," he spat. "You are in no position to make such demands."

He lifted a fist well above his head.

And he cracked her cheek so hard she flew backwards in her chair. The back of her head knocked hard against the tile below.

"I'll heal her, Brooklyn!" I heard Liam cry out from behind me. "Don't –!"

But it was too late. I'd already sprinted ahead of him, leaving them both in the shadows.

Before any of them could react, I lifted a forgotten bench from the floor, and I hurled it right at the man who had hit my mom.

It contacted his head with a crunch I found both satisfying and repulsive.

His body fell limply to the ground, and his knife spun wildly in a circle on the tile beside him.

My eyes widened in surprise at what I'd done and locked onto the remaining terrorist, who had instantly lifted his semiautomatic rifle, pointing it directly at me.

56

"YOU. YOU STUPID CHILD." THE LEADER SAID IT
like an insult, but he was smiling as if he had won the
lottery. He was striding confidently toward me, his
weapon aimed directly at my face.

"And which one of us would you be referring to?"

Liam had crept up behind me and stood confidently
at my side. I shot him a reproachful glare. "He wants us
ALIVE," he whispered.

Of course. Major McCoy had told us the terrorists
wanted us alive. He wouldn't kill us. Our gifts were no
good to them if we were dead. But we had to keep from
getting trapped.

I skirted to the left, and Liam maneuvered right.

"STOP! You stop now, or I shoot!"

I dove for a large banquet table, which was perched on
its side against the wall, and tucked myself behind it.
Making good on his promise, shots rang off as the
terrorist aimed his weapon at the light above me. Sparks
showered down, and the whole room dimmed.

Silence.

Uncertainty hovered over me like a rain cloud that threatened to break.

"It's shame, you know," the man said with grit in his voice, shuffling around the room. "You born here, born of bad men. You, girl. You're very pretty. Maybe…maybe someday I show you how pretty I think you are."

I shuddered. Like hell, he would.

Silence again.

"Marco…" he whisper-yelled, giggling softly. "That is game you like, right? Marco Polo? I heard you in forest, through radio…"

He chuckled. "MARCO!" He said it louder this time – mocked me with it.

"Hmmm… Perhaps this 'Marco'… perhaps it's the name of someone, yes? Your brother perhaps?"

I peered around the end of the table. In the silence, he'd taken Bryce as collateral. He held my brother in front of him like some kind of shield, pointing the end of the rifle precariously at his throat.

My mom was still on the ground behind them. Liam was at her side in the corner of the room, his hands at her head. A tube of light above them flickered on and off again, reminding me of the healing power Liam was radiating through my mother's body.

"Come on out, children!" the bastard taunted as I ducked behind the table again. He was inching closer to me. "Come on out and save 'Marco'!"

I had to think of a plan to keep him from Liam and my mom, and I had to get him away from Bryce.

I didn't know if it was possible to keep him away from me, too.

The man's face broke into a sinister grin, as if he could feel me wanting to surrender. "MAAARRRCCC – "

"POLO!!!" Out of nowhere, Liam tackled him from behind.

He knocked Bryce out of the man's arms. Then, pinning the terrorist against the wall, he hit his elbow repeatedly – over and over and over again – until the semiautomatic rifle flew out of his hands. It landed on the floor about fifteen feet away from the skirmish.

The man snarled in anger and threw himself at Liam, who deftly avoided contact and brought him to the ground instead, straddling him and punching him in the head repeatedly, doing a move we called the 'ground and pound.'

My mom rushed to Bryce.

"Get out of here!" I screamed.

She hesitated, as though she didn't want to leave me behind.

"Get the hell out, Mom!" I commanded, sprinting to Liam, who had been pushed off the man, but was still exchanging blows with the terrorist.

"LEAVE!"

She and Bryce scurried out the door just as I reached Liam.

I didn't just need to help.

It was my calling.

The terrorist had gained the upper hand. He was on top of Liam now, his hands crushing Liam's neck.

Liam's beautiful ivory skin was turning a deep shade of purple.

I felt that rage again: the same rage I'd had when the other man had hit my mother. It was hotter than lava and more potent than poison. It bubbled up from inside and shot out of me, before I could even think about what I was doing.

With an animalistic shriek, I lifted them from the ground: the man and Liam.

The man's eyes rounded in shock as I pried his fingers from Liam's neck.

I threw Liam to the ground beside me.

Then I twisted slightly, still holding the man. I focused all of my attention on the far end of the room. Without even thinking – and without an inkling of compassion – I hurled the bastard into the concrete wall fifty feet away.

Drywall crumbled behind him as he slammed into the barrier. His body slumped to the ground.

And I stood there, trembling with rage.

57

I WAS STILL SHAKING WHEN LIAM CRAWLED OFF
of the ground and clung to me in an embrace. He was
wheezing, but other than that, he seemed okay.

Different, but okay.

And I felt different, too. Altered, somehow. Like I was
an actor cast in a part I never wanted to play.

I studied him, exploring those eyes that had grabbed
hold of me from day one and refused to let go.

And I saw something new.

I saw *hate*.

His jaw clenched. He left my side and walked
purposefully toward the body of the man trapped under
the bench. He grabbed the knife that was resting on the
ground next to the body and without hesitating, he strode
toward the man who had choked him and had threatened
to hurt me.

"Stop, Liam," I commanded.

He wasn't listening.

"STOP!"

I ran to him now. He was still intent on reaching the
monster.

Finally, I caught his elbow.

"You're a healer, Liam. Not a killer."

That role had been filled by me.

"You are a healer," I repeated, making him look me in the eye.

And just like that, Liam stopped. His look softened, as if he was seeing what he was doing for the first time.

"Christ," he mumbled, first dropping the knife, then dropping to his knees.

And instead of trying to reach the body of either man, he reached for me, instead.

We stayed like that for a moment, lost in a place we'd never visited before: one where we'd done the worst kind of things.

Jacob shuffled out from the shadows and walked briskly to the first man I'd attacked, who was trapped under the bench.

I'd almost forgotten he was there.

Jacob kneeled, pressing his neck for a pulse. "He's gone," he declared.

I didn't know if I was relieved or upset.

"I- I'll go find someone to come help," Jacob offered. He seemed thankful when I nodded my assent.

"I'm sorry," Liam said as Jacob left. He'd turned his back to me, and his voice was a quieted whisper. His shoulders fell forward as he spoke. "I'm sorry I was going to – to do that to him– in front of you. What I was feeling – what I was thinking when he threatened to hurt you – I-I'd never felt or thought those things before. When he said that about how he was going to show you how pretty you were…" He spun toward me, his face masked in pain.

327

"That image was worse than anything I could ever imagine."

"Liam," I insisted. "You don't have anything to be ashamed of. I do. I'm the one who killed them." The last sentence came out stronger than I meant it to, as if I completely owned my actions…as if I were proud of what I'd done.

Damn.

"I don't know what's happening to either one of us — who we're turning into," Liam remarked. His eyes looked more silver than green, as if he'd been shocked into becoming someone — or something — else. "But I do know that I never want to see you in danger again."

I closed my eyes for a moment and considered how nice that sounded — a danger-free life.

He grabbed my hand. "But Brooklyn, if we have to be in danger, if we are going to be part of this world, then I'm glad I have you by my side."

In that moment, I wanted more than anything to kiss him, to reassure him I felt the same way.

But I never got the chance.

Jacob returned. And just as he entered the room — before he could warn Liam, and before I could even utter a word, a knife flew into Liam's back.

"Sorry I break up this… this romance," the man whom I'd thrown into the wall snarled, tearing the knife out of Liam's flesh, catching his body and holding it hostage. "But I've got job to finish."

58

THE MAN IN FRONT OF ME HAS A KNIFE.

He has a knife, and he has Liam.

Isaac. Bree. Adrianna. Major McCoy.

Everyone.

Everyone was outside fighting a different battle.

In here, it's me.

And Jacob, standing by my side.

"Jacob, tell me what he's thinking," I said.

He stared straight ahead.

"DAMMIT, JACOB!" I screamed. The man had Liam. Liam. "TELL ME."

"That's not going to happen, I'm afraid."

It was the man talking – the man with Liam.

Not Jacob. He was still staring straight ahead.

"Go ahead and tell her, Jacob," the man instructed. He was walking toward me now, Liam in tow and wielding the knife wildly.

"Wait. Wha…What?" My eyes skirted from the man to the boy, the boy to the man. "Jacob," I demanded. I reached over to shake his shoulder, to get him to snap out of it.

But his hand caught mine before I could finish the act. "Don't. Touch. Me."

His eyes were different behind the lens of his glasses – different than I'd ever seen them.

Normally they were dark in color.

Now they were dark in intent.

THE BACK OF THE MAN'S HEAD WAS BLEEDING

profusely. He winced as Jacob wrapped an old cloth around it, clamping it tightly against the wound to slow the bleeding.

How could it be? Jacob, the informant? Jacob, who had always seemed so much younger than us? More innocent, even? How could he betray us like this?

Liam was forced to kneel at his feet, his hands bound behind him, and the man's rifle pointed at his back. He looked like he was going to pass out any minute.

I was worried about him. I knew he was weak from the healing he'd done this week, then from healing my mom, and now, from his own knife wound.

His body wouldn't be able to take much more. He could die, just as his mother did.

He could die.

My hands were wrenched behind my back, held by something strong. Maybe, if I tried, I could break free.

But with their rifle trained on Liam, if I attacked – or even attempted to get to Liam – they'd shoot him for sure.

So I waited.

I could hear bullets peppering the grounds outside. Explosions seemed to shake the building, and men were frantically shouting to each other over the walkie-talkie.

The man left to speak into the machine.

"Why?" I asked Jacob as the man retreated.

It was his turn to hold the weapon, and he held it resolutely to Liam's back.

"Why, after what terrorists did to your dad, would you help them hurt us? Why would you help them hurt the innocent people out there?"

Jacob rolled his eyes. "My dad had it coming," he answered smoothly. It was as if he were emotionally detached from the topic. "He worked for a corrupt organization, for this stupid country."

"That's not something to be ashamed of, Jacob. Being in the Army is something to be —"

"Spare me the patriotic protest, Brooklyn," he interrupted. "America is power-hungry, and our military is the most gluttonous in all the land. It preys upon a stupid populace and feeds it bullshit in order to keep it content." His demeanor was different than I'd ever seen. His chin jutted out, and he squared his shoulders, as if he were daring me to argue — or even fight — with him.

"They find people like you, like your father — like mine," he said, his tone dripping with insolence. "Idealistic morons who think they're actually doing something courageous instead of dumb, and talk them into 'fighting for the good of our country.'"

His fingers were too close to a trigger for him to talk like this and stay calm, but he pressed on.

"You have to ask yourself, Brooklyn: 'How many soldiers have a say in the war they fight? How many of them actually start that war?' Did my dad? Did yours? Huh?" He spit on the floor. "They gave up everything to help a government that wanted to use them. They gave up *us*. And you're stupid enough to follow in their footsteps. You're all ridiculously weak pawns in the hands of the greedy, rich, and powerful elite. All of you."

His face was a dark red, an enraged mask that chilled me to the core. "My dad was an idiot," he spewed. "He had this – this gift – that could have allowed him to change the course of history. And he could have changed it on his terms, not the terms of a government who didn't give a crap about whether or not he survived."

"So you're saying you wish your dad was a dictator," Liam chimed in.

"I'm saying I wish my dad had a freaking mind of his own, that he was man enough to call his own shots in his life instead of be a stupid sheep," Jacob retorted.

"I...I hate bullies," he continued, shaking as he said it. "And our government is the biggest bully of all. I found the letters they sent him. They spent years brainwashing him into thinking he had to use his gift in order to protect the country."

He laughed inappropriately, as if he were an out-of-control child at a funeral. "AND LOOK WHERE IT GOT HIM, LADIES AND GENTLEMEN," he announced theatrically to the empty room. "HE'S DEAD!"

"But not me," Jacob bragged. "I'm not going to end up like him. I wasn't born with this gift to be bossed

332

around and given impossible tasks." His eyes gleamed. "I was given this gift to have power."

"And you have power now, do you?" I asked, jerking my head in the terrorist's direction. The man's face was masked in urgency and panic. The voices on the other end of the walkie-talkie were equally frantic.

"At least your dad worked for a country that had an honorable cause," I accused. "You're working for murderers."

A slow smile spread across Jacob's face. "Oh, Brooklyn," he admonished. "You really are a moron. They're not using me to get to you. They're enlisting my help as an ally. We have a common goal, you know."

"Which is?"

He grinned. "Chaos." Seeming thrilled at the very word, he giggled. "Developed countries will be the worst off during a world-wide attack – an attack that's going to happen, regardless of my part in it. Looting, killing, starving to death… it's all going to add to the drama. And when those attacks occur and they want order restored," he confided, "they're going to look for someone different to lead them. They're going to want someone powerful. Someone who can decide exactly what direction they should go and how they should be led. Someone with –"

"A gift of prophecy?" Liam interrupted.

And Jacob beamed. "Yes," he answered without hesitation. "Someone who can lead them to a sure and secure future. Someone like me." He shrugged nonchalantly. "It's too bad you don't want to join the cause."

"I'd rather die," I declared.

"You might," Jacob said indifferently. "Or you might not. There's a good chance you'll become what we want you to be after being in our care," he said. "We have ways to make you change your mind."

I shuddered at the thought as Jacob's partner in crime returned and spoke directly to him. "There is... helicopter coming now," he said simply. "But must hurry. We have no time."

"Then let's go," Jacob decided, hammering Liam in the ribs with the barrel of the gun.

And we marched out into the unknown.

59

EVERYTHING WAS DIFFERENT AS WE EMERGED from the basement.

Night time had fallen, and the fires had stopped. I could no longer hear bullets or explosions.

It was as if West Point was mourning and cloaked in black, the tragedy from earlier in the day silencing the campus. Even the loud roar of a lone helicopter, attempting to land on the field, didn't seem to break the heaviness that hung in the air.

No one was around. No cadets. No families. No tanks or guns or grenades.

The commotion from earlier was completely erased from the scene.

I could see the pilot's face as the helicopter wavered over the landing spot – as it hovered for just a moment. It was as frantic and frightened as a man facing a firing squad.

It didn't take me long to realize why. I could almost feel the line of soldiers behind me.

In less than a second, they attacked.

THE MAN WHO I'D THROWN EARLIER PRODDED
me to sprint with him to the aircraft – through the bullets and everything, but I hit the ground instead. Liam did, too, and he lay exhausted at my side.

I looked into the helicopter. The pilot was pressed against his own seat. He was wildly grabbing at the air and at his neck, as if an invisible force was strangling him. After a few seconds of struggle, he slumped to the side, his face expressionless, and his eyes, vacant.

My heart and my hand reached for Liam, who was pale but lying by my side, his hand protectively on my back. "Stay low," he commanded weakly, wincing as the man who had held us hostage stepped on him in an attempt to run away.

I thought he was trying to get to the helicopter, but I looked up to see the terrorist, running alongside Jacob, reach out for him at the last minute.

Jacob's eyes widened in terrified surprise as the terrorist clutched his body in front of his own, holding it as he'd held Bryce earlier, as a shield.

He hadn't been able to see enough into the future to know that his was about to end.

And it did.

While the man held Jacob in front of him, a bullet found its mark, right between his eyes, above the spot where his glasses rested on the bridge of his nose.

And the man who had turned on him – the man who had reigned over us with terror – his future ended abruptly, too, when an invisible force lifted him high into the air.

His body was thrown into the helicopter's rotors – got tangled in them. And the body was no more.

I buried my head in my hands and screamed, wanting it to end. Needing it to end.

Major McCoy ran to us. "Cadets! Cadets! Cadets, are you okay?"

I couldn't answer. I burrowed my head even deeper to escape him… escape here…escape everyone.

"Brooklyn, Liam. Are you okay?" We couldn't answer, let alone move.

"Adrianna! Isaac!" the major continued. "Get over here!"

Faster than I'd ever seen, Adrianna arrived at our side. She draped me with a blanket, and covered Liam, too.

"Was that – who – I mean, how did that man and that pilot – how did they –?" I could barely form the words.

"Remember when you said it was like Major McCoy had a gift, too? A gift of inducing pain? Kind of like an invisible force?" She shook her head. "I think you may have been right."

Isaac joined Adrianna. He helped lift me by my elbows, and he told me to stand and be strong.

But all I wanted was to be weak.

60

WHEN I'D FIRST ARRIVED AT WEST POINT, THE Plain was beautiful and majestic.

Now, it reeked of smoke and tragedy.

Nighttime hid nothing, because there was nothing to conceal. The field was deserted, completely barren of the robust cadets that had once marched its green surface with significance and purpose.

We never asked for war.

And as I made my way across the field, my heart cried out to God, begging to know why war was being demanded of us.

Liam and I, flanked by Major McCoy and the other Crest members, gingerly made our way across the grass. I walked carefully, shivering because of the cold and because of the killing.

I tried my best to ignore the wet, sticky blood that blanketed the place, and I tried even harder to forget the pain that was inflicted.

"I want to go home," I heard from behind me.

It was said softly, but it punctuated the silence. We kept walking, though.

Adrianna was crying now. "I- I don't think I can... I need – I need –"

She collapsed to her knees and wailed.

Maybe Isaac could have used his gift on us, but he didn't. He sank to the soil, too, and covered his face in his hands. And before I knew it, we were all there with him – all of us but one – hugging and crying and wiping our tears.

WE EVENTUALLY FOUND THE STRENGTH IN

1each other to finish our walk to the dorms.

Eyes fixed ahead on our barrack, we wove in and out of the crowds of cadets and their families as they huddled together, away from the central area and evidence of violence from the day.

Liam's hand found mine, and we walked in silence until I reached my room. With some kind of quiet understanding, without speaking or any questioning at all, Liam released my hand and retreated to his room.

My mom and Bryce were there waiting. They sprinted to me, as if this were the kind of warm reunion you'd see on a Dateline special or something. They opened their arms for an embrace, then let their arms drop awkwardly when I didn't give it to them.

"Brooklyn, I –" my mom began.

I started to walk toward the bathroom.

"I'm sorry!" she yelled from behind me. "I shouldn't have left you."

I turned slowly and read the scared expression on her face. She looked like she'd aged ten years in a day.

"What kind…what kind of mother leaves her child?" She found my bed and sank onto the mattress, rocking slightly. "What kind of mother does that?" she wailed.

Bryce sprinted to her side, protectively draping an arm over her shoulders, soothing her and quieting her cries.

"I guess," I began with a crack in my voice. I cleared my throat. "I guess the kind of mother who knows she can. The kind who knows her daughter is different."

Bryce met my gaze with a wide-eyed expression, as if he had a million questions of his own.

"That's all I'll ever say, you know," I explained calmly. "But I am. I'm different. You've always known it, and I have, too. And Mom?"

She raised her chin to meet my stare.

"You don't have to be sad about that. Because Dad was different, too. And he was a good man… He was a hero."

She didn't nod. She didn't shake her head. It was as if we were in some kind of silent poker game, where we knew all the cards the other was holding, but preferred to be polite about it rather than call the bluff.

I wondered if we'd be playing this game forever.

I turned from them again and entered my bathroom.

I shut the door. I thought about the sprinklers on The Plain and how they would make the grass clean again.

And I stepped into the shower. I let the scalding water run over me until it became lukewarm, then ice-cold.

And when I got out, I put on a warm robe. I walked past my mom, who was sitting at my desk, and walked past my brother, who was sitting on the floor, and I crawled into bed.

I fixed my eyes above me, at the ceiling, for just a moment. And then I fell asleep with no shame, and no regrets.

It was a beautiful, terrifying place to be.

61

Two Weeks Later

IT'S FUNNY HOW A CHANGE IN SOMEONE CAN lead to a perceived change in environment.

It'd happened to me before. In middle school, I'd visited my old kindergarten classroom. Ms. Thorpe was still the teacher. Her rocking chair was still set up in the corner by all of the books, with a rug of primary colors still stretched under it. The carpet was the same, the desks were still set in groups of four or five, and colorful posters still adorned the walls.

But because I'd grown – because I'd changed – the classroom had, too.

That's how I felt about the van we were in, the same white vehicle that had delivered us to West Point, just months before… the van that was now driving us away from it - back to our families in New York City.

The exterior was the same, and the interior was, too. The driver was still Major McCoy, the person who had driven us to the prestigious military academy. And all of us were the same, as well.

But we weren't, really.

The others undoubtedly felt this difference, too. Our voices were unusually silent, and when we did speak, it was an awkward attempt to fill the void. We tried desperately to avoid looking at the empty seat in the back, where Jacob once sat as one of us.

We tried. And failed.

We were headed home for a week-long sabbatical from the Army.

After the attacks, we'd had to wait two weeks before they allowed us to leave the protection of the U.S. Army at West Point.

In those two weeks, the Army had sprung into action, at home and overseas. Major McCoy had grilled all of the surviving terrorists from the battle at The Plain, using both his gift and "the gift of others we didn't need to know about." According to him, the Army was confident all terrorists involved in targeting The Crest members had been arrested or killed, and we were safe to go home and visit our families.

I was looking forward to it. I knew it'd probably be awkward at first, since my mom and Bryce had been through so much, and since they had witnessed a change in me, too. But I wanted a new normal with them, even if it entailed a few growing pains.

Growing pains.

We'd had them at West Point, especially in the last two weeks.

The rest of the cadets were given the option of going home to their families after the attack on the base.

But I don't think a single one took the academy up on their offer. They attended classes, did extra PT, and dove into their studies with a reinvigorated tenacity.

The tragedy had only served as an invitation to commit even more of themselves to the country.

And for once, we'd been allowed to interact with them. It was like we belonged there, now that we had truly sacrificed, too. And I think the normal cadets felt the same way. We'd played on sports teams together, eaten meals with some of them, and even had normal conversations.

"Why do you think the terrorists came after you?" a short blonde cadet had asked. We were walking to our barracks from Jefferson Library. She looked at me, and then to Liam, with curiosity and awe.

It was Liam who had answered. "I guess they came after us because of our parents," he explained. "They died as heroes in the 9/11 attacks, you know. It must have been symbolic for them."

She had nodded, had said she understood.

But she didn't. Because she had only been told a partial truth. The reality was, they had attacked us for much more than who our parents had been.

They attacked us because of who we were becoming.

62

WE PULLED UP TO A FAMILIAR SPOT.
Skyscrapers towered all around us, and yet the expansive space in front of us was a stark reminder of what was missing.

I knew exactly where we were.

The city block had been completely decimated in the attacks, full of twisted iron and ash. But in the years that followed the 9/11 attacks, life had sprung forth from the wreckage, and the 9/11 Memorial had been created.

The trees that had been planted around the buildings' foundations were young and small, but they were thriving. And the foundations of the buildings themselves had been filled with water, creating two square, reflective pools. Each one was coated with granite and engraved with the names of the thousands of 9/11 victims. The water was in constant motion at the site, muting the sounds of the city, and falling into where the towers had once been.

…Where my father had once stood.

My legs shook as they always did when I approached the site. I thought nothing of the others. My feet crunched the dried leaves at a faster and faster rate as I ran along the path that led to the spot on the memorial that held my father's name.

I found it.

And I reached out with trembling fingers and traced the letters of his name – the letters of mine – as if it were his epitaph and the granite was his tombstone… as if this were his true resting site.

But I knew better.

As I watched the water cascade down into the deep, hollow, pool, only to resurface and cascade all over again, I knew my father was not resting here, under granite and soil.

His soul had gone on to a different assignment, and his legacy was resting in me.

And in my heart of hearts, I knew he'd be proud I'd embraced it.

I felt tears on my cheeks and a few hands on my shoulders. I turned to see the other Crest members, and after sharing hugs and tears, we spent a few minutes darting to areas all around the site, showing one another where exactly our parents were honored. It was a sad and happy celebration: with each other, and with people we'd never met.

It only ended when a familiar figure arrived on site.

General Richards – looking as stern as ever and flanked by Major McCoy – addressed us with a quick nod in our direction. "Cadets."

"Sir," we responded. Standing at attention in our uniforms, we followed our greeting with a salute.

"At ease," he instructed. Surprising me, he took a seat on a long bench by the site and invited us to do the same. We followed the casual order. A few civilians passed by us, quickly and shyly thanking us for our service. I blushed. Receiving words of gratitude would take some practice.

"I asked Major McCoy to bring you here for three reasons," the general explained after the civilians left. "First, in times of trouble, and especially after an attack on our soil, I believe in honoring the dead. When we're surrounded by evil, we need to remember people like your parents, who sacrificed everything for the greater good, for the people they served."

"But also," he continued, "I wanted to make sure you took the time to look into the reflection pool today. See more than the names etched in stone. See more than the water and the empty space it fills. In that water," he explained, "search for yourself. See *your* reflection among the wreckage."

"You see," he said simply, "in hard times, soldiers will often study their reflections for the first time. At times, they'll want to convince themselves they're monsters, simply because they've had to do what many could not. Other times, they'll see imposters, someone who they don't think can quite fill the uniform and the status it inherently brings with it. But what I hope you see... is pride."

He swept a broad hand to the landscape behind him. People were milling around everywhere, snapping pictures and crying softly...and even eating lunch in this now peaceful part of the city.

"Those people," the general continued, "are safe because of *you*. You are young." He chuckled. "Incredibly gifted, but incredibly young. Despite your youth, however, you still worked together to defeat evil – the same evil that took your parents' lives all too soon."

He straightened. "And that brings me to the final reason I came here."

He reached into his pocket, pulling out five medals. Each was the size of a silver dollar – a perfect circle made of lustrous gold and hanging from a thick, royal-blue ribbon.

"These medals are awarded to members of The Crest – the Chosen, Rare, Elite, Superhuman, and *Triumphant* division of our military. They receive it when they earn their wings, so to speak– when they fulfill their destiny and are triumphant in battle, rising above the ashes to ensure the safety of everyone around them."

He gazed intensely at each one of us. "These medals once belonged to your parents. They've been in our possession for almost twenty years, taken by us after their deaths to keep their identities secure. It's an honor to present them to you."

He walked to each of us, taking great care to pin each medal and salute each cadet. His hazel eyes were flanked by wrinkles as he peered into mine, and for a moment, I wondered what they had seen in his decades of service – how many Crest medals he had pinned to the uniforms of young soldiers like us.

The medal gleamed on my chest, showcasing the silhouette of the phoenix – the symbol of The Crest that I had seen for the first time just two months ago.

"You know the new tower they built? The Freedom Tower?" General Richards asked suddenly, changing gears and motioning toward the newest skyscraper, just northwest of the grounds. "A lot of people report light reflecting off of that building at all parts of the day. Rainbows seem drawn to it, too. People are captivated by it."

"And that's because that building is like you, Cadets. It reflects goodness and light after being born into a tragic situation."

"A place like this," he commented, "is a good place to adjust one's perspective." He stood and straightened his cap.

Then, suddenly and without saying goodbye, he turned and left.

We sat there for a moment, digesting his words. Then Bree stood up. She nudged Liam, who gave Isaac a hand, who gave Adrianna and me a hand, too.

And we all walked to the reflective pools together.

Jacob's absence was obvious, a missing limb from the body we'd trained to work together. And even though what remained was stronger, it still felt incomplete.

In the past two weeks, I'd wondered how Jacob had let the roots of hatred overtake him. It was hard to comprehend that it was the same person behind both the boyish grin and the murderous, mirthless laugh.

When did he decide to partner with that level of hate and evil? What did he allow himself to partner with that would poison his heart beyond repair? Did the venom not taste bitter simply because he'd labeled it as justice and righteousness in the name of revenge?

I looked at the others and prayed we would be different, that no matter what came our way, we would see hate and evil clearly. I made a solemn vow to defeat it, even if it donned a mask of justice or legitimacy.

Major McCoy cleared his throat when we arrived at the pool. "Your parents will be here soon, Cadets, so I'll get out of the way." He stood uncertainly, putting his weight on one foot, and then the other. "I hope I'm reassigned to this mission, Cadets, but I don't know what tomorrow brings. And in case this is the end of the road for us, here's my unsolicited advice: Stay together and stay strong.

He met each one of our eyes. "You never know where the missions of this life will lead you, but wherever that is, one thing is for sure: you'll want the best by your side."

With that, he turned on his heel and walked away.

Liam squeezed my hand. His other was thrown over Bree's shoulder. Isaac knocked my elbow slightly with his own. And Adrianna laced her arm in his.

And together, we leaned over the edge and gazed into the reflection pool.

And where most people would see five,

We saw one.

ACKNOWLEDGMENTS

IN THE COURSE OF WRITING FOR ALMOST A DECADE, there's a lot of people you need to thank, and inevitably, there's a lot of people you'll overlook. If you find yourself in the latter group, I want to apologize. Please know that while my memory clouds over time, the impact of your uplifting advice and support never went away. Thank you in advance for your grace.

To my students, past and present: Thank you for allowing me the honor of teaching you. Thank you for showcasing your talents and gifts every day, for giving me hope for the future when I feel like all hope is lost in the present. Thank you for letting the words God gave me about your identity land on your hearts, and for speaking truth about my identity, too. You were the first to tell me I was a great writer and that I should write books, and I'll never forget it.

To Amanda K. Morgan and LS Hawker, my fellow authors and close friends: Thank you for believing in me enough to not only encourage me, but to deliver hard truths as well. You not only guided me through this crazy industry, giving me tips and tricks you've learned along the way, but you guided me in improving my craft. Thank you for believing in me enough to do that.

To Ali Aman and Emily Kuczek, the wonderful sisters from my hometown who both went to West Point: Thank you for your advice and critique. I know I probably took a lot of poetic license in this final fictional version of what could and couldn't happen at the academy, but the basic information you gave me was invaluable and help shaped my characters and the plot.

To all of my beta and sensitivity readers, thank you. The insight you gave me into your hearts as you read helped me hold the hearts of all readers as well.

For Sarah Anderson, thank you so much for the layout and design of this book cover and its interior. You were the best I could have ever asked for and were a gem when collaborating. I feel as if a fast friendship was formed, too. Thank you for all the tweaks and adjustments, the marketing advice, and the overall enthusiasm you showed me from day one of working on this project. You are not only an astrophysicist, but an amazing artist- a beautiful juxtaposition and an inspiration for all.

To Mick Silva, my rock star content editor: Thank you so much for pushing me to develop Brooklyn more, for pointing out where there were some heart issues in the messages I was trying to convey. This was never a religious novel, but like me, you wanted to make sure God's hand could be felt in it, and you demanded I reflect His nature accurately. I'm so grateful.

To Bethany Anderson, my amazing copy editor and multi-talented friend: Thank you for being the peanut butter to my jelly, for noticing everything I'd missed when you read my book. You made it shine for everyone holding it now. You believed in me and spoke life into my spirit when I needed it the most. You are a jewel, and I am lucky to know you.

To my tribe of women: You know who you are. Thank you for calling me to rise up, for telling me I wasn't made to play small. Thank you for loving me. You call out the gold, but you don't ignore the grime, either. Instead, you help the gold shine and cover the grime with your grace. Thank you for doing life with me, for making sure I'm partnering with truth and love. I don't know where I'd be without you.

For my sisters and mom: Thank you for teaching me to use my talent as a gift for others. I may not have known her at the time, but Brooklyn was listening, too.

For Aubrey and Rylan: Thank you for being patient as your mom spent her spare time doing this work. It required your sacrifice, too, and I never want to overlook that. Thank you for inspiring me to be and do better, and for showing me the very best of God's nature every single day.

For Jason: Thank you for being the solid structure where my wild spirit lands. Thank you for providing a cocoon of safety when my world feels out of control. Thank you for believing in me enough to release me out into the world to do the work God wants me to do, but welcoming me back into our world with open arms. Your spirit is the match to mine, and when I'm with you, I'm home.

To the admins and moderators of the 9/11 Memorial social media groups who volunteered to read and share their stories and their hearts with me, thank you. I will never forget your words, your stories, or your impact.

To the families of those who perished on 9/11, who were impacted forever on that horrible day, I have no words. Just admiration and pride and love. Thank you for shining bright when the world went dark.

And to you, dear reader: Thank you for saying 'yes' to this book. Thank you for believing in these characters' gifts. And now I ask you, as you close it for good:

What do you need to say 'yes' to as you go out into the world? What gifts do you have to make it better?

Much love,

Amanda Deich

AUTHOR'S NOTE

THIS WAS A FICTIONAL STORY WRITTEN BY SOMEONE who wasn't directly involved in the attacks of 9/11. Because my own dad died when I was just a baby, I was able to identify with Brooklyn in a very sad and real way, but this doesn't mean my grief is the same. It doesn't mean I belong in their community. It doesn't mean I get to be their voice.

From the moment I started to write this book, the victims of 9/11 and their families, the policemen and first responders, and the soldiers who defend our country weighed heavily on my heart. Every single time I sat at my computer, I acknowledged my inadequacies and asked God to fill the holes, to anoint me in areas I could never achieve with my own talent. I reached out to a few survivors and family members of the victims and asked them to read the story, wanting more than anything to hold their hearts well during this process.

What I found is, in many ways, their voice and their grief has been ignored. In general, people find the topic to be too raw and too wounding. They feel like it's too much.

And that, my friends, is not okay.

There are a few charitable organizations that seek to help these families in a completely honest way, to hold their grief and attempt to make life easier for them. I'd like to point you to one right now.

If this story touched your soul and reminded you that heroes of the 9/11 attacks still walk among us, I would encourage you to give to THE STEPHEN SILLER TUNNEL TO TOWERS Foundation. Not only do they seek to empower and honor our heroes, but they also educate our youth about the attacks on that horrible day. They give a voice to a pain that has been ignored for far too long.

WWW.TUNNEL2TOWERS.ORG

Photo Credit: Mary Elizabeth Graff Photography

Amanda Deich is an author out of Littleton, Colorado.

In her other life, she is a mother to two children and a teacher to hundreds. She loves every single kid she knows: the imagined ones in her novels and the real ones at home and in the classroom.

AMANDADEICH.COM
TWITTER: @AMANDADEICH
INSTAGRAM: @AMANDADEICH
FACEBOOK: AUTHOR AMANDA DEICH

CPSIA information can be obtained
at www.ICGtesting.com
Printed in the USA
LVHW051143100121
676048LV00001B/9